TAMESIDE LIBRARIES

3 8016 01515 0404

KV-184-550

WITHDRAWN FROM
TAMESIDE
PUBLIC LIBRARIES

SPECIAL MESSAGE TO READERS

This book is published under the auspices of

THE ULVERSCROFT FOUNDATION

(registered charity No. 264873 UK)

Established in 1972 to provide funds for research, diagnosis and treatment of eye diseases. Examples of contributions made are: —

A Children's Assessment Unit at Moorfield's Hospital, London.

•

Twin operating theatres at the Western Ophthalmic Hospital, London.

•

A Chair of Ophthalmology at the Royal Australian College of Ophthalmologists.

•

The Ulverscroft Children's Eye Unit at the Great Ormond Street Hospital For Sick Children, London.

You can help further the work of the Foundation by making a donation or leaving a legacy. Every contribution, no matter how small, is received with gratitude. Please write for details to:

**THE ULVERSCROFT FOUNDATION,
The Green, Bradgate Road, Anstey,
Leicester LE7 7FU, England.
Telephone: (0116) 236 4325**

**In Australia write to:
THE ULVERSCROFT FOUNDATION,
c/o The Royal Australian College of
Ophthalmologists,
27, Commonwealth Street, Sydney,
N.S.W. 2010.**

Joanna Erle was born in Plymouth and convent educated to matriculation. She always wanted to write and began with poetry at the age of seven. She has worked variously in the accounts department of a film studio, on film publicity and as the secretary to a criminal lawyer.

SCANDAL'S DAUGHTER

Summoned to a first meeting with her grandmother, the Dowager Countess of Emmington, Kezia Aston is surprised by the hostility of her reception and shocked to be told she is illegitimate. Being spirited, sparks fly. Later, however, she agrees to spend a year as the old lady's companion, unaware that the Dowager is seeking to avenge an old grief. Lucius Sellon, to whom the earldom has recently passed, comes to Emmington from a country where a woman is of less value than a camel. Caught in the schemes of these despotic Sellons, Kezia fights for survival — and love.

Books by Joanna Erle
Published by The House of Ulverscroft:

FALSE ECHOES

JOANNA ERLE

SCANDAL'S DAUGHTER

Complete and Unabridged

ULVERSCROFT
Leicester

First published in Great Britain in 1998 by
Robert Hale Limited
London

First Large Print Edition
published 1999
by arrangement with
Robert Hale Limited
London

The moral right of the author has been asserted

Copyright © 1998 by Joanna Erle
All rights reserved

British Library CIP Data

Erle, Joanna
 Scandal's daughter.—Large print ed.—
Ulverscroft large print series: romance
 1. Large type books
 I. Title
 823.9′14 [F]

 ISBN 0–7089–4146–X

Published by
F. A. Thorpe (Publishing) Ltd.
Anstey, Leicestershire
Set by Words & Graphics Ltd.
Anstey, Leicestershire
Printed and bound in Great Britain by
T. J. International Ltd., Padstow, Cornwall

This book is printed on acid-free paper

For Bill

1

'So! . . . I am at last privileged to see you, miss!'

The pale, bleak stare which had watched her walk the length of the lovely panelled room, the words, the tone, were all part of a reception meant to overwhelm, Kezia recognized, as she halted before the old woman. She held the stare unwaveringly, her delicately arched brows lifting a little above fine grey eyes as she curtsied gracefully to a depth exactly appropriate to the rank of Cornelia Sellon, Dowager Countess of Emmington.

Such self-possession did not please. With no reciprocating courtesy, the dowager snapped, pointing, 'Come nearer. Be seated there,' and when her words had been complied with, leant back in her throne-like chair, marking her displeasure with a long, deliberate silence.

Serenely, Kezia made her own study of the dowager. Age had robbed her of the beauty for which, long ago, she had been famous, the once brilliant blue eyes were faded, the smooth skin heavily netted. But the elegance of finely drawn bones still remained, an elegance thrown into sharp relief by the mourning black of her handsome gown, its sombre richness emphasized by the gold and pearls of one or two superb ornaments.

Conscious that she herself was being coolly observed, the dowager's thin, beringed fingers began to tap the arm of her chair.

'Your refusal to attend my first invitation was a rich impertinence, and so I tell you, Miss Aston,' she said now.

Kezia's head, in its modest interpretation of the latest Wellington bonnet, remained unbowed. 'No impertinence was intended, ma'am. I was, as I wrote, unable to come.'

'You were not too ill to pen a letter. I take it no one about you was dying. What should keep you?'

Kezia remained silent. Why add to the dowager's hostility by saying she had not wished to come, or that that her reluctance had been strengthened by the phrasing of the 'invitation'? Even the differently worded second letter had not induced a quick change of mind.

The old lady snatched furious breath. 'You go from bad to worse. Returning the money I sent for your journey here and now not answering me!'

Again Kezia's brows lifted slightly. 'My

presence affords you so much annoyance, ma'am, I am puzzled to know why you wished me to come. Should I not leave before I disquiet you more?'

As Kezia made a movement to rise, the dowager drew a breath of pure outrage. 'Sit down, miss! I will decide when you go. Your behaviour is so much above your station, one would think you were Countess of Emmington and I . . . and I — ' Her mouth snapped shut on the unfinished sentence.

With wicked demureness, Kezia supplied, 'Her great-granddaughter?'

'Certainly not! I do not recognize the relationship!' was the instant, freezing reply.

It left Kezia unmoved.

Silence hung heavily in the room until the dowager asked abruptly, 'What is your age?'

'I was nineteen at my last birthday, a month ago.'

'And you teach in some school in Putney Village?'

The tone invested both school and location with an aura of disrepute so far removed from the actual that Kezia's lips twitched, but all she said was, 'Yes. For three years now, though two were as a pupil teacher.'

Minute by minute — as though the simple fact of her existence was not sufficient affront — the girl's quiet composure was adding to the dowager's annoyance. This was not the low, vulgar, easily over-awed creature she had anticipated, and the adjustments she was being forced to make served only to increase her impulse to punish. Her eyes narrowed unkindly: she would breach that composure yet!

In a thin, cold, rapier-sharp voice, she asked, '*And were your parents ever married*?'

The question, so totally unexpected, so destructive in its implications, slid home to its mark. That her parents had eloped, Kezia knew, but never had she doubted their legal status. In the world in which she had grown up, parents were always married: what the dowager countess implied was not easily to be believed. Staring back at the fierce old face before her, she returned, 'Why should they not be?'

'*Oh, why indeed!*' Contempt was loud in the dowager's voice, but her triumph was bitter. 'Charlotte — My granddaughter had not reached the age of consent when she left her home, and certain it is that your father made no attempt to carry her to Gretna. Indeed, despite long search, no record of a marriage *anywhere* has ever been found! So, young woman, you have a very doubtful right to your father's name — for what little that may count!'

4

It was more the slur cast on her father than her own injured pride that brought Kezia to her feet now. Her promise to Hallie to keep command of her tongue vanished from her mind.

'If I am here simply to be taunted with doubts of my legitimacy, then I hold you cheap for it, ma'am! Be sure that even if it should prove my parents did not marry, I would still be proud to be the child of two such people as they were! I bid you good-day.' With the briefest of curtsies, she turned to walk back the way she had come.

Before she reached the door, the dowager called, '*Wait*! Come back. Such lack of respect! Of consideration!'

Kezia turned, the gates of her anger flung wide. 'I came with deep reluctance, but it was consideration of your age and our relationship that brought me. What is due to you on the score of age I have paid. Our relationship you have disowned. As for respect — *that* you have destroyed in me.'

'Indeed and indeed! *Such words to me*! Am I to care for your opinion?'

There, she stopped. The girl must not go. The interview was not to end as *Miss Aston* chose! Snatching breath, the countess swept her hand in a severing motion 'Enough! Do not go. Let us begin again. My purpose in sending for you was not what you suggest. No more will be said regarding your parentage. Consider if you will, that the memories you bring are painful and age is a time of infinite vexation!'

When Kezia did not immediately respond, she added pithily, 'Now I have come as close to an apology as I am ever like to do, so do not be pettish!'

Had her feelings been less ruffled, Kezia would have smiled at the arrogance of that quittance. Debating the wisdom of staying, she found she could not ignore her relationship to the old lady with the same ease as did the dowager. In the end, she returned to her chair, saying gravely, 'I trust your word with regard to my parents, ma'am.'

The dowager's gaze made another assessing sweep over her visitor. Miss Aston's appearance suggested neither riches, nor the poverty which would have accorded better with her feelings: the blue bombazine walking-dress and beige shalloon pelisse, though simple, were as fashionable as her bonnet. Much against her wish, the dowager was also forced to acknowledge that the girl had both good looks and good style.

Complainingly, she said, 'You are not at all what I expected. So young and so sure!

Who brought you up so hardy?'

'Do I appear so? Then it must be that Hallie — Miss Halsinger, my principal — completed what my parents began.'

'An oddity among schools that trains up its girls to be so fearless. Since you are so, you may tell me plainly why did you not come when you were first invited?'

'Your letter, ma'am, did not read precisely like an invitation.'

'Such particularity! And the money beneath the seal put you more securely on your high horse, I suppose! Well, Miss Hoity-toity, I thought you might need it to pay for your journey. However, my steward's letter brought you . . . was the offer of a crested carriage more to your taste?'

'Mr Osborne's letter asked that I visit someone of great age and indifferent health. A crest was not mentioned and the carriage sent was a plain one.'

'An answer for everything! I am not used to such forwardness!' Hooding her eyes, the dowager sank into thought for several moments before saying sombrely, 'I am in my eighty-fourth year. How can you, at nineteen, possibly understand what it is to live long and endure so many losses . . . ? What can you know of the bitterness of seeing an old and honoured line wither

7

away and all that has given life purpose come to nothing?' She turned a blind gaze to a nearby window that looked out on a splendid view of parkland lying richly green beneath golden June sunlight. The thrust of memory, slackening the irascible lines of her face, allowed in an expression of deep sadness.

The warmest affection had once existed between her mother and this woman, Kezia remembered, and seeing the dry lips begin to quiver, her compassion awoke.

Blinking water from reddened eyes, the dowager looked back at her visitor. 'Are you aware that the mourning I wear is for my grandson, Lawrence, the seventh earl?'

'Yes. I read of his death in The Times. I'm sorry,' Kezia said gently.

'Charlotte never saw her brother, born as he was three years after she went from this house. Sickly always, and dead at seventeen! Husband, son, grandson, all gone and the direct line ended! Now a stranger is to come to take the place of those I have loved . . . A man of dubious honour, from a far, heathen country, knowing nothing of Emmington people, Emmington lands . . . A man from whom I have had just one letter since his inheritance and of whom I know no good beyond his appearing not to have forgotten the English language after thirty years in Egypt!'

Anger was conquering sorrow now. 'It was Piers's marriage to that pallid, sanctimonious creature, Sarah Buckley, that set disaster in train! That my son should choose so awry! Should mistake frigid religiosity for sweet innocence! A duke's daughter she may have been and well-endowed, but what did she breed out of her piety? Only a headstrong girl and an over-late, weakly son! All her prayers and prudery led nowhere but the destruction of this family.'

With some anxiety, Kezia noted the two spots of high colour now visible in the dowager's sallow cheeks, but suspected she was finding some relief in spilling out her bitterness.

'Pious she was, but cunning, too!' the old lady continued. 'Waiting until I was out of the country to compel Charlotte — my darling, sparkling girl! — into marriage with a man nearly three times her age and a canting crop-ears into the bargain! To think of linking *Sellons* with a tribe that supported that regicide, Cromwell! Small wonder Charlotte was driven to — ' She broke off, closing her eyes and rested her head against the chair-back.

Presently, she said wearily, 'To return from

9

Scotland to find such rout, such *scandal*! But worse, to find my granddaughter lost to me forever! Gone to a sordid life with a man who held her too cheap to marry! And then, after fourteen empty, silent years, to receive two barren lines announcing her death and signed simply *Kezia Aston*. With no address to which I could write for better information.'

Kezia flushed. 'I see now that it was not well done. But *then* I was just twelve years old and in a rage of misery at losing both my parents.' Lost with brutal suddenness in an accident while being ferried across the Thames, she remembered desolately. 'Miss Halsinger persuaded me it was my duty to inform my mother's family. I was too young to understand . . . What I knew was that my mother grieved deeply that her letters were never answered. For that, I hated you all. I did the least I could.'

The dowager shook her head, said painfully, 'If there were letters, they were kept from me. For it was to me Charlotte would have written, not to that pious bigot, her m — ' She broke off. 'Well, the woman's dead, too!' With visible effort, she cast off wounding memories and turned a piercing look on Kezia.

'Six years it has taken to trace you! Six

years in which you have grown up. Knowing Charlotte's connections, why have you made no attempt to approach us?'

'It is better I do not say, ma'am.'

'Such coolness!' The faded eyes measured the girl anew. She had been so sure that Kezia Aston would be a thoroughly plebeian creature, reflecting only her unknown father. Locked in a strange dichotomy, even now her mind refused to accept that Kezia was, in any real sense, Charlotte's child. She had carefully avoided examining her reasons for summoning the girl to Emmington. Wealthy, privileged, powerful, life had still dealt her heavy blows. Sorrow acting as a harsh corrosive on a strong and passionate nature, she had been left with an abiding sense that some requital was her due. Some half-formed idea of exacting it from Kezia Aston was disturbed by the reality of the girl. Almost to herself she said, 'So quick and bold in speech as you are . . . so unlike what is expected of a lady's companion.'

'So I imagine, ma'am,' Kezia agreed, wry amusement breaking through her sober mood. 'Fortunately, I have no thought of being one.'

'Have you not! Could you indeed ignore opportunity to be companion to someone of high rank . . . dismiss the chance to live in the comfort of such a house as this?'

'I cannot say.' Demurely wicked again, Kezia added softly, 'So much would depend on the person of high rank.'

'*Ha!*' Hastily the dowager clamped down on a responsive chuckle. 'Well, miss, it happens that my companion of thirty years has gone from me and I am left alone to face both the coming of this new man and removal to the solitude of the Dower House. Suppose, Miss Aston, I tell you I am prepared to disregard certain facts and accept you as my companion? What then? In time I might even be prepared to find you a husband. What have you to say to *that*?'

Kezia looked her astonishment. This, after all that had passed between them! Checking an impulse to laugh, she said, 'I'm obliged for the thought, ma'am, but I do not think the position would suit me — nor I, it. I am content as I am placed and not at all anxious for a husband.'

'You don't say!' The dowager's tone of lofty benevolence vanished instantly. 'Nameless and unconnected, how likely are you to come by one do you think?'

'If a husband has to be *found* for me, I shall prefer to remain single! If I marry at all, it will be in the hope of finding as much love and happiness as my parents shared.'

'Love and happiness!' The words were an explosion of angry scorn. 'How can you know the truth of what you saw? You were a child. Do not tell me that Charlotte, born in this house, enjoying the privileges of high position, never regretted all she threw away! I do not know who, or what, your father was. I do not ask! But certain it is that you are in no position to treat my offers — my *notice* even — with such disregard!'

'For what you intended in kindness, believe me grateful, ma'am. But, with respect, you must see how impossible your suggestion is. Thinking as you do, how could we find the least pleasure in each other's company?'

'That is for me to decide. I desire you to come.'

'Indeed, I cannot.'

'Cannot?'

'Will not!'

'*Girl, I am Countess of Emmington!* Who and what are you?' Snatching a hissing breath, she leaned towards Kezia. 'I will tell you, miss! You are less than nothing, for you are *scandal's daughter* and despised by society for being so! At eighteen, Charlotte was underage and could not marry without consent. It's a rare man who marries his mistress after the passage of three years! Even if it had been done, it would have

13

conferred no legality on you, miss, for by your age, you were born in the second year of their liaison.'

Kezia broke the short, tense silence which followed, with an angry laugh. 'It was *my father* who taught me to honour my word, ma'am.'

She had risen again, but the dowager, already regretting the emotions that, lately, slipped so easily out of control, threw out a detaining hand.

'It was not my intention to break my word regarding your parentage, but you vex me so!' To her chagrin, the humiliating weakness of age overtook her and her head bowed to hide the angry, brimming tears. Her voice muffled, she said, 'Well, go if you must, and pray loneliness does not overtake *you* in your old age.'

Her weakness held Kezia in a way her imperiousness could not. 'I do not care to leave you as you are. Is there no one I may call?'

'Oh, indeed! A whole houseful of *servants*! Shall *they* comfort me?' Scorn was the dowager's defence against the outrage of irrepressible tears.

Kezia went to kneel beside the old woman, taking one thin, veined head into her gloved ones. 'It was not my wish to upset you. I am truly sorry we cannot agree. It is just that you — That I — Please do not weep.'

'I have not wept in sixty years!' the dowager declared against the evidence. But alert to Kezia's softening towards her, in a gentler tone than she had yet used, she said, 'Come to Emmington as my companion for a time . . . for six months. No . . . Come for a year, until I know what manner of man this eighth earl is. Can we not agree together for a twelvemonth?'

'But is it likely, ma'am, when I vex you so? You have seen how little meek I am.'

'To practise humility can only be of benefit to a junior teacher!' returned the countess tartly. Then, hastily replacing tartness with pathos, added, 'Who is to say how long I have left in this world? Cannot you bear me company — endure a few petty rippets — for a year? You, who have a lifetime before you?'

More than 'petty rippets' had passed between them, Kezia knew: feelings had run deep on both sides. Nevertheless, the appeal touched her. She remembered the dowager's smothered laugh a short time ago, the almost shared moment of humour. She found, too, that her long-held animosity had diminished now that the grievance of her mother's unanswered letters had been removed.

Hallie had urged her to make this visit as something her mother would wish her to do. That Hallie also hoped that it would lead to the Sellons openly recognising Lady Charlotte's daughter, Kezia guessed.

Her glance skimming the room, she thought, this is the Lily Room, named for its plasterwork frieze. I know it, as I know so much about this house my mother loved so well, but I never visualized how very beautiful it would be. There would be pleasure in exploring it fully, sharing for a while something of the fairy-tale life her mother's stories had woven into her childhood memories . . .

She was surprised to find herself tempted. She looked back at the dowager: could she really spend a whole year with this imperious, abrasive woman without coming into serious conflict with her? Had enough of the poison of their different resentments drained away in their exchanges to make it possible?

She said doubtfully, 'Miss Halsinger's convenience would have to be consulted . . . '

If the woman had a morsel of worldly sense and a touch of goodwill towards the girl, she was unlikely to put obstacles in the way, the dowager thought.

'Consult if you must. Arrange how you will — only *come*! And do not be too long about it, I cannot live forever. But' — her eyes narrowed — 'you will not expect to be other than plain Miss Aston, my companion. Good sense will tell you why. Charlotte's disgrace is not to be resurrected; her reputation again made a torn rag by scandalmongers! There will be enough threat to the family name attendant on Theodore Sellon's arrival! Hurried out of the country in his youth for some unsavoury reason, and returning with an outlandish Egyptian wife — or worse, with *wives*! It is more than enough to bear!'

'If I come,' but decision had been reached, Kezia knew, 'I shall be happy to be plain Miss Aston. Nor shall I trouble you with *expectations* of any kind.'

That last assurance gave the dowager no satisfaction. Something deep within her stirred dark malevolent coils. Such insolent independence required a curb. Miss Aston had much to learn — not least that there were those who had the power to crush upstarts. But first she must ensure the girl came to Emmington.

She said in a weary voice, 'Well, we shall see . . . Now I am tired. Go; make your arrangements — but do not fail to come.'

Rank and privilege made no effective barrier against the limitations of age, Kezia thought pityingly. This was her own great-grandmother and her only known living relative: with goodwill on both sides, they might find a little friendship. Even if it ended badly, what would be lost? Her decision now firm, she allowed herself a little amused curiosity concerning the incoming earl. Theodore Sellon must be fifty and more — might he really have several wives? And what could he have done to have been hustled out of the country when young? And now, was he better or worse for having spent thirty years in Egypt?

Diverting as these questions were to her, she could understand the dowager's apprehension. Raising the thin hand she held to her lips, she murmured, 'Adieu, Great-grandmama. I give you the name for the first and last time, do not fear.'

She stood up and meeting the dowager's faded eyes, smiled down at the old woman. 'It may surprise you, ma'am, but so far, I have quite enjoyed being 'plain Miss Aston'.'

2

'So nauseous a concoction makes me wonder if you and Powlett are in collusion to poison me!' the dowager complained sourly, handing back a reluctantly drained glass to Kezia.

'But of course, ma'am. We are astonished you have not yet succumbed,' Kezia returned with a smile.

Setting down the glass, she wondered if the old lady had any idea how close to death her recent illness had taken her. It had taken all her own fortitude to nurse someone so desperately sick: whether her patience would be equally enduring throughout the dowager's crotchety convalescence, she doubted. Nor was the old lady's present testiness likely to be lessened when she was told — as soon she must be — that three uninvited guests and their several servants were now resident at Old Hall.

Taking up the book she had been reading a little earlier, Kezia returned to where the dowager sat in a cushioned chair, October sunlight falling on her with pleasant warmth through the leaded casements of her bedroom.

'Shall I continue reading, ma'am?' she asked.

The dowager, however, had another, familiar, grievance to air and ignored the question to say, 'Four months since first I saw you, three since you came to stay and still we have had no notice of that wretched man's intentions! What manner of man can he be! One might wish him never to come — '

A knock on the door interrupting her, elicited a sharp exclamation of exasperation and a testy, 'Enter.'

Betty Bassett, the newest and youngest of Old Hall's housemaids and the one assigned to wait on 'the companion', squirmed nervously into the room and directed an imploring look at Kezia.

Laying the book aside, Kezia went to meet the girl and was told in an urgent whisper, 'Sorry, miss, but the baroness would have it I asked you to attend her at once, her knowing you was usually free at this time.'

'But I am not so today, Betty,' Kezia returned quietly. 'Please give Lady Holford my apologies and tell her — '

'I am no longer at Heaven's gate, so no one has need to whisper,' intruded a waspish voice.

Flustered, Betty took a backward step and

the dowager, snatching at the silver-topped stick resting against her chair, thumped the floor with it. 'You, young woman!' she called. 'Come here!'

Despairingly, Betty crept forward, tripped on the carpet's edge and forgot to curtsey.

'Now, girl!' the dowager said petrifyingly. 'What message do you carry in this house that I, its mistress, may not hear?'

Crimson-faced, Betty mumbled to the floor, 'None, m'lady, I'm sure.'

'Indeed, ma'am, it was a small matter meant for my ear,' Kezia interposed.

'A small matter you say, yet both so adverse to having it spoken aloud! Do you arrange an assignation, perhaps?'

'No, ma'am,' Kezia returned with a slight smile, only to be told quellingly, 'It will be no laughing matter if so it proves, miss!' The dowager swung back to Betty. 'Now, girl! Repeat your message without delay.'

Close to tears, knowing that the household was under orders to keep knowledge of the presence of visitors in the house from the convalescent, Betty mumbled unhappily, 'Please, m'lady, Lady Holford says will Miss go to her in the library this minute.'

The dowager drew a quick breath, threw a gleaming look at Kezia and told Betty, 'Convey my compliments to the baroness

21

and inform her that Miss Aston is engaged with me.'

With Betty gone from one ordeal to face another, the dowager, narrow-eyed, demanded, 'Well, and just how long has this house been favoured with Cynthia Holford's presence?'

'Four days, ma'am.'

'And I not told!'

'Dr Powlett thought it inadvisable.'

'Did he! He extends his prerogative, I think. But if he has kept my niece-in-law from despatching me with her attentions, no doubt I must think myself grateful. The baroness has not come unprovided with company, I may guess!'

'No. Miss Holford and Miss Melissa are also here.'

'And a rabble of Holford attendants disrupting the running of my household, to boot! But why should her ladyship be sending for you?'

Impossible to explain that within minutes of her arrival, Lady Holford had made use of the dowager's companion as a substitute for her daughters' maid who had broken her arm just before the Holford cortège set out and had continued to make use of her services more generally since. Less timid out of the countess's presence and possessed of an unruly tongue, Betty Basset had revealed to Kezia that the servants were very much aware that the baroness always made the old lady 'mad as fire'. For that reason Kezia had hesitated to challenge the woman for fear of provoking a rumpus that might disturb the sick dowager.

While Kezia hesitated, the dowager pounced. 'You do not need to tell me. Vexacious woman that she is! What was Giles about to marry her! The men of these late generations have no judgement. And which busybody do I have to thank for informing her of my indisposition, I wonder.' Her cane struck an irritable tattoo on the floor. 'Using my companion as a waiting woman . . . How could you allow it, miss? No, no, do not trouble to answer — it is not beyond my imagining.'

She continued to express her displeasure for some time, found fault with her noonday meal, and was still declining to take a nap when her physician, Dr Powlett, arrived.

The doctor was a well-made man of middle age and middle height, with a broad intelligent face and thick, silvery hair brushed smoothly to the shape of a bob-wig. His manner had all the genial assurance of one whose professional services were eagerly sought by the high and the mighty. Having pronounced himself well pleased with his patient's progress, he observed that she owed her careful nurse a considerable debt and, with a slyly quizzical look, added, that a certain acidite in her present mood was pleasing proof of returning vigour.

'I'm glad you think so!' The pale eyes glittered at him. 'In that case you will not quarrel with my intention to take my dinner in proper form in the dining-room today. And that I mean to ingest something other than a mess of baby pap.'

The doctor bowed ironical acceptance of this announcement before countering with a ruthlessness to match her own, 'But you will remain below for longer than two hours at your peril, dear ma'am, and you will rest before you make the attempt. More importantly, if you venture beyond the lightest food, little different from what you have been having, I shall expect to see you nailed into your coffin a week from now.'

'Am I to be so bullied, sir? I wonder why it is I continue you as my physician?'

'Perhaps because you are alive at a count of years I will not be so ungallant as to mention?'

'And deuced lonely do I find it!' was the snappish reply.

'Well, your favourite dish of lampreys

in vinegar would undoubtedly solve the problem, dear lady, and so I warn you. But if you are to feel sorry for yourself, then the world is about to end in any case.'

Regarding him from beneath drooping lids, the dowager's mouth turned a little askew. 'We are too long acquainted, I think. However, it will not be my fault if I am not here a week from now.'

Another smiling bow, and the doctor turned to Kezia. 'And now you, Miss Aston . . . It is nearly a week since your patient was out of danger and I recommended you to take as much air and exercise as possible. What have you been about, for I see no sign of the bloom returning to your cheeks?'

Kezia's evasive murmur caught the dowager's attention at once. 'I see how it has been!' she interposed. 'Well, that will change!' The light of battle glowing brightly in her eyes, she gestured towards the tray standing on a nearby chest. 'When Dr Powlett has drunk the Madeira you will now pour for him, I shall rest until four o'clock, when Rudge may dress me. Meanwhile, you shall walk through the park to young Osborne's house and deliver a message of the greatest importance — for so it will be when I have thought of it. That being settled, depend on it, more will be settled before tomorrow.'

With good understanding of the nuances of the situation, Dr Powlett said amusedly, 'I see, ma'am, you have a tonic in preparation that will do equal good to any of mine if not over-indulged.' Taking the glass of wine Kezia now offered him, he saluted the dowager. 'Your improving health, ma'am, and unabating powers!'

★ ★ ★

The afternoon was bright with a brisk, erratic wind when Kezia set out for her walk wearing an old but warm grey cloak over a plain blue dress. The message she had been given to carry to Harry Osborne, the young estate steward, had astonished her.

'I recollect you saying you ride,' the dowager had said. 'And there is not now a horse in our stables trained to take a lady's side-saddle. You may tell young Osborne to purchase a suitable mount for your use.'

It was a royal provision for a mere companion and Kezia guessed it was intended to acknowledge the dowager's obligation to her nurse. A simple 'thank-you,' spoken with sincerity, would have been enough, but smoothly as the three months she had spent at Old Hall had passed, the dowager still kept her at a determined arm's length.

Why the old lady had pressed her to come to Emmington remained a mystery. But, once or twice, looking up suddenly from book or needlework, she had found the faded eyes fixed broodingly on her, provoking an uncomfortable feeling that some dark purpose lay maturing in the dowager's mind. Always, she had dismissed the idea as nonsense.

Resolving to count her blessings, she concentrated on enjoying her walk. It was not difficult: the first hint of autumn's brilliance was beginning to enrich an already beautiful landscape and in a nearby tree-top, a robin was rehearsing his winter song. Twenty minutes brisk walking brought her to the steward's substantial stone cottage which was set among trees not far from the working centre of the estate with its blacksmith's forge, carpenters' sheds, clerks' offices and storehouses. Here, Harry Osborne lived with his widowed aunt, Amelia Robby, to keep house for him, as she had done for his father.

Harry's father had been Emmington's steward for many years and Harry, when he left Oxford, had become his assistant. Mr Osborne's untimely death four years later had left Harry with full responsibility at the age of twenty-four. Any thought of engaging a man with longer experience was quickly dropped: obvious ability, good looks and a quite unconscious charm of manner, had quickly won him the dowager's favour.

Friendship between Kezia and Harry had grown quickly and to a point of easiness which permitted them an unconventional use of first names when alone. Kezia did not expect to find him at home at this time of the day, but as she opened the gate into the pretty garden surrounding the house, she saw him coming towards her down the flagstoned path, his brown springy curls glossed almost to gold by the sun. She watched him pleasurably as he quickened his pace towards her, thinking how lightly he carried his very considerable responsibilities.

His tone matching the warmth in his hazel eyes, Harry said as he reached her, 'Well met! So rare a pleasure it is of late, I had begun to despair of seeing you out and about again.'

'I am come with a message from the countess, but little thought to find you at home in daylight hours.'

'Is that to imply that if you had known I was here you would not have come?'

'Oh, I think I should. The message is all in my own interest you see.' Kezia's teasing smile answered his.

'Unkind! I looked to be given a better answer. But what am I to do for you?'

She told him, ending, 'Do not put yourself out. There is no great hurry.'

He laughed. 'Don't tell me the countess said that. Her wishes do not wait upon anyone's convenience! But I'm delighted she has made this provision for you, particularly as I see advantage to myself in it. There will surely be occasions when we can match times and ride together?'

'Oh, Harry, of course! I should like it of all things.'

'So what is your riding experience?'

'Nothing great. Once past pony age, I rode only livery hacks, so I cannot claim to be a remarkable equestrienne, much as I enjoy riding.'

A groom driving up in the light chaise Harry sometimes used, interrupted them and, learning that he was taking a rare holiday in order to drive his aunt into Westerham village to visit a friend, Kezia said goodbye. Harry gazed after her as long as she remained in sight, his smile unconscious and revealing.

Beginning a circular route back to Old Hall, the broad, grassy track Kezia was following soon began to ascend a tree-crowned hill. The wind opposed her now with increasing force, tossing back the hood of her cloak, whipping her hair into a tangle and buffeting her like an over-playful child so that she reached the hill-top breathless but exhilarated. Here, where the trees flanked the windward side of the track before pouring down the back of the hill in a dense woodland, she found some protection.

A short distance along, a rutted cartway branched left into the woodland, and soon after that the wall enclosing the Dower House gardens began. The handsome iron gates of the main entrance were set centrally in the front wall and finding one leaf open, she stood in the opening to catch her breath, to admire the house, and to try in vain to order her blown locks.

This was where she and the dowager countess would come when the eighth earl came to take up his inheritance — if ever he did! Set back in a sheltering indentation of the woodland, the graceful lines of the house showed the Dutch influence of a hundred years ago. But the remoteness of the house's situation, Kezia knew, robbed it of all charm for an old lady who delighted to be at the centre of things. Though the house was kept always ready for her, the dowager would only suffer removal from Old Hall at the last possible moment.

The site for the Dower House must have been chosen for someone who loved the quite magnificent view it commanded over a large part of Emmington's 1,200 acres of parkland, Kezia thought, as she turned her gaze to its splendidly disposed woods and gardens, its lakes, fountains and water-courses, and the superb mile-long avenue of chestnuts. All beautiful, but what caught at her heart was the chief jewel in the landscape, the centrally placed house. Beginning as a hall-chantry with land and endowment enough to support a priest and four monks, it had been one of the many seized a hundred years later in Edward VI's name and sold for secular use. The house that had then risen, had been built mostly of the new and costly brick, the largest part of what Kezia could see being completed by 1555. What alterations and additions had been made through the centuries had done no more than give it an enchantingly complex outline of tower, gable and courtyard, while leaving it pleasingly low in height and blessedly harmonious. House and Sellons had belonged one to the other for 260 years now, and Kezia found herself suddenly overtaken by something within herself laying wistful claim to a share in that belonging.

Lost in a dream to which the clamour of the wind in the trees made a half-heard background, she was startled out of it by the crunching of gravel behind her.

Swinging round, she saw a man who appeared to have come from behind the house, leading a horse of no particular breeding across the wide carriage sweep. Wearing a shabby fustian jacket, his boots and riding-breeches as dusty as his nag's hide, the man looked equally rough-bred. He was hatless and his over-long black hair was as tangled as her own. Because his head was bent, she could see little of his features but enough of his sun-browned skin to suspect he was a gypsy — and a gypsy should certainly not be wandering within Old Hall's walled domain! The bulging satchel he carried over one shoulder widened her suspicion: it looked to her as though he might have broken into the Dower House, broad daylight though it was. If so, he was bolder than most of his kind who generally chose darkness and stealth for their depredations.

Her first thought was to raise the alarm and she was poised to hurry away when his head lifted and she found him staring at her. It was a stare of arrogant intensity, holding no hint of being daunted at seeing her. Several unpleasant tales concerning gypsies nudged her memory. They were a strange race, unaccountable, alien, wild . . . She suddenly had the strongest wish to be elsewhere. Pride and the knowledge that, mounted, he could overtake her in moments, held her where she was.

He had neither checked nor hurried his approach, and gathering up her courage, Kezia demanded in a tone she had used in the past to quell unruly young ladies all too close in age to herself, 'What are you doing here?'

It was astonishing to discover brilliantly green eyes in the dark, fine-boned face with a jetty swathe of hair falling untidily across its wide brow; it was disconcerting to witness the swift change her words induced in those same eyes which now subjected her to a slow, inimical inspection from head to foot and back again.

'Who asks?' was the answering demand made with curling lip and a show of white teeth in a smile that was surely more menacing than a scowl.

Alarm prickled Kezia's skin and her voice sharpened, her words coming in tight little bursts. 'One who has the right. You should not be here! Gyp — Travellers are not allowed inside the park. Fox Spinney on Emmington Heath is set aside for them. And what have you in that satchel?'

Beneath thick, straight, shadowing lashes, the aberrant green eyes narrowed, and something darkly mischievous came into his face, deepening the unkind smile.

'Such dangerous questions the pretty lady asks . . . '

What was faintly foreign in his deep-toned voice had a more noticeable Romany lilt now, but more disquieting even than his effrontery was the way in which his bold gaze continued to hold and appraise her.

'But it is not a lady from the great house walking all alone with no one to guard her,' the insinuating voice went on. 'Her maid perhaps . . . a foolish maiden, who walks unwary and speaks so bold to a stranger and a . . . a traveller.'

He was laughing at her. How dared he! Kezia thought furiously: laughing at her while his strange eyes held her captive under their intimidating, speculative gaze. He had reached the gateway now and she realized he was taller than most gypsies. Jerking back as from a threat, her mouth dry, she blurted, 'My . . . my brother is not far away!'

Lazily his glance swung left and right over the visible length of empty track. Eloquently silent, he returned his wickedly smiling green gaze to her face.

The nervousness she felt was quite foreign to her. There was the oddest kind of trembling deep within her and she seemed quite unable to turn her eyes away from his.

But her spirit firming to meet the challenge, she tilted her chin and lied bravely, 'He is in the woods behind you. I have only to call.'

'And what does the gorgio do there? Does he poach the lord's game? Will he share his catch with a poor Romany?' the alien voice taunted softly. A moment's pause, and then more softly, more insinuatingly, 'Perhaps the pretty maid will give the gypsy a fee for her safe passage?'

'*No*! I mean I — I carry no money.' But instinct told her he had not been speaking of money, and in an oddly desperate way, she ended, 'I have nothing to give you.'

'*Oh, but you have!*'

Suddenly he was so close she was even more devastatingly aware of him; shockingly aware of his maleness, as she never had been of any other man; aware of the supple, sinewy power of the body under his rough clothes. Her breathing grew shallow and the strangest feelings quivered through her, feelings which took still more force from the look he had fastened on her mouth. *He couldn't — surely he couldn't actually be thinking of kissing her!* Shaken and shaking, she took another jerking step backwards.

What might have happened then if they had not both caught the creak and rattle of a wagon laden high with faggots lumbering out of the woods on the branch track, Kezia was never to know. Reaching the main track, the wagon turned away from them to go the way she had come.

With a snicker of laughter in his throat, the gypsy took in the hunch-backed old woodsman and the young boy perched on the driving bench. Looking back at Kezia, he jeered softly, 'You didn't say *two* brothers, lady, and both as strong as brandy!'

But though laughter still glimmered in his eyes, in the pause that followed, Kezia sensed that the interruption had made a change, perhaps by reminding him of the dangers of trespass.

'So . . . ' Again the curling smile. 'I'll take myself away.' But before turning to swing up into the saddle, he reached out with easy grace to lay a brown finger on her lips.

It was a statement of intent, a kiss by proxy that seemed to sear Kezia's lips as though it was the Devil's own fiery touch. She stood rooted, watching him ride unhurriedly down the path she must herself follow to return to the house, the faint odour of leather that had clung to his fingers lingering with her.

The familiarity of his last action and what it implied was shocking, as everything about the encounter had been shocking. It accounted for her present breathlessness and the total confusion in her mind. She picked what she could from her whirling thoughts and found herself reminded by her careful upbringing that she had every reason to feel outraged. But was outrage what she felt? There was an angry alarm still trilling along her nerves, but mingled with it was a strange, pleasurable excitement. *As though*, she thought astonished, *she had not been entirely averse to being kissed — and kissed by a gypsy!*

It was not to be believed! The unexpectedness, the singularity of the encounter, was disordering her senses. But she was not so far astray as to allow herself to think there had been anything romantic in meeting an impudent rogue, or that she had felt a thrill of attraction towards the threat he had conveyed.

Shaking herself out of her trance, she began to hurry down the homeward slope of the hill. But still her pulses raced, still her thoughts scuttled this way and that: she must let it be known that a gypsy man was roaming the estate . . . must see that someone was sent to check the Dower House . . . must —

'*Such dangerous questions the pretty lady asks . . .* ' the deep and mocking voice seemed to whisper again in her ears. And her breath caught again remembering his '*Oh, but you have!*' and all it had implied.

That, and the brazenly intimate touch on her lips which had followed . . .

3

Her reflection in the cheval looking-glass in her bedroom brought Kezia to a dismayed stop when she saw how the wind had blowzed her. Her cheeks were scarlet and her hair blown into the wildest disorder. Small wonder the gypsy had behaved so insolently towards her when she looked as dishevelled as a woman of his own kind.

The encounter refused to leave her mind and an uneasy sense of change possessed her, as though the gypsy's touch had marked her indelibly. Stripping, she washed with an oddly compelled thoroughness, though quickly because she expected to be summoned to attend the dowager at any moment.

Walking naked to take a clean shift from a drawer, she paused again before the long mirror. '*Pretty lady . . .* ' an insinuating voice whispered again in her ear. *Gypsy patter!* she told herself sharply: he would have said it if she was cross-eyed and crooked. But thank goodness she wasn't! Her skin was creamy and unblemished; large eyes and a well-shaped nose and mouth made her looks at least passable. She might wish her hair was either fashionably brunette or appealingly blonde, but she was lucky that, though only brown, it curled naturally.

'*Pretty lady . . .*' the words whispered through her mind again and her lips seemed to burn with the memory of a predatory finger laid against them. Hastily walking on, she snatched a shift from its drawer, covered herself and gave her attention to deciding which gown to wear that evening.

Until the dowager's illness, she and the old lady had always dined in formal state in the dining-room even when there was no addition to their number by way of Harry Osborne or the elderly widowed rector. But what would be expected of her now? The dowager was preparing to meet Lady Holford in a combative frame of mind and might prefer not to have 'Miss Aston' witness a family row. The irony of that did not escape her.

The doubt of her legitimacy the dowager had planted in her mind had nibbled away at previous certainties over the months. The stigma bastardy carried was real. Except where royalty was involved, those whom it touched were despised, branded inferior. The enquiries she had made had led nowhere. Neither Hallie, nor Mr Staiton, a lawyer and

Kezia's official guardian, had been able to throw light on the matter, but the latter had reminded her that he held a sealed packet in trust for her until either her betrothal or her coming-of-age, whichever occurred first. The suggestion that there might be information to come seemed to Kezia to lend weight to the dowager's charge.

Her childhood had been happy, but, looking back on it, she was made aware of the total absence from it of aunts, uncles and cousins, and though her parents had lived very comfortably, they had entertained only occasionally and within a narrow group of acquaintance. She had known her father's profession had to do with the law, but she had been too young then to be interested in its precise nature. Often, she recalled, he had remained in London for a week or more — and lately that had prompted the unbearable thought that he might have had another home . . . wife . . . family . . .

Soberly now, from her three evening dresses, Kezia selected the mulberry-coloured mousseline with its rather prim neckline and plain sleeves. The gown had the fashionable outline, its waistline coming just below the bust and the skirt falling straight to the ankles but fuller than skirts had been for some years. The hem was modishly stiffened and decorated, but the beading was mulberry-coloured, too: it was a gown made to support the dignity of a young teacher among Miss Halsinger's older parlour boarders.

Her only ornament was a simple gold chain with unusual twisted links, a gift from her mother on her twelfth birthday, but since fashion at present insisted on evening head-dressing, she threaded a narrow gold ribbon through her curls. Her toilette was just completed when Nancy Rudge, the dowager's pleasant, middle-aged abigail, came to summon her.

The dowager was regal in a gown of black *gros de Naples* with quilted sleeves and several rows of black filoselle on the skirt. Adorning her head was a lavender silk turban bound with a black silk cord and having a diamond clasped aigrette of black feathers on one side. The base of her neck was circled by a triple rope of pearls banded at intervals by more diamonds, and an imposing assemblage of rings glittered on her fingers. Though looking a little fragile, she was girt for battle and appeared quite as impressive as she intended, Kezia thought appreciatively.

Rising with Rudge's help from her dressing-stool, the dowager turned to inspect Kezia.

'H'mp!' was her reaction. 'That is a dress

I have always thought passable for a second-year widow but decidedly thereabouts for a gel of your age! What's the matter with your pretty green grenadine gown? Or the white and rose muslin? Well, it's too late to change now. Give me your arm and we will go down.'

This they did slowly and cautiously, entering the drawing-room only moments before Lady Holford and her daughters appeared.

The baroness was a tall, strong-featured woman and the gown of olive-green twilled silk she wore admirably set off her dark-eyed, haggard handsomeness. Whatever her thoughts were on a dinner-hour restored to 5.30 from the hour of 7 to which she had changed it, nothing but pleasure was visible in her face as she swept forward, first to curtsy and then to embrace the dowager.

'How glad I am to see you at last, dear Countess, and to know you are recovered. So very odd as it has been not to be permitted to visit you, laid on your sick-bed as you were. I cannot help but wonder if you have known of our presence here, or if Powlett — *and others*' — her black eyes stabbed a fierce look at Kezia — 'have not been very wrongly officious. So necessary as it is to have the comfort of *family* about one when brought low. At least you may be comfortable in the knowledge that your household has been well in hand these last few days.'

The dowager, settling herself into her high-backed chair close to the banked-up fire, regarded Lady Holford enigmatically and said dryly, 'After thirty years I should hope Sopworth might be trusted for that.'

'Oh, in the *domestic* way, of course!' the baroness hastened to agree. 'I am forever in envy of you for his possession. But for the rest — how much more easeful to the mind to know one has one's *own* about one.'

'No doubt you're right,' conceded the dowager blandly and then asked with wicked emphasis, 'How is my nephew? Am I to have the felicity of a visit from Giles, too?'

A necessary diplomacy forced Lady Holford to swallow the stinging retort that sprang to her lips. Unfortunately, she told the dowager, before news of her illness reached them, her husband had gone into Gloucestershire to shoot over Lord Moston's coverts.

Receiving this news philosophically, the dowager turned her attention to Miss Holford who, though having features similar to her mother's, somehow lacked the older woman's handsomeness. An expression of peevish superiority was no help to her.

'Well, Sophia, no suitor in your sights yet?

Twenty-five is late in the day to hang fire,' said the dowager unkindly.

'I'm twenty-three, Great-aunt,' Sophia snapped.

'You surprise me!' said the dowager even more unkindly, before turning to poke her stick in the other sister's direction.

'You're the younger gel grown up of a sudden, I suppose. Melissa, is it? Seventeen and about to go on the town, I suppose.'

Petite of figure, pertly pretty, Melissa had nothing in common in looks or character with Sophia. Unawed by her autocratic great-aunt, her head of black curls held high and a glint in her eyes, she advanced to make her curtsy.

'Blessed with true *Holford* eyes, I see. Such a *particular* blue! But that saucy look is wasted on *me*, miss. Keep it for the men. Well, by the look of you, you should take well enough to marry better than respectably!' She swung her gaze back to the baroness. 'What's her dowry?'

'Really, Countess!' Lady Holford shot a meaningful glance at Kezia.

Sopworth's entry to announce that dinner awaited her ladyship's pleasure made a timely interruption.

Convention required the dowager to accept Lady Holford's arm, the two sisters followed

45

and Kezia, deciding her presence was expected in the dining-room, walked into the hall behind the rest.

Looking back, Lady Holford halted abruptly.

'Is that person joining us *at table?*' she demanded in astonished displeasure.

The dowager glanced back, too. 'If you mean Miss Aston, naturally she is joining us. Where else should she eat?'

'I thought — It had not occurred to me she was on such a footing.'

The dowager straightened. 'Does the Countess of Emmington choose a companion too low-bred to dine in company?' she demanded awfully.

'No, indeed, Countess! A misunderstanding — nothing more! You must know I would not imply — ' For once at a loss, Lady Holford floundered into a silence that afflicted them all as they continued across the hall.

The pall deepened rapidly when the Holfords realized that Head Cook had taken revenge for recent annoyances. The dishes she had provided for this meal, though plentiful, were all of the kind Dr Powlett had prescribed for the dowager. In addition to milk soup flavoured with the merest hint of nutmeg and fillets of sole in white sauce, there was nothing more robust to follow than the most delicate slices of breast of chicken, a dish of creamed cauliflower and another of sweetbreads with side dishes of the lightest fluff of *oeufs Chantilly* and other such invalidish foods. Nor when the *entremets* arrived did they have either greater substance or more colour, being all of the order of white pudding, *bevaroix à la vanille* and *crème au café vierge*.

The dowager observed this pallid repast with grim amusement, guessing the reason for it and refraining from the scathing observations she would otherwise have had conveyed to Head Cook. Breaking the silence, now heavier than before, the dowager, having uttered no word herself, sent a glance like a flicker of lightning over her silent guests and enquired outrageously, 'Has the world stood still while I have been laid on my bed? Or has the art of conversation been quite forgot?'

Constrained by her hope of her children ultimately benefiting from the dowager's substantial personal fortune, the baroness again bit her tongue and said only, 'One hesitates to weary you with words, dear Countess, when you are only just restored to us.'

'It will weary me a great deal more to sit mumchance for an hour or more, and so I tell you,' was the unaccommodating reply.

Drawing careful breath, Lady Holford

launched into an account of a recent visit to Scotland. When that subject was exhausted she found herself unable to resist introducing one which promised a little retaliatory amusement.

'It is hard to credit you are still without news of Lord Emmington's arrival!' she began in a honeyed tone. 'But he comes from a branch of the family held in poor esteem, I believe.'

'Just so.'

'I feel for you. You must suffer the gravest concern. Only recently Sir Victor Cowan told me — ' She hesitated delicately. 'But perhaps I should not say . . . '

The dowager gave her a look of dislike. 'Having said so much, pray don't be backward on my account.'

Lashes hid the gleam in Lady Holford's black eyes. 'Sir Victor was at Harrow with the in-coming earl when he was no more than Theodore Sellon. They were friends for a time, though Sir Victor was of the opinion young Theodore was a rake in the making before ever his intrigue with the wife of a divine became known. It was *that*, of course, which resulted in his being thrust out of Oxford. And it was being sent as aide to a merchant adventurer that caused him to be in Cairo when the Ottoman Turks briefly

48

occupied it in '86. But did you know that during that troubled time Theodore saved the life of a native Egyptian? And that was how he acquired a wife, because soon after he married the man's daughter. Which must mean that the earl's wife is a — a *paynim*. Unfortunately, Sir Victor's correspondence with him fell into abeyance and he could tell me no more.'

'How romantic it all sounds!' breathed Melissa, agog. 'Just imagine if the new countess comes veiled in black from head to heels, as I've read Egyptian women do!'

'One must hope she will be the *only* wife,' sighed the baroness pleasurably. 'I believe as many as *four* are countenanced in Egypt. How should we address them? And just think what a tribe of children there may be! And the earl no more than two and fifty, so possibly more to come!'

Being baited with her worst fears was having visible effect on the dowager, Kezia saw with concern. The withered skin had stretched tight over jaw and cheekbone and two hectic spots of colour gave clear signals of stress. Though the dowager was still capable of dealing adequately with Lady Holford, the effort would, undoubtedly, take further toll.

Deliberately drawing the baroness's fire to

herself, Kezia said, 'I think matters may not be so bad. The Egyptians have preferred generally to absorb their invaders rather than resist them, with the result that they have been influenced by many different cultures. More than one religion favouring monogamy has taken root in the country, including Christianity, so there is every reason to hope the earl is both monogamous and Christian.'

Astonished indignation that *Aston* should not only volunteer speech but also a contradictory opinion, held the baroness silent just long enough for the dowager to seize opportunity and say acidly, 'At least, if there is a number of children the succession should be adequately ensured.' She rose to her feet as she spoke signifying the end of the meal and obliging Sophia to abandon her unfinished grapes. The dining-room was vacated in a silence as deep as it had been entered.

By the time they reached the Lily Room, Lady Holford had reflected on the foolishness of having indulged her natural inclinations. Before she could attempt repair of the damage done however, the dowager, settling into her chair, said pointedly, 'Now that I am restored to health, Cynthia, you must not allow me to detain you beyond tomorrow. Obliging as your visit has been, you will be anxious to return to Queenswood and your own affairs. I would not for the world keep you from them longer.'

Almost breathless with indignation, Lady Holford began, 'Why as to that, Countess — '

The rest of the sentence was lost as the door opened wide and Sopworth announced sonorously, '*The Earl of Emmington, your ladyship* . . . '

4

Five pairs of eyes turned to the man who now entered and a tense, astonished stillness descended on the room.

Kezia's mind reeled with disbelief. *This was not the 52-year-old man expected: this was the gypsy of her afternoon encounter!* It could not be — yet it was!

But how could one man be so differently both? It was not just the obvious differences of neatly trimmed hair and clothes proper to a gentleman: gone altogether was the sly, menacing affability of the gypsy, in all outwards showing this man was patrician, with a presence that radiated authority — a cool, subtle but unremitting authority. Just by entering the room he seemed to take command of it.

Yet the sun-browned face, lit by those singular green eyes now surveying the room's occupants with such dispassionate interest, was so much the gypsy's as to make Kezia close her own eyes momentarily on a surge of unwelcome memory. When she opened them to look again, it was in the foolish hope of finding herself mistaken. Surely the gypsy had been a younger man than this? And surely the mind that had chiselled such resolute lines into the face before her, that had graven a hint of cruelty into the line of the shapely mouth, must have had a longer, deeper, harsher experience of life than had the Romany's?

The stranger's polite bow served to wake the women from the trance into which they had fallen and they rose to their feet almost as one.

In a tone of formidable scepticism, the dowager countess spoke. 'Can you be that same Theodore Sellon who went into Egypt in '86 and from whom I was in receipt of a letter decidedly more than a year ago? I think not!'

Something flickered across the stranger's face, gleamed in the green eyes. Untroubled by the doubt expressed, he advanced towards the dowager and bowed again.

'You, madam, must be the Dowager Countess of Emmington. *I* am Lucius Sellon. Theodore was my father's name. He was a sick man when he wrote to you — had been so for a number of years. For all that, his death, just six weeks later, was unexpected. It has been the cause of delay and difficulty aggravated by the fact that Egypt is a troubled country where the safe sending and receiving of letters is not to be relied on. If, however, you have doubt of my being legitimately the ninth Earl of Emmington, your lawyers, Bursey and Garth of London, will confirm my rightful claim.'

Such a show of aristocratic self-assurance! Kezia thought indignantly. It would not be difficult to believe he had been reared from birth to occupy high position and that a certain shabby gypsy had never existed! For a brief moment she wondered if he could be an impostor, but common sense told her how unlikely it was that a man could walk into an earldom without proper proofs of his identity. Earl or not, his behaviour this afternoon promised an uncomfortable degree of awkwardness when he recognized her, and her annoyance deepened.

Yielding as much to his manner as to his words, the dowager said stiffly, 'If it is as you tell me, pray accept my condolences for your father's death. I regret that you find your house so much occupied. Had notice of your arrival preceded you, it would not be so. Be sure the place will be made your own tomorrow.'

His lordship waved a careless hand. 'It is no matter for concern, Countess. Will you not now make me known to your company?'

The introductions ended with, 'My companion, Miss Aston.'

Curtsying perfunctorily, it added to Kezia's vexation to know she was blushing.

'Miss Aston . . . ' the earl acknowledged, no hint of a gypsy lilt in his deep-toned voice.

She had been careful to keep her gaze lowered, but now, against all intention, it flew up to meet his. There was no recognition in the green and brilliant eyes. How could he not recognize her! In some way, it seemed to add insult to some obscure injury, and for a moment her eyes blazed back at him. But he was already turning away and at once there was a general movement to be seated.

With no need to enter the conversation, Kezia had time to think over the past moments. He *must* have recognized her, and that being so, she had reason to be grateful that he had not done so openly. What a stream of tiresome questions would have followed any mention of an earlier meeting! What capital Lady Holford would have made from it! Very probably, anticipating some such inquisition, his lordship had acted in self-defence.

If their earlier meeting had not so shaken her, the resentment she felt might not have had so much depth and her sense of humour would not have deserted her so completely, she thought. But would this upstart gypsy-lord have gone so far as to kiss her if the woodsman's wagon had not chanced to rumble out of the woods just when it did? Had chance alone saved her from even greater embarrassment?

She slid a baleful glance towards the source of her annoyance. There he sat, entirely at ease, the centre of everyone's attention, the supple grace and power of his figure as evident in repose as in movement, and, to judge by the gleam in Lady Holford's black eyes and her elder daughter's avid gaze, a lodestone of attraction to other women, if not to her. Even young Melissa looked entranced.

Lady Holford's voice broke in on her thoughts, saying, 'How strange you must find it to be here, Lord Emmington, after having lived all your life in Egypt. And how astonishing that you have such a command of English!'

'English is not unknown in Egypt and was in common use between my parents,' she was told levelly.

The baroness showed surprise. 'Oh! Was your *mother* English, then?'

'My mother was — and is — Egyptian. Perhaps, though, I should tell you I was at

56

school and university in this country.'

'Indeed! I had not heard that.'

'No, Baroness. How should you?'

Undaunted, Lady Holford pursued, 'And may we hope to meet a countess?'

'If you are prepared to wait some time for the fulfilment of your hope.'

This reply, smooth, smiling, and cryptic, left the baroness uncertain whether the earl had a wife (or even wives), or whether he was, more usefully, a bachelor. In either case, he remained a valuable connection and she went on to inform his lordship, 'You will wish for acquaintance, no doubt. You must allow us the pleasure of welcoming you to Queenswood before too long.'

'You are most kind.' Lord Emmington inclined his head in princely acknowledgment, but left it unclear whether or not he intended to avail himself of the invitation.

It astonished Kezia that Lady Holford, insensitive though she was, did not perceive how misplaced was the patronage implicit in everything she said. It seemed dazzlingly clear to herself that Lucius Sellon would not consider he needed help from anyone, socially or otherwise. Such ease and confidence as he was displaying carried no hint of his being impressed either by his elevation to the peerage or by the value of his inheritance.

Unawed by the first, she thought, and fully prepared to be master of the other . . . How would Emmington and its people fare in his hands?

That thought switched her attention to the unnaturally silent dowager with an anxiety that was immediately increased by a striking clock reminding her of the limit Dr Powlett had set on his patient's time downstairs. More than two hours had passed and strain was visible in her face. Lucius Sellon's unheralded arrival must have upset her all the more because of her weakened state, but the dowager would never willingly admit to weakness, and Lady Holford, pursuing her own ends, would never notice. Quietly, Kezia rose from her chair.

She had hoped simply to whisper a reminder in the dowager's ear without drawing too much attention, but the baroness destroyed this hope by suspending what she was saying in mid-flow and glaring pointedly at her. All other eyes were at once centred on her and, by ill-chance, Kezia found her own gaze trapped by Lord Emmington's.

His slightly raised brows expressed only polite enquiry but because, to her, everything about him was suspect, she was provoked into saying with gritty starkness, 'I feel obliged to remind the countess that she has already greatly exceeded the two-hour limit her physician set on this her first coming downstairs after severe illness.'

She heard the dowager's hissing intake of breath, could guess the expressions worn by the Holfords.

'*Miss Aston forgets herself* — ' began the dowager in a tone of icy reprobation.

But Lord Emmington was already up and crossing the room with fluid grace. Looking down into the proud, unyielding old face, he said, 'I can only be grateful to Miss Aston for allowing me to know you have been ill. To keep you from your rest and set back your recovery at the beginning of our acquaintance would be the poorest way to recommend myself to you and your friends. My baggage is at the Sellon Arms where I propose both to sup and to lie this night. I shall hope to see you none the worse when I come again tomorrow.'

Also rising to her feet, the dowager said austerely, 'It is quite improper that the Earl of Emmington should not be received into his own house at whatever hour he comes. I cannot be the cause of such — '

'I shall not stay to dispute it with you, Countess.' The earl bowed over her hand, carried it to his lips, then turned to take leave of the rest of the company collectively.

Briefly, his eyes rested on Kezia, a bright, unhallowed light in their depths, and then he was gone from the room.

At once a storm burst about Kezia.

'How dared you take so much upon yourself, miss! Ordering a man of rank from his own house!' the dowager fumed.

'Indeed, it was not meant so, ma'am.'

'How else it should be described I cannot think!'

'So objectionably officious and coming from whom it might be least expected,' Lady Holford happily contributed.

The evening had taken heavy toll of the dowager both physically and mentally. Ragged with nerves, she rounded on the baroness. 'I am not yet in need of help in ruling my household, Cynthia! I bid you all goodnight. Miss Aston, your arm!'

The stairs were climbed slowly, and in glacial silence. At the door of the dowager's bedroom where Rudge waited in fidgeting concern, Kezia was dismissed with an abrupt, 'I shall have more to say to you tomorrow, miss.'

Glad as Kezia was to reach her own room, tonight its firelit comfort was unnoticed. Understanding the several stresses the day had laid on the countess, she was not unduly troubled by the old lady's scolding. Her preoccupation was with the quite unexpected mischief the long-awaited earl's coming had brought her. Her anticipation of the event had never held more than mild interest and a readiness to be amused: that it could have any appreciable effect on herself had never occurred to her. But then, who could have foreseen the arrival of such a *mountebank* — one who had acted gypsy and earl so convincingly she could readily believe him to be a member of a group of strolling players!

Making an effort to control the continuing riot of her thoughts, she bade herself view what had happened with less heat. So the man had made a fool of her and was now probably laughing at her . . . annoying though it was, why gratify him by allowing it to disturb her? Tomorrow she and the dowager would remove to the Dower House and thereafter she was unlikely to see very much of Lucius Sellon, ninth Earl of Emmington and sometime gypsy.

It was cold comfort: nor did she find it any great aid towards promoting sleep after she had climbed into bed.

5

Kezia woke next morning prepared to take a calmer view of the previous day's events.

If Lord Emmington chose to ignore their hill-top meeting, it was probably better so. With a little luck, she might not even meet with him again before she and the dowager removed to the Dower House . . .

About to go down to breakfast, she found Rudge at her door to report that the dowager was awake.

'On the fret half the night, too, for all the the doctor's draught I gave her,' said the abigail worriedly. 'One moment intent on being up and away to the Dower House and next saying she will not survive the removal a month.'

Kezia nodded understanding. 'Ring for her chocolate, Nancy,' she said. 'She will feel better if she takes some breakfast.'

Approaching the dowager's bed with its handsome blue and gold needlework hanging, Kezia saw at once that the old lady's eyes were fever-bright and there were two spots of hectic colour on her withered cheeks.

'Such a scramble as everything is in!' the

thin, complaining voice began at once. 'No word from Bursey and Garth to warn me that Emmington was come and by their negligence I am found in occupation of his lordship's house! As for *you*, miss! — making all so much worse by such gratuitous impertinen — ' Her voice cracked on the last word and she began to cough in a dry, painful way.

Kezia hurried to raise her from her pillows and hold a glass of water to her lips. The spasm past, the dowager threw aside the bedcovers, saying peevishly, 'I must remove from this house. Call Rudge to me.' She jerked herself upright, but fell back with a gasp, breathing fast, her eyelids fluttering.

Drawing the covers back into place, Kezia laid her fingers to a wrist and found the pulse weak and hurried.

'I beg you calm yourself, ma'am,' she urged. 'You cannot leave your bed today without making yourself thoroughly ill again. Lord Emmington will have no wish to be the cause of that. Nor, if he wishes for credit with his neighbours, will he want to be seen hurrying a sick woman from the house the moment he arrives.'

The thought slid pleasantly home. The dowager's breathing steadied and after a moment, with an air of conscious suffering, she mourned weakly, 'I have lived too long . . . become a burden to all! You must meet with Emmington at the earliest moment and offer my apologies. Inform him that only my body's weakness compels my continued presence in his house but that it shall not be for long.'

Rudge came in with the chocolate then, and having seen the dowager accept a cupful with only a token demur, Kezia went downstairs.

Having hoped to escape to the Dower House without further meeting with Lord Emmington, it was disquieting to have to actually seek him out. How very soon that meeting might take place she learned on reaching the hall. There, she found Sopworth supervising the disposal of a number of travelling boxes being carried in by the lesser servants.

The boxes were as new as the clothes worn by his lordship the previous evening, Kezia observed. It reminded her of the need to exercise tolerance towards a man newly ennobled and made rich. His lordship was to follow his baggage in about an hour's time, Sopworth told her when she mentioned her need to speak to the earl as soon as was convenient to him. Entering the breakfast-parlour, Kezia hoped that a cup or two of coffee would supply the stiffening of which she felt in need.

Melissa Holford was already at table and carefully polite 'good-mornings' were exchanged. There was silence for a time, though Melissa's bright blue eyes observed Kezia's meagre liquid breakfast with interest.

Recently released from the schoolroom, and inheriting buoyant good-nature from her father, she was further blessed with a natural confidence and a goodly portion of determination. Having found little in common with her older sister, from an early age she had allied herself with her brothers and absorbed more of their independence than her family yet realized.

Her inclination to be friendly towards Kezia had been given little opportunity for expression so far but now, she remarked airily, 'The devil was in it last night, wouldn't you say, Miss Aston?'

Startled, Kezia looked up to meet the young girl's mischievous gaze. She smiled wryly. 'I must agree. Though perhaps I would not express it quite so.'

Melissa laughed. 'Well, my brother Jeremy would say it was 'dashed apt!' ' She straightened in her chair, looked down her pretty little nose and in fair imitation of her sister, intoned, ' '*Quelle confusion!*

Si vexant!' Now *that* is to take Sophy for a model.'

She had caught Miss Holford's supercilious voice and expression so exactly Kezia had difficulty stifling her amusement. Shaking her head, she said, 'You shouldn't, you know. It isn't at all the thing to mimic your sister. It isn't kind.'

'Well, nor is Sophy,' Melissa returned irrepressibly. 'But didn't it set us all about when the new earl turned out not to be the one expected? And then he was so tremendously grand in his manner I think even Great-aunt Emmington was nearly overpowered. Still, you well-nigh equalled him when you said '*I feel obliged to remind the countess that she has already greatly exceeded . . .* ' et cetera . . . '

Kezia stared in horror at the talented young mimic before her. 'Did I really sound like that?'

Melissa nodded, her eyes dancing.

It had been nervousness combining with annoyance at finding herself forced to say aloud what had been intended for the dowager's ear alone. But how had his lordship regarded it? The question did nothing to make her coming interview with him easier to face.

'Well . . . ' Melissa rose to her feet — 'pray

excuse me, but I must attend Mama. We are off this morning because we have no wish to begin at the wrong end with his high-and-mightiness, though I cannot think we shall actually be gone before Mama has further word with him. Our baggage was all loaded last night, causing a great bustle, as you may guess.' She held out her hand to Kezia, saying more seriously, 'I go now to take leave of my great-aunt, but I should like to say goodbye to you here, Miss Aston. Later it may be less easy.' She grimaced. 'I expect you have found us all a bit *much*! I for one am sorry for it.'

Taking her hand, Kezia said, 'You have nothing with which to reproach yourself. I hope you will have a safe and comfortable journey.'

'Oh, Mama will see to *that*!' the imp replied cheerfully. 'I just wish it will not be too tediously slow!'

Leaving the breakfast parlour soon after Melissa, Kezia again met Sopworth who told her that a parcel of books, newly come from the dowager's London bookseller, awaited her attention on the table in the library.

Entering that room, she found scissors laid ready to hand beside the package.

String and paper removed, she checked the contents against what she knew to have been ordered. She was glancing through Lord Byron's *Corsair* published the previous year but new to her, when Harry Osborne entered the room.

'Sopworth told me you were here,' he said with his engaging smile. 'I came to see how you are bearing up under the shock of the earl's sudden arrival in our midst. No doubt the Countess was set all about to find he is not the man expected.'

'It is extraordinary how much he has managed to surprise us all when we have waited so long for his coming,' Kezia agreed, her tone tart.

Harry nodded. 'For me, his coming was particularly ill-timed. My aunt's Westerham friends persuaded us to remain with them far longer than was intended, so it was not until this morning I learned Lord Emmington had summoned me to attend him at the Sellon Arms. I fear I cannot have made the best start with the gentleman.'

'Well, it will be wonderful indeed if he does not soon discover how much is owed to you for your care of his properties!' Kezia declared warmly.

Harry smiled. 'Perhaps I should ask him to apply to you for a recommendation . . . Tell me, what sort of man do you judge him to be?'

Struggling with memory of her two diverse encounters with the new earl, Kezia was slow to answer, and Harry exclaimed, 'Heavens! You make me fear the worst!'

'N-no . . . ' The word wavered. 'Impossible to say what like he is. We were all so fluttered by his arrival, we — I — ' She broke off, ending lamely, 'He has a very grand manner.'

'I begin to wish I had not asked,' Harry said, halfway between real and mock apprehension. 'Clearly you have formed no golden opinion of him.'

'Oh, pray do not be influenced by me. There has not been time to make sensible judgement of the man,' she urged guiltily.

'Then I shall continue to hope.' He smiled and shrugged the subject aside, saying lightly, 'Yesterday was an eventful day in several ways. Sopworth tells me you encountered a gypsy near the Dower House. Nothing there appears to have been disturbed, so you must have frightened him away before he could get into real villainy. I hope the rogue offered you no insolence?'

To Kezia's annoyance, she felt herself colour. 'Oh, no,' she told him untruthfully. Anxious to leave the matter she held out the small volume she held. 'Have you met with Lord Byron's *Corsair*? It has only just come my way.'

Harry looked a little puzzled by the swift change and she babbled on, 'Though Lord Byron is said to be so disreputable, I have been told his friends hold him in high esteem for his kindness and generosity. How difficult it is to know the truth! One of the countess's correspondents reports that his marriage is already foundering though not yet out of its honeymoon year and Lady Byron is in an interesting condition. How sad if it is so!' Nervously, she opened the book. 'Do look at this illustration. The artist appears bent on outdoing his lordship's invention. Is it not absurd?'

Harry's head was close to hers and both were laughing when the door, which stood ajar, was pushed wider and Lord Emmington walked into the room. Startled, they almost jumped apart.

The earl's green gaze went in sharp interrogation from one to the other. Kezia, making her curtsy, was annoyed to find herself blushing again.

A brief inclination of the head acknowledged them both, and as Harry straightened from his bow, his lordship said crisply, 'Osborne? How do you do. Will you be so good as to wait elsewhere for me. I understand Miss Aston has first claim on my attention.'

What a gift the man had for unexpected appearances! Kezia thought crossly as the door closed on Harry and was unhappily aware of being still unready for the tete-a-tete ahead of her.

'Will you not sit, Miss Aston?' his lordship invited, in a tone that did nothing to set her at ease.

Unlocking her tongue with an effort, she said, 'Thank you, no, sir. I do not mean to detain you. I am here only to convey the countess's apologies. Regrettably, she finds herself too unwell to leave her bed today but is anxious that you should believe she will not delay her removal to the Dower House a moment longer than necessary.'

Lord Emmington was disappointed. He had assumed that she wished to speak to him about their hill-top meeting, and with slightly wayward amusement, he had looked forward to discovering how she would broach the subject. Finding the glowing Diana of that meeting was an inmate of his new home had been a surprise, though he had quickly realized that he might have supposed she lived somewhere on the estate.

In teasing her as he had, he was aware of having stepped back in time, of having reverted to the light-hearted Lucius Sellon of his student days. Days before change had come to him with a heavy burden of responsibility and the everyday dangers of simply living through the perilous intrigues always rife in Egypt. Perhaps the freer air of England had gone to his head . . .

But he had caught a note in Miss Aston's voice that was unlike any directed towards him in a long time. He had travelled sufficiently to be tolerant of meeting women with uncovered faces who were not members of his own family; even so, he found he was not always prepared for a woman daring to raise her eyes to a man's face and allow her thoughts to show. At this moment, Miss Aston's very beautiful grey eyes were not only meeting his but making no secret of their owner's disapprobation. His amusement fled.

Noting the sudden hardening of his expression, Kezia mistook the cause and felt impelled to enlarge upon the dowager's reasons for remaining where she was.

'The countess is old and has been very ill,' she said stiffly. 'Indeed, it is not long since her life was despaired of. She has, too, long been in dread of leaving this house which has been her home for so many years. Your arrival without notice was a considerable shock for all that she knew you must come at some time.'

She had only stated the facts, but even in her own ears her words suddenly took on the character of an accusation. She had the strongest sense of having mismanaged something that should have been perfectly simple. If only he did not have such an extraordinarily disturbing effect on her! That she had angered him was obvious. The eyes looking at her were cold and hard. She shivered, feeling threatened.

Lucius, too, had thought he was accused. For once the anger that jolted through him was not immediately clamped under the control of his cool mind. What was the matter with this damnably impertinent young woman! By God, she should learn her place! Off balance, he made an unworthy descent into sarcasm.

'I see you anticipate my urgent wish to throw the countess instantly out of doors. How am I to forego the pleasure? After all, we are no more than distantly related — and even that only by marriage! But you may take some comfort, Miss Aston, from the fact that I shall be too much occupied to attend to it immediately.'

The venomous words spoken, he was appalled by them — but even more appalled that she had broken his control and reduced him to vulgarity.

Kezia stared at him. Had she deserved so much? The colour that had first flushed her face drained away leaving her unnaturally pale. Pride kept her head high. In a voice tight with strain, she said, 'If what I have said has given offence, I apologize. It was not intended. I meant only to explain the countess's indisposition.'

If more was needed it was beyond her power to say it. Her throat closed and, infuriatingly, she found herself close to tears. She could not bear for him to witness her weakness, and she turned towards the door.

Furious with himself but even more so with her, Lucius was there to open it. Looking down at her, his expression unrelenting, he said, 'Will you be so good as to convey my regrets to the countess for her relapse. Tell her, if you please, that now is not the time to concern herself with thoughts of removal. I shall hope to offer my reassurances in person when she is well enough to receive me.'

A gracious message for the dowager but no acknowledgment of her own apology. But why should she have expected it? What was she in his lordship's eyes but an unimportant underling? Her tears dried. Inclining her head, she murmured a queenly 'Thank you', and passed through into the hall.

Mounting the stairs, it seemed to her that she could still feel the dark force of his anger and small tremors of distress continued to run through her. Reaching the upper gallery, she stood for a moment before entering the dowager's room. How silly to allow herself to be so shaken by a man's scowl and unmannerly words . . . a man moreover, who was probably doing no more than ape what he thought were the manners of the great!

But as her hand grasped the latch of the dowager's bedroom door, she was praying earnestly that it would not be many days before the countess was well enough to go to the Dower House.

Because she did not think she could long endure living in close proximity to Emmington's new lord and master . . .

6

Receiving the earl's message from Kezia with satisfaction, the dowager then remarked austerely, 'I trust you made use of opportunity to offer Emmington an apology for having thrust yourself forward as you did last night?'

That Kezia had not was evident and aroused instant irritation.

'Really, girl! To be so remiss! Scarcely do I begin to come about from having endured Cynthia Holford's goodbyes than I have another cause for vexation!' She glared fiercely at Kezia. 'You hold yourself altogether too high, and I recommend you to remember that what Sellon blood runs in your veins counts for nothing in the circumstances by which you came by it.' Reading a warning in Kezia's changed expression, she waved an imperious hand. 'You may leave me. I am too seriously displeased to be in want of your company this morning.'

The attack took Kezia by surprise. Until now they had jogged along evenly enough but suddenly it seemed they were back at the beginning. Closing the dowager's bedroom door behind her she had a sudden longing to be back at Putney where she had been valued both for herself and as a teacher. What value did she have here at Old Hall?

The ill-starred day had not finished with her. She was on her way to collect the books she had left in the library when voices rising from the hall told her the Holfords were just leaving. Pausing out of sight, she waited. Lady Holford's incisive tones rose clearly as she again pressed Lord Emmington to make an early visit to Queenswood. His lordship's replies were briefly courteous but he made no commitment and he said nothing to delay the baroness's going.

When it seemed to Kezia that everyone had passed out of the house she began her descent of the stairs. But the baroness and Lord Emmington must have paused at the threshold for now she heard Lady Holford say in a voice pregnant with significance, 'My Lord, I cannot go from here without saying a word to put you on your guard . . . Recently, the countess has made a most unsuitable choice of companion as you will have observed last night. There is a strange reticence on both sides as to her background. I fear the young woman wields a mischievous — possibly even a sinister — influence on a woman of advanced age. With the fortune in jewels the countess keeps so carelessly about

77

her . . . well, I think I need say no more.'

'Indeed, you need not,' Lord Emmington agreed sparingly.

Wicked woman to pour out such poison! Kezia thought indignantly. Heaven knew, his lordship was already sufficiently intent on thinking ill of her without being given additional cause! Hurrying back to her room, she roamed angrily about it until, feeling the need of greater space, she changed into outdoor clothes and going downstairs by one of the lesser stairways, went out by a side door.

Heedless of time, she walked through the shrubberies trying to subdue her wrathful feelings. For the countess's sake she had endured the annoyances Lady Holford and her elder daughter had inflicted on her in the past week. Her reward was to have a legacy of distrust bequeathed her! Even removing to the Dower House could not restore her peace of mind.

She turned back to look at the house. The day's cold light did nothing to diminish its romantic beauty, but how different was the life she lived in it from the golden girlhood her mother had described to her! She could have little regret in leaving it. The thought brought her to a full stop. To leave under a cloud? To run away? *She would not!*

Kezia Aston was not to be driven off by an ill-disposed woman's spite! She would stay to meet what came and, if necessary, Lord Emmington should learn her mettle!

It was past noon when she re-entered the house and having neatened her appearance, she went to see if the dowager's disgruntled mood had passed. The old lady was sitting up in bed, looking frail, but radiating triumph.

'Emmington has not long gone from me,' she announced the moment Kezia entered, all previous disaccord conveniently forgotten. 'He stayed a full half-hour and, with the greatest civility, entreated me to continue to regard Old Hall as my fixed home. Furthermore, he asked as a favour that I should remain its chatelaine and in the kindest way, observed that it was only proper that my comfort and welfare should be under his care and surveillance.'

Aglow with pleasure at being released from her dread of removing to the Dower House, she pronounced complacently, 'He shapes better than I have ever dared hope and may yet prove worthy of his high destiny.'

Kezia thought Lucius Sellon's use of the phrase *under his care and surveillance* nothing less than ominous. She suspected that it was towards the dowager's companion his surveillance would be directed. It seemed to her that from a bad beginning, worse was promised.

* * *

To Kezia's relief, however, before the countess was well enough to leave her bed again, his lordship rode away with Harry to make a tour of Emmington possessions in the nearer counties before winter made travelling unpleasant if not impossible. Besides the farms, woodlands and hop fields, there were breweries, a gunpowder mill, chalk and clay pits, and a prosperous fishing village to be visited: the travellers were unlikely to be seen again under a month.

With the threat of the Dower House removed, the dowager's health and temper improved together and life at Old Hall resumed its former uneventful pattern. There was, however, one event of note for Kezia: the beginning of the second week of the earl's absence saw the arrival of Hebe, the pretty little mare from the Hombury stables which Harry had commissioned the head groom, Cossick, to buy in his absence. Whatever the dowager's motive had been in ordering the mount for her use, Kezia could not be other than truly grateful for the delight Hebe gave her from their first meeting.

As the quiet days passed, it was easy for her to forget that Lord Emmington would return. So when one evening nearly four weeks later, she looked up from the *gâteau des châtaignes* she was eating to see him entering the dining-room, she saw him as though he were a stranger. Though no bustle of arrival had been heard, he was already in evening dress, the stark black and white giving emphasis to the dramatic quality of his appearance. Beneath his brown skin, the bones of his face drew lines as positive as the intense black of his slightly waving hair. The hawkish outline added a strength to his looks that took them beyond mere handsomeness; else, she mused, the unexpected green of his eyes must surely be thought an over-plus. But even beyond his looks, what would mark him out in any company was his air of purposeful command.

It was then that recollection's admonitory finger touched her. This was Lucius Sellon, Earl of Emmington, who had taken her in hearty dislike and had it in his power to make life decidedly uncomfortable for her. It had been easy to sink back into peace during the past weeks: in his lordship's formidable presence, that peace had little substance.

Hastily, she looked away, quite unconscious that her sigh, though not audible was visible, and that her expression was that of someone braced to endure.

7

That sigh and that look undid most of the benefit three and half weeks' separation from Miss Aston's provoking presence had bestowed on Lucius.

She had intruded on his thoughts with disturbing frequency during his recent travels, his recollection of their meeting in the library renewing an irritation uncomfortably harnessed to guilt for his heavy-handed response to her. Time and harsh experience had educated him in the need to control an impatient temper: to have that control wrecked in a moment by the tone of a young woman's voice, the look in her eyes, bit deep into his pride. His early years in England and his Western education made for some ease in adjusting to English culture, but not without an occasional sense of dislocation, particularly in regard to the freedom allowed English women.

Miss Aston was a very particular case, scraping raw male sensitivities he had not known he possessed. He had not missed the way her smile faded when he entered the dining-room, or the way the soft curve of her lips had set so firmly. He suspected she sat in judgement on him. Miss Aston, he thought grimly, might be judged to be wanting in a proper humility! He had long deplored the iniquities under which women suffered in Egypt, but it would do *her* no harm to be transported to that country for a time and discover that there, as a woman, she was simply an item of property whose value did not equal that of a good horse or camel. Moreover, she would be considered less able than either beast to form an opinion — and certainly less entitled to have one!

He had already dined, Lucius told the dowager, sitting down at the table, but he would take a glass of wine while the countess finished her meal. After a lordly nod at Miss Aston, he gave his attention exclusively to the dowager but found to his annoyance, his awareness of Miss Aston's presence increased with every minute that passed.

Abandoning her pudding in favour of what remained of her wine, Kezia tried to hide her interest in Lord Emmington's answers to the dowager's many questions. It was obvious that he had been a keen and intelligent observer during his tour. Surprising her, his praise of those tenants and employees achieving good results was generous and where he thought there was room for improvement he seemed to have shrewd ideas already forming. With a cynicism unusual to her, Kezia wondered if this merely pointed to an ingrained clutch-fistedness, a determination to wring as much as possible from what he owned with little consideration for the people under his hand. Recalling his appearance when she had first seen him, she questioned his knowledge of what was due from *him* to those who were now his dependents.

It did not escape her that she was being excluded from his lordship's notice. She guessed he was attempting to teach her her place and her feelings divided between pique and amusement. Very well, if a self-effacing, self-abasing female slave was what he looked for, she would, she decided, present him with the personification of conscious insignificance. In Lord Emmington's presence, she would do what Shylock had disdained to do 'bend low . . . with bated breath and whispering humbleness . . . '

She could not know that her inward laughter chimed loudly on a mental ear grown peculiarly aware; nor what further and considerable inroad it made upon Lord Emmington's goodwill towards her.

★ ★ ★

Delighted to find Harry waiting at the stables for her next morning, Kezia greeted him gaily. 'Harry! How noble of you after nearly a month in the saddle! Are you not heartily sick of sitting a horse?'

Harry laughed. 'Not so. I am now so hardened to it I shall find difficulty in adjusting to another way of life. But what I am anxious to know is how you and your mount agree?'

'Oh, Hebe is impossible to fault! I don't think a sweeter-tempered mare exists, or one more comfortably paced. I cannot thank you enough for such a clever choice.'

'That was largely a matter of the Hombury misfortunes being our good luck. But I'm glad you like her. Now, which way shall we ride?'

Kezia having suggested the green gallops, they set off at a companionable walk. The November morning was pleasantly crisp with a light frost stiffening the grass and a red sun just beginning to edge up into the sky beyond the furthest trees. Conversation naturally turned towards the expedition from which Harry had just returned and Kezia was surprised to discover Harry had taken a very favourable impression of his new employer.

'He was less foreign than I expected him

to be. Though there were moments . . . a particular one when a rather lively young woman interrupted her husband and his lordship looked — I hardly know how to describe his look, but it was as though he expected the man to strike the woman and he was preparing to intervene. There were times, too, when he took on an air of such *absoluteness* I felt as though I were in the presence of a pharaoh.'

Kezia's lip curled a little. 'Heaven-born . . . king of kings?'

Harry nodded smiling agreement. 'Just that! To the point of suspecting that if I really displeased him, I might be one of the unlucky slaves chosen to be buried alive under the next pyramid.'

He caught her look of ready belief and laughed. 'Don't worry, as yet there are none planned for. Speaking sensibly, I found him generally a very pleasant companion and surprisingly knowledgeable about estate management. I think he will not demand any unreasonable changes . . . which will be a relief to our tenant farmers.' He looked at her shrewdly. 'I confess to liking him, but you, I think, were not so favourably impressed at first meeting and have hardly had time since to revise your opinion.'

Kezia murmured vaguely in reply, wondering

what Harry would say if she told him that Lord Emmington and the gypsy she had encountered were one man — wondering, too, why she did not tell him. But now they had reached the gallops where their mounts could be given their heads and the subject of the new Earl of Emmington could be abandoned.

★ ★ ★

It was the middle of the following week before Kezia and Harry could ride together again. A new moon had brought a spell of mild, damp weather and on this day a white mist shortened the view to a hundred yards. They intended this time to follow one of the broad rides through the extensive eastern woodlands, but barely had they entered among the trees when they were overtaken by Lord Emmington.

Because the mist had muffled the sound of his approach, his arrival startled them. After a brief greeting, he said, 'Sorry as I am to deprive you of your ride, Osborne, I must ask you to return to the house to meet Sir Joshua Rowland. He sent word of his intention to call to discuss a matter of access to water for some of his cottagers. It appears there is difficulty with a spring on his land and the nearest alternative supply of water is a stream on Emmington land. You will know best what accommodation can be made. Make my excuses for being absent and keep him entertained until my return.' He turned a cool, expressionless face towards Kezia. 'Miss Aston will, I hope, accept my company in place of yours.'

A lively instinct for self-preservation prompted Kezia to begin to turn her mare as she said hurriedly, 'I could not allow you to put yourself to so much trouble, sir. I shall return to the house with Mr Osborne.'

The iron grip suddenly laid on Hebe's bridle, brought the mare to a fidgeting stand. 'You will not be so unkind as to deprive me of the pleasure, I am sure.' Words and tone were smooth as cream but the green eyes fixed on her held a glittering determination that was far from reassuring. Harry, unable to see that look and unaware of Kezia's unease, was already pulling his mount round and a moment later the mist had closed on him.

Now they were alone, his lordship showed no haste to ride on but sat gazing at Kezia with a disagreeable little smile twisting his lips. 'Your reluctance to accept my escort is sadly unflattering, Miss Aston,' he observed silkily.

Something about him — a visible tension — warned her that this was a man in a temper. Though Kezia's conscience was not entirely easy, she could not believe that she was the cause. Since his return she had, as she had promised herself, shown him always a face of nunlike meekness, retiring from his near presence into any available shadow with a humility that skimmed the edge of outright parody. Her reverent curtsies and his stiff nods had been their only coin of exchange.

Warily now, her eyes modestly downcast, she murmured, 'I have no wish to inconvenience you, sir.'

So meek! So unassuming! So false! Lucius ground his teeth. He had no belief in the sudden eclipse of Miss Aston's personality. Her recent parade of slavish subservience had mocked the care with which he had ignored her and her guessed-at amusement had added an extra barb to the provocation. And then this morning, entering the stableyard at the moment she and Harry Osborne were riding out, he had heard her light-hearted laughter, seen the smiling, teasing look she gave his steward . . . Goaded, but without pausing to wonder why, he had set out in pursuit of the pair, abandoning his plan to ride for a brief while only before returning to meet Sir Joshua.

With no precise idea of what he intended towards Miss Aston even now, he spoke the first lofty words that presented themselves. 'It will admirably suit my convenience to have that discussion which is overdue between us. I suggest we dismount.'

Dismayed, Kezia glanced up at him again and found no more reassurance than she had before. To stand on solid earth might be preferable though, for she was all too much aware of what an intimidating picture his lordship made astride his horse. Man and beast shared a like aura of physical power and dark arrogant splendour.

She remembered witnessing the crow-black stallion's arrival: was, indeed, unlikely to forget the display of snorting irascibility he had provided as, with nostrils flaring, head tossing, he had been coaxed towards an unfamiliar stable. Faced with the very embodiment of power-charged intolerance, even Cossick, experienced head groom though he was, had not challenged the right of the quiet Egyptian attendant who accompanied the animal to keep sole charge.

Oh, that Lucius Sellon had a like keeper! she thought with a quiver of apprehension as she slipped to the ground and turned to face the stallion's rider.

8

The mist was thickening; now, even the nearer trees were beginning to fade behind its pale, damp veils. Kezia had an uneasy impression of being islanded with his lordship in a small and rapidly decreasing space.

Thinly smiling, Lucius saw there was little meekness visible in Miss Aston now. Head up, she stood with the skirt of her neat brown velvet riding-dress looped over one arm, small beads of moisture trapped among the hairs of her jaunty, cockaded beaver hat and pearled in the shining curls showing below its brim. The flush of colour in her cheeks had been deepened by the coolness of the morning air and even in the shadow of her hat, her eyes were lucent and lovely. Impatiently, he shrugged away his awareness of Miss Aston's charms. It was not the loveliness of her eyes that brought him here, he told himself, it was her falsity. In a voice harsher than he knew, he launched into speech again.

'Well, Miss Aston, let us come to it. You were critical, I think, of my failure to acknowledge a prior meeting between us when I first entered Emmington Old Hall. That being the case, I must suppose you lacking in imagination not to have seen what awkward and lengthy explanations would have been forced on us by the company we were in had I done so.'

Kezia stared. Was this why Lord Emmington had come galloping into the woods instead of sending a groom to recall Harry? Was this a punitive expedition? If so, she did not mean to be bullied, but with a clear memory of the first occasion she had felt the lash of his temper, she counselled herself to caution.

'At the time I was confused. Later, I saw things differently and was grateful,' she said quietly.

'Were you?' His disbelief was patent. 'Why then do I suspect that something has continued to rankle? Was it my playing the gypsy? As I remember it, you *thrust* the role on me.'

And how quickly he had taken advantage of it! She stiffened, colour burning in her cheeks. 'My mistake was a natural one. Your use of it was not . . . not kind.' Virtuously, she withheld the word *ungentlemanly*.

The little flicker of militancy in her eyes, however, was enough for Lucius. False again! By God, he'd have the truth from her yet! What particular truth he was seeking, he could not have said. His smile a deliberate offence, he taunted, 'You made the role irresistible. Are you so sensitive to a small piece of teasing that it is past forgetting?'

Recollection of how shaken she had been by the turmoil he had induced, swept away caution and she flashed back, 'It was a memorable performance!'

'Memorably received, as I recall.'

So he had known how she had felt! Her last remark had been a foolish indulgence, she knew, but yet had to fight against telling him plainly what she thought of him. Cold reason won the day with the warning that the sooner this meeting ended the better.

Lucius's intentions were unclear: what he was chiefly aware of was of being exhilaratingly awake and impatient to strike more sparks from the flint of Miss Aston's contumacy.

In his grandest manner, he said, 'Bear with me, Miss Aston, for I am little practised in having to account to others for what I do. Your own position — dependent on the goodwill of others — is rather different, I think. You should reflect on the unwisdom of continuing in the counterfeit role you have been playing lately.'

As soon as spoken, the words sounded unbearably pompous even to him. To make

94

things worse, it appeared clear that Miss Aston thought so, too. Far from looking in any way diminished, the set of her shapely mouth, the quirk of her eyebrows, conveyed a subtle scorn. Furious with himself, more furious with her, mischievous instinct handed him the means to wipe that look from her face as he added with smiling malice, 'As an actor, I think I showed a more convincing skill.'

'Oh, indeed, my lord! And made shabbier use of it!' she thrust back at him, all sensible intentions forgotten.

That stung his pride and he took an involuntary step towards her. 'You go too far!'

'Do I? As the gypsy, you meant to intimidate. Beyond that you . . . you — ' Impossible to finish that particular sentence! Hurriedly she substituted, 'Had you said who you were — '

'Oh, don't be foolish! If I had laid claim to an earldom just then, you would have added fear of dealing with a Bedlamite to the alarm roused in you by the rest!' He halted there. That had sounded uncomfortably like an admission and a defence. It was not for *him* to excuse himself. And then Baroness Holford's warning regarding the dowager's companion crawled obligingly into his mind.

'But let us consider *you*, Miss Aston. Are you all you seem — or wish to seem? Is there no mystery about you warranting investigation?'

Kezia was silenced.

Lucius saw the shadow of uncertainty darken her eyes and his own narrowed sharply. With rather more objectivity, he said, 'You came to Old Hall some four months ago, and before that you were employed as a teacher at a school in Putney . . . a very young teacher, but one who was paid a salary, I imagine.'

'Yes, of course.'

'Salaried employment then, that you gave up for a position which — as yet — has paid you nothing. Or, at least, nothing that is shown in the accounting books of either house or estate.' He took another step towards her, looming over her, as much menace in that as in his next, coldly incisive words. 'I am interested to know, Miss Aston, why you should surrender independence and — young as you are — be content to share the dull, retired life of a very old woman. I cannot believe the comforts of Old Hall, even taken with the purchase of a mare for your use, can truly compensate you for the tedium you must suffer.'

Even with his suspicion coiling about her

like a fowler's net, she had a moment's wonder that he should have grasped such trifling details of his household affairs so soon. But her thoughts switched quickly to the difficulty of answering him without breaking her promise not to reveal her connection to the Sellons. As head of the household, he had the right to question her background and to be given information. Uneasily, she said, 'I came to Emmington at the countess's invitation. It was — is — a temporary scheme. The question of salary has not arisen.'

'Oh, then that shall be rectified. The countess's former companion received forty pounds a year, paid quarterly. If you are to continue, I will see that you are remunerated at the same rate.'

If she was to continue . . . *That*, and his insistence on payment, brayed aloud his intention to demean. The knowledge that as much Sellon blood flowed in her veins as in his brought her head up a little further. Consciously and unconsciously, it was the daughter of Lady Charlotte Sellon who said with cool, unfeigned dignity, 'The matter is between the countess and myself. I beg you will not concern yourself with it, sir. All my needs are met.'

Her look, her tone, her stance, gave him for one disagreeable moment, a picture of

Lord Emmington stooping to put Miss Aston in her place. Then rage like a fireball surged through him uniting the several smaller fires that had been steadily gathering heat. Snarlingly, he flung at her, 'In my household, service receives payment. You are not the countess's guest. You render service. You fetch and carry. For that you will be paid. So do not play off your pretensions on *me*!'

She drew in a small, hissing breath. 'I . . . will . . . *not* . . . accept!.'

'How then, I wonder, are you rewarding yourself!'

Her heart had begun to bucket so fiercely as to make her feel sick. *Why* was the man so determined to bring her low? Ghost-white now, she managed to say with only the slightest tremble in her voice, 'You have said enough, sir. I will arrange my going with the countess.'

Now, when she had accepted defeat, was the time for generosity. But the devil riding Lucius drove him on beyond all reason. He reached out to grasp her arms.

'*You* will arrange! It is *my* roof that shelters you. It is *I* who will decide when you leave. And if I say you go today — go you will! I am not deceived by the fine airs you parade.'

His grip was painful, but the insult of being so held acted to contain her panic. Her gaze came back to his and with icy clarity she said, 'Sir, you are insufferable!'

The last vestige of temperate thought left Lucius and he shook her. 'But what are *you*, Miss Aston, *what are you?*'

With the courage of the damned, Kezia gave a small, choking laugh and, shrugging contemptuous shoulders, flung back disastrously, 'What I am *not* is a slave to be bullied. You should remember, my lord, that you are no longer in Egypt.'

His face bleached queerly under the fading gold of his skin. There was a moment of deadly stillness in which she almost expected his hands to fasten on her throat. Instead, with the speed of a striking snake, she was jerked into his arms, her own held fast to her sides, and his mouth descended on hers in vengeful assault.

When the first cataleptic moments of shock had passed, she tried to wrench herself out of his grasp and found that against his iron strength her utmost effort was humiliatingly ineffective. Tears of outrage filled her eyes. And when the hard pressure of his lips began to move on hers as though to force them open, she clamped her mouth limpet-tight and felt the soft flesh tear. All she could do then was to stand rigid in that merciless embrace and endure to the end.

But Lucius's wrathful need to master and subdue was rapidly combining with a quite different need. With her soft curves grappled relentlessly to his own lean length, his body was demanding more . . . was telling him that there was a more positive conquest to be made . . . a surer way to overcome this contentious woman. Without thought, he had freed one hand to make a swift, predatory exploration of those curves, caressing her throat, her breasts, tugging ineffectually at the tightly buttoned jacket. Her hat fell off as he bent her back to move his mouth to her throat and it was now that her rigidity broke and she began to tremble. To Lucius, it signalled surrender and he was too far beyond thought to question it as he pressed her downward . . .

It was her sobbing gasp of sheer fright that struck through to his clouded mind. His blind gaze sharpened into focus on her face and the look of horror in her eyes slew passion on the instant. So nearly, he realized, *so very nearly*, he had borne her to the damp ground to take her, willing or unwilling. What was it about her that shook him out of all self-control, letting loose demons that he supposed safely chained? Powered by self-disgust, he thrust Kezia away from him so fiercely she tottered and he was forced to throw out a hand to steady her.

Fingers pressed to her abused mouth, Kezia snatched herself out of this less firm hold. Nothing had prepared her for the violence of this encounter. Had he really meant to bear her to the ground and ravish her? Shocked and still trembling in the aftermath, she stared at him. Surely a man who had behaved so monstrously should wear something of the look of a monster! To treat her so, simply because his verbal attacks had failed . . . But she would not let him think she was routed. Groping for the only weapon available to her, she said with all her heart and what strength she had left, 'Not only insufferable but despicable!' But her voice so nearly failed, she feared all she had done was let him know how close he had come to destroying her.

Hurriedly she turned away to hide her distress, wanting, needing, a swift escape. The quivering legs that carried her to her horse seemed hardly to be depended on. One explosive, incomprehensible word escaped the man behind her as she reached the mare. But with the reins in one hand and the other clutching the saddle, she realized she could not mount without his help. It was the last mortifying straw.

Lucius had followed her. Now he said gratingly, 'It was not meant to happen.' He then nullified what little value that had by adding, 'You may, however, think it a not altogether undeserved lesson.'

Her jaw clenched, but she had no strength left to battle with him further. Without turning her head, she said frustratedly, 'I must ask your help to mount.'

In the long moments that passed before he bent with linked hands to take her foot, she had begun to think he would not do it. But settled in the saddle at last, she took the hat he handed her and, still careful to avoid his gaze, said with studied flatness, 'It will suit us both, I think, sir, if I leave your house today.' She touched her heel to Hebe's side on the last word, but instantly Lucius gripped the mare's bridle again, making the mare dance with annoyance.

'We will return to the house together, if you please.' It was an order given in a tone that forbade any appeal. He did not tell her the reason was because she looked as though she might faint before she got there.

But he did not immediately move away, and though she did not look, Kezia knew his hard gaze was fixed on her. At last he said in a vexed tone, 'It was, after all, only a kiss — '

She closed her eyes briefly, shaking her head in silent denial.

Dark colour running up under his skin, Lucius turned and strode towards his own horse.

9

All Kezia remembered of their silent ride back to Old Hall was the urgency of her wish to reach its end and her relief when she saw Lord Emmington's Egyptian servant waiting, with his usual uncanny percipience, to take his master's horse. Abandoning Hebe to Ahmed's care, she slipped from her saddle and hurried into the house, stumbling when she sensed purposeful movement behind her. Sir Joshua Rowland and Harry chancing to come into the hall as she entered it made possible her escape to the stairs.

With the door of her room safely closed on her, she stood with her hands pressed to her temples willing herself to calmness. She felt dazed by the awfulness of what had taken place. Almost as shocking as Lord Emmington's physical assault on her, had been the fierceness of the emotions that had raged between them. Echoes of her own feelings at the time returned again and again to astonish her. And what intense dislike he must have for her to inflict such punishment! She saw now the impropriety of her game of pretended subservience. Even so, it astonished her that his self-love had been so wounded he had come in search of revenge. But to take it in such a way! Handling her as though she was a woman of the streets to demonstrate at what level she stood in his estimation.

The tumble of unhappy thoughts and recollections pouring through her mind fixed finally on one that perplexed as much as it troubled her: when, with her body clamped to his, Lucius Sellon's lips had swooped down upon hers, the nerves of her stomach had convulsed in the most extraordinary way, and when his kisses had reached her arched throat the strangest sensations had set other nerves thrumming in the strangest places, as though . . . as though . . .

Her thoughts reeled away, scattered, refocused on what now lay before her. There could be no going back from what had happened. She had thought once before that she could not long endure living in close proximity to the new Earl of Emmington, now she knew it to be impossible. She would — *she must* — leave Old Hall before the day advanced too far to think of travelling.

Fingers fumbling at buttonholes, she changed out of her riding-habit, washed her hands and face, and put on a plain green shalloon gown warm enough to travel in. Her bottom lip felt both sore and bruised and the looking-glass revealed it to be swollen. It hardly mattered; far more bruised was her self-esteem.

A glance at the clock told her that even before she packed her boxes she must face the ordeal of telling the dowager she could remain at Old Hall no longer. The old lady would resent the inconvenience, but there would be no blow to her affections. The biggest problem lay in deciding what explanation she was to give. Not the true one, that was certain! Unable to conjure up any reason the dowager was likely to find acceptable, she left it to the inspiration of the moment.

The dowager was comfortably ensconced in her usual chair beside the fire in the Lily Room. Her ladyship was in a state of unusual complacency for she had woken with an idea so appealing it had already hardened into fixed intention. Her original offer to find Miss Aston a husband had been flung out on impulse, but the particular marriage she now had in mind came with a promise of serving her still nebulous purposes. Ready to present her notion to her companion, it was annoying to see her looking less well than usual.

'You're very pale, miss. Are you sickening?'

she said accusingly. 'Or have you taken a toss from your horse?'

'Neither, ma'am. I am perfectly well but — '

'What then?' the dowager cut her off, grimly suspicious of her plan being thwarted. 'Have you been quarrelling with young Osborne?'

'No, indeed. Not at all.'

The girl's surprise carried conviction and the dowager relaxed. 'Good. I should not like to think it. He is a very estimable young man with a secure future. Emmington has no thought of making any change.' She regarded Kezia more closely. Something was amiss, but she saw no reason for further delay. 'I have come to think you find his company agreeable?'

'Indeed, yes.' Too abstracted to be surprised, Kezia hurried the subject aside. 'Ma'am, there is something I must tell — '

'Then,' continued the dowager, ruthlessly pursuing her purpose, 'you might consider he would make a very satisfactory husband. You appear to have caught his interest, and it would be a better match for you than you have any right to hope for. He knows nothing of the scandal attaching to you and it behoves you to make certain of him before he does.'

She had Kezia's full, startled attention now. 'I have no thought of doing so! Nor has Mr Osborne given me any hint that he has the kind of interest you suggest.'

'Oh, don't be foolish, girl! He likes you well enough to seek your company. It is your part to turn liking to attachment. I tell you again, you will be fortunate above your deserving to secure him! He is nephew to General Sir Henry Osborne and while there can be nothing to come to him from that direction, he can offer you all the benefits of living securely here at Emmington. What better can you possibly look for?'

On a note of desperation, Kezia said, 'It is all beside the point, ma'am, for I came to tell you that I am leaving Old Hall today.'

Shock silenced the dowager momentarily. Then, her eyes snapping with anger, she demanded, 'What nonsense is this? What has happened? Have you been called away?'

'No, ma'am. It is just that I *must* go. I am sorry I cannot give you my reason — '

'No reason and such suddenness! It cannot be allowed! You are not yourself. I am not listening!'

'I beg you will. I cannot stay. Indeed, I cannot!'

'I will remind you, miss, that you gave an absolute promise to remain a year — '

It was the dowager's turn to be interrupted. Sopworth entering, said, 'His lordship's compliments, ma'am, and if not inconvenient, he would be grateful for a few minutes of Miss Aston's time.'

Kezia stood as though paralysed, thought and feeling shrieking protest. What more could the wretched man possibly want to inflict on her?

The dowager seized a welcome breathing space. Waving an imperious hand, she snapped, 'Well, go, girl. It is not for you to keep Emmington waiting. We will finish this other matter later.'

Sopworth held the door for Kezia and, as she passed through, said with the kindly smile he always had for her, 'You will find Lord Emmington in the Cabinet, miss.'

10

The small oddly shaped room known as the Cabinet, lay at the end of a short flagstoned passage. Originally the monks' buttery, it had seen a number of changes, but early in the previous century had fallen into disuse. Something about the ancient room had appealed to the ninth earl, however, and recently it had been furbished up to a high degree of comfort and dignified with its present title.

Today, more light came from the logs flaming in the open stone fireplace than fell through the single large window with its dim old leaded glass inset with the Sellon coat-of-arms. The room was tremulous with shifting light that gleamed and glowed on silver candelabrum, on the handsome writing-table, on crimson velvet curtains and on gold-tasselled, crimson cushions on two Jacobean chairs flanking the hearth. Lucius, his back to the room's warmth and colour, stood gazing out into the grey-white mist which now almost totally obscured the small green court hedged with yew which the window overlooked.

Having freed himself from Sir Joshua as quickly as courtesy allowed, he had spent the last twenty minutes facing the disturbing fact that he knew himself less well than he had thought. Bleakly, he had accepted that it had been sexual jealousy that had raised the storm and sent him in hot and imprudent pursuit of Harry Osborne and his companion.

Considered in absence, he could not rate Miss Aston's charms as being utterly irresistible: the mistress he had left behind in Egypt was more beautiful, her temperament more accommodating. And yet, there remained in his mind, icon-like, the image of perfection Miss Aston had presented when, on Nob Hill, he had looked up to see her standing sun-gold and wind-blown against the blue of the sky. In those first moments, his every sense wakened to vibrant life, he had stepped back through time to the Lucius Sellon of his carefree student days . . . days before he had learned the need to probe every man's purpose, to discover every man's price . . .

In dealing with Miss Aston, had he ever re-established his equilibrium since? It had been no cool, reasoning man who had found himself faced by Miss Aston with a pride to match his own; a Miss Aston who answered him as a scornful equal. What else but primitive instinct had lurched him into responding with fury, hell-bent to humble, to punish, to prove himself her indisputable master? His prized liberal views had vanished in a storm of sexual frustration so that he had handled the girl as he had never before handled a woman. Worse still, he had been carried to the edge of an action that, taken any further, would have made him despise himself forever.

But having reached the nadir of self-reproach, like most sons of Adam, he began to think that quite as much blame belonged to the temptation as to the weakness of the tempted. If Miss Aston was not as she was, *he* would not have behaved as he had. From that came the thought of how differently everything would have proceeded in Egypt. *There*, had he seen her unveiled, the probability would have been that she was for sale, could have been purchased from whatever male — father, brother, or other — whose possession she was. That he would never have made such a purchase, he dismissed as irrelevant: it was pleasing that it could have been so. Further, Miss Aston, there, would have learned to be submissive to masculine will almost before she left the cradle, or else would have been bent to it. Never, in that country, would she have dared to look at a man with contempt and say as she had — *not only insufferable but despicable.* That rankled. By God it did!

Perceiving a certain duality in that line of thought, he turned to considering Miss Aston as a problem in need of a solution. That was simple: she must go! He was no rake-hell, but if she remained at Old Hall, the probability was that he would eventually seek to take her to his bed — to her ruin and the dowager's outrage. All too vividly he recollected how it felt to hold Miss Aston in his arms and to have the tantalizing sweetness of her mouth under his.

The frown this produced was still on his face when, hearing a slight sound behind him, he swung round.

★ ★ ★

Kezia saw the frown and braced herself anew. She had no fear of his assaulting her again, but somewhere deep within her there was a vague, quivering apprehension that it lay in his power to inflict a hurt with which she could not easily deal.

Lucius had determined his course: he would see that she had the necessary funds for her journey and a safe destination and then she would be sent on her way. But her

113

pallor, and something that lay hauntingly in her eyes, made him say abruptly, 'Come in and sit down.' He indicated a chair by the fire.

Reluctantly, Kezia obeyed, sitting down with graceful neatness, her back straight, her head held high on her slender neck.

'Have you told the countess you intend to leave?' Lucius asked.

Kezia murmured assent.

'You told her the reason?'

She shook her head. 'I was called away before I could say more.'

'Shall you tell her the truth?'

Her brows arched slightly and he wondered what she had read into the question.

'I do not see the necessity,' she said.

'Generous!' He thought then that she must have heard the clipped word as a sneer because he saw her bruised lips press together. Brusquely, he asked, 'Where will you go?'

'I shall return to Putney.'

'There will be no difficulty in that?'

'None. I shall be welcome.'

'Good,' he said with a snap that seemed to contradict the word. 'I cannot think the countess received news of your departure lightly?'

Control of her voice was growing increasingly

difficult but Kezia managed to say fairly evenly, 'She does not like change, of course, but — ' She closed the sentence with a faint shrug that implied the dowager would not be made unhappy.

The truth of that, made Lucius pause. A swift review of the dowager's attitude to her companion showed it to be a strange one: he had an impression of a close and feline watchfulness; of claws hidden but ready for use.

His lengthy silence prompted Kezia to rise from her chair. 'The day is advancing, sir. The sooner I complete my preparations to leave the better.'

She was right. Now was the time to offer to pay the charges of her travel and be done with her. It was not the time to admire her valiantly maintained composure, her burnished curls, the delicate bones under the visible flesh tantalizingly limned by firelight. Above all, it was not the time to discover that, against all reason, he did not want her to go.

'Wait. Sit down.' His authoritarian tone stung his ears seconds later and he added, 'I mean, if you please.'

He recognized the reluctance with which she complied. She, it was clear, was still firmly resolved on leaving, while he was more than halfway to surrendering a reasoned solution to impulse. Less than ever did he want her to go.

His voice strained, he asked, 'Are you quite determined to leave us?'

The question made no sense to Kezia. From the moment she had entered the room, she had been certain that he was as determined upon her going as she was herself.

Her silence hurried him on. 'If you choose to stay, what happened this morning would not happen again. Of that you may be sure.'

The shift in his attitude was bewildering. She said, 'I *cannot* stay! It is not just what happened — it is the contempt that inspired it. I cannot live with that.'

'*Contempt*! Good God, how can you think it!' The words exploded from him. 'Several things inspired my behaviour but contempt was nowhere among them, I assure you!'

Kezia shook her head.

Frowning, Lucius declared fiercely, 'You can know very little about the nature of men if you are not aware that when women throw out a challenge — consciously or unconsciously — they do so at their peril.'

She supposed that any woman who was not wholly obsequious in his presence must be a challenge to him. 'That apart, my lord, you made plain your distrust of me,' she said.

Looking into the clear grey depths of her remarkable eyes, he thought that only a fool could really do so. He had used Lady Holford's insinuations entirely in anger and now, unable to remember just what he had said, he brushed the matter aside.

'One says more than is strictly true when feelings get out of hand. I must suppose the countess to be satisfied as to who you are.'

It was too sudden a conversion and not quite to the point, though why she felt compelled to correct trivial details of their quarrel, she could not think. 'It was not *who* I am you questioned, but what,' she reminded him.

Impatience flooded through him. How like her not to grasp gratefully at the proffered olive branch! And how unlike the lady-companions he had met in the past: they, most notably, had clung to security at whatever humiliating cost.

'I think you must concede you are sufficiently unlike the common run of paid companion to occasion some curiosity,' he said.

'Perhaps because I am *not* paid! In this house I — ' She stopped abruptly, having nearly said 'I prefer it so'. A little awkwardly she substituted, 'It is a privilege I am able to claim because I have a small income of my own.'

He sensed the significance of that 'In this house' and reached for what she had left unsaid: *In this house I choose not to be paid*. Was that it? Then why particularly *this house*? Everything about her bespoke her quality and the very things that had so provoked him, he saw now as virtues — virtues that would have become a daughter of the house —

The thought arrested him. *A daughter of the house!* Old Hall has no living legal daughter: the family records made that clear. But if she were a Sellon bastard, provided for but not recognized, much would be explained. A bastard then, but whose? The most likely candidates were Piers Sellon, the sixth earl and the dowager's son, or her nephew, Baron Holford.

Miss Aston's illegitimacy gave him certain advantages. Base-born, she was outside all usual categories of society. Her chance of a marriage commensurate with her quality would be almost nil, while chances of being made offers of another kind were likely to be multiplied.

At nineteen, Miss Aston could have few

illusions regarding her position. There would be less reproach to him in offering to make her his mistress — and less to her in accepting. It was most satisfactorily in his power to give her such compensation well beyond her likely dreams. It seemed to him he had found a reasonable solution to the problem of Miss Aston after all!

His gaze concentrated on her. It was strange to him to be so in thrall to a woman; to feel so intense and particular a desire, so fierce an anticipation. But she had yet to be persuaded; yet to be brought to look on him as something other than a satyr and a brute. With their recent encounter in mind, he would need to begin slowly.

He said, 'Let me show you something.'

Moving to a cupboard, he took from it the scuffed and shapeless satchel he had carried when she had first seen him. Unbuckling it, he poured out its contents on to the small table at her elbow.

Kezia's breath caught on a gasp of wonder at the tumbled heap so carelessly displayed: beautiful and strange, new and old, the assorted jewellery and artifacts made a fabulous display. Collar-like neckpieces heavy with lapis lazuli and other stones lay mixed with ruby-eyed snake-bracelets, every scale of which showed distinct and perfect. Necklaces of many periods, brilliant with gems, carelessly tangled about rings, enamelled brooches, and small, ancient, golden ornaments.

Such brilliance of colour, such a prodigality of riches, were hard to imagine.

'That was what I was carrying when we first met. As you see, it is not a fair responsibility to pass to a servant. Egypt is a troubled country. Travelling is neither easy nor safe. A wise man does not advertise his wealth, but makes himself as inconspicuous as possible, appearing, if he can, as one of the poorer hangers-on of a caravan or some other group moving in the direction he wishes to go. That was the semblance in which I came to England.'

As he watched her staring down at the table, he was half hoping for a sign of covetousness that might make her conquest easier. All he saw was wonder.

With a quizzical smile, he said, 'I cannot help that part of me which is Egyptian, you know. Nor do I deplore it. I was content to be my father's heir in Egypt and expected no other. There, I knew my world . . . knew that the prudent possessor of property makes both covert and overt enquiry into any part of it administered by others in his name. If he does not, he is likely to find himself outrageously robbed and — what may be worse — more dangerous even — credited with an oppressive tyranny of which he knows nothing but which is imposed in his name. I was enough of a cautious Egyptian when I first arrived here to think it sensible to discover how things were managed at Emmington before I made an official appearance on the scene. I believed the countess to have transferred to the Dower House and I instructed Bursey and Garth not to inform anyone of my coming.'

'Oh,' she said rather inadequately. It was a reasonable explanation of what had so perplexed her, but what did it matter now?

Selecting a necklace of delicately wrought gold set with diamonds and emeralds, he said, 'This is Italian Renaissance work and said to be of great value.'

Glancing briefly at it, Kezia said politely, 'It's charming,' but she was already reaching for a small gold figurine with the beautifully fashioned head of a hawk, its black and amber eyes looking intimidatingly alive. 'But *this* is fascinating — exquisite.'

He let the necklace fall back among the rest. 'That's Hor, a god of ancient Egypt. Giver of the day, god of the rising sun and son of Orisis and Isis. You would probably call him Horus.'

How strange, she thought, to represent the god of the life-giving sun as a predator. 'Beautiful but deadly,' she murmured and, glancing up, saw in the eyes of the man looking down at her something that matched with both the image of the hawk-headed god in her hand and the live hawk in her mind. Her breath snagged in her throat and she stilled like a mouse beneath the raptor's shadow.

Sensing her momentary chill, he offered quickly, 'Hor appears in a number of different guises — sometimes as a child rising from a tree.'

He swept the treasure back into the satchel as carelessly as he had shaken it out and shut it away in the cupboard. Turning back, he said, 'Is it not possible to begin again, Miss Aston? Think of the difference your going will make to those you leave behind. I'm told you are teaching the maid who waits on you to read and write and that several of the Sellon pensioners have cause to be grateful to you. I think, too, that the countess would be more upset by your going than you imagine.'

Half-beguiled by the smile he now gave her — warmer than any she had received from him before — Kezia still mistrusted the change in him.

He leaned down towards her, his green eyes intent. 'Come now, be generous. Say you will stay.'

She felt the pressure of his will and though vague misgivings slithered like small poisonous snakes through her mind, the coaxing warmth of his voice poured like honey on her senses. Her resolution weakened. As from a distance, she heard herself say, 'Very well, sir, I will.'

Careful to hide any hint of triumph, he bowed. 'Thank you. But now you are left with the need to explain your change of mind to the countess. Can you think of a reason that will satisfy her?'

'I must hope so.' She rose again as she spoke, no more sure of herself than of him. With a curtsy, she turned to the door.

He was there to open it for her. '*Roh-es-salaam*,' he said as she passed through.

She looked back questioningly.

'I said, go in peace. To which you should properly respond *Ma salaami* — which is to give me your blessing. But perhaps that is too much to hope for yet.'

It was said with a charming degree of lightness and release from tension making her feel a little light-headed, she threw back at him, 'If you have need, sir, my blessing is yours.' Briefly, she gave him her lovely smile, dipped a second curtsy, and was gone.

He stared after her, wondering why he had ever thought she fell short of true beauty. Yet it was not her looks alone that drew him so strongly. Something in her that was essentially *Miss Aston* teased his mind, was provocation to his senses, was threat to his peace. As a sensible man, he meant to overcome that threat.

It was an inconvenient moment for conscience to stir and question his coolly made plan for her. A jumble of words from some forgotten verse came into his mind, something to do with 'reason' and 'hunting'. He supposed they had relevance but the words would not take order and he shrugged them away.

11

Hiding her relief at Kezia's change of mind, the countess accepted her obscure explanations with no more than a few acid remarks on the volatility of the young. She ended, however, on a plaintive note, saying, 'I must remind you, Miss Aston, that at my age it is distressing to be subjected to uncertainty. I trust you will not again suggest leaving here before a year is up.'

Kezia, herself relieved to escape a searching interrogation or any reference to Harry, made no demur.

The countess had not forgotten Harry. Her desire to keep her companion under her eye and thumb had grown: marriage to Harry Osborne would ensure the continuance she desired. She was not to be thwarted; the mere possibility had caused the deep-hidden thing that lay at the heart of her dealings with Miss Aston to stir again and emit a dark displeasure. She would bide her time.

★ ★ ★

Opportunities for Kezia and Harry to ride together now became extraordinarily rare. Lord Emmington required his steward to be available for consultation at an early hour; Harry therefore, must hold himself in readiness each day for a summons that might or might not come.

Setting out for another lonely ride, Kezia's mind was troubled. A letter just received from Hallie, though written with all that lady's usual warm affection, had contained items of Putney news that gave Kezia an uneasy sense of a door being closed. A gratifying influx of new pupils had obliged Miss Halsinger to engage another teacher in Kezia's place. This, she stressed, would make no difference should Kezia choose to return to Putney: Hallie's home was hers for as long as Kezia wished it.

It came as a shock to Kezia to realize how much she had depended on the world she had left behind remaining unchanged. Hallie, she knew, hoped for great things from Kezia's stay at Old Hall. It was a hope Kezia was certain would not be fulfilled.

The early December day was coldly bright. Having given Hebe a good gallop over open ground, once in the shelter of the woods, she allowed the mare to settle to a walk. It was here, following the curve of the grassy track around a clump of splendidly berried hollies, she found Lord Emmington approaching her on Moorsi.

Since the interview in the Cabinet his behaviour towards her had been exactly what it should — pleasantly detached and gentlemanly. Consequently, she had begun to feel that when time had dimmed the recent past a little more she would be perfectly comfortable in his company. With the common courtesies exchanged, she expected they would continue in their chosen directions, but surprising her, his lordship turned his mount to ride with her.

The conversation he initiated was sufficiently commonplace to dispel any awkwardness and a comment on the abundance of holly berries led quickly to a discussion of what might be done at Old Hall to celebrate Christmas, at the end of which Kezia asked, 'How different your life in Egypt must have been! Do you miss it? Will you ever go back?'

He was slow to answer and Kezia sensed that the questions had ramifications beyond her guess. At last he said, *'Lishrub moyet en Nil* — who drinks the waters of the Nile must return. I shall go back because I must.'

The words had an odd undernote and, as if conscious of it, he added, 'I miss what is best in the Egyptian people: their peculiar subtlety and humour, their determination to wring advantage from the worst of circumstances. Only an Egyptian, at a grievous day's end, would thank Allah that never again can he know such wretchedness.'

Kezia's smile was partly for her doubt that Lucius Sellon was enough of an Egyptian to accept outrageous fortune quite so philosophically.

Launched into reminiscence, his lordship continued, 'Egypt has a beauty quite unlike England's. To see the sun rising through the mists over the Nile, or the full moon lifting above the Mokattam hills behind Cairo are sights never to be forgotten. And there is no more exquisite pleasure than a walk through the scent of bean-flowers. Even sounds have their magic. The *shadoofs* that irrigate the fields creak endlessly day and night but always are woven through with the unutterable sweetness of the watchmen's pipes. And all around the desert lies red-gold and — ' He broke off suddenly, looking startled, as though he had caught himself out in an unexpected foolishness. 'Well, no more of that!' he said.

Kezia was disappointed. She had been fascinated as much by what he had revealed of Lucius Sellon as of Egypt. The ride however, continued pleasantly to its end without further revelations. Only once, glancing up, she found him regarding her with an intensity that sent a flutter along her nerves, but his expression changed so swiftly she was left unsure of what she had seen.

She had no suspicion of the care with which Lucius had arranged that fortuitous meeting and was equally unsuspecting of others that followed at careful intervals. Even less did she suspect the ever increasing delight he found in the game he was playing. As time passed, she found it hard to believe she could have mistaken him for a gypsy, or that the deplorable encounter in the woods had ever taken place. It was a comfort to her that she could now be aware of his charm while observing quite dispassionately that this, allied to good looks and sensual appeal, must make him dangerously attractive to many women. She could perceive the potency of the combination and was thankful to be in no danger from it.

★ ★ ★

Christmas came to absorb everyone's attention. Harry was busy with lists assigning gifts of wood and blankets, pork, beef and rabbit where they would be most appreciated and devising suitable entertainments for the entire village.

By now, the neighbourhood had woken to the fact that the new earl was not the 50-year-old married man expected but a young man with no visible wife — facts particularly gratifying to mothers of eligible daughters. Fathers were prodded into making formal first visits and there was an increase in the numbers of ladies calling on the dowager countess which resulted in Kezia finding herself with more notes to write and errands to run than was usual.

The earl's lack of a wife was prominent in the dowager's mind and, attentive to the claims of her own family, Melissa Holford was invited to return to Old Hall for what time remained before her come-out. Having as little liking for Sophia Holford as she had for the baroness, the dowager saw no necessity to invite the older girl. Melissa, as it happened, was already in London having been despatched to the care of her godmother to be given a little polish in advance of the Season. Her return to Old Hall was promised for the first reasonable travelling day after Christmas Day.

Christmas Eve brought an unexpected visitor. A little before the dinner-hour, Kezia, the earl and dowager were gathered about the fire in the Lily Room when the Duke of Mawdsham was announced.

For a brief moment even the dowager's face showed astonishment. The duke's residence, Staneflete Castle, was no more than four miles distant, but six years ago, following the death of his young wife, the duke had withdrawn entirely from the social life of the neighbourhood.

Kezia saw a man of medium height and compact build, with a fresh complexion and attractive features. His eyes were brown as was his hair which had greyed a little at the temples, balancing with a touch of distinction his rather boyish look. His age, Kezia guessed, was a few years past thirty.

His manner was easy, his voice pleasing, though his delivery had a slight and quite individual abruptness. Shaking hands with Lord Emmington, he said, 'Haven't gone about much since my wife died. Time to change, though. Time to bid a new neighbour welcome. Christmas, too. Must offer the compliments of the season.'

Then, crossing the room to kiss the dowager's hand, Kezia was astonished to hear him say as to himself but in a perfectly audible voice, *'Not a fool . . . no!'*

She hardly had time to recover before she was making her own curtsy to his grace.

His bow and his smile, she found, were in no way diminished by the dowager's stiff, 'Miss Aston, my companion.' He surprised her again then, by looking at her more closely and saying, 'We have met before, have we not?'

'I think it unlikely, your Grace,' Kezia told him.

'Oh? Well, perhaps not.' He nodded at her, but as he moved away, he said in the same self-communing way as before, 'Dashed pretty! Something about her . . . '

The duke remained just long enough to make himself generally pleasant and to toast the season in a glass of wine before excusing himself from remaining to dine, saying in his friendly and unassuming fashion he was 'promised at home' but that he and his sister hoped to see them at Staneflete before long.

Dinner being served close upon the duke's departure, it was inevitable that he should then be discussed.

'The want of a sense of proportion must be the reason for his having shut himself away for so long!' the countess pronounced dourly. 'But the Delarives have always been an unconformable race. His wife was the Marquis of Hildewick's second daughter. It was a love-match and her death when her second child was born completely sank him.

Hermione, his unmarried sister, alone saved the household from descending into chaos. She made better work of it than anyone could have expected, though it is to be hoped that the two little girls' governess will have corrected whatever peculiar ideas Hermione may have passed on to them. As for Mawdsham — it is past time for him to be looking out for another wife. He has yet to provide himself with an heir!'

There was a sourness in her tone that made Kezia wonder about the dowager's relationship with the duke and his sister.

'If the duke frequently reveals his private thoughts in the way he did this evening,' remarked the earl, 'one must hope they are always as favourable. Does his sister share that eccentricity?'

The dowager sniffed. 'No, but she is singular in her own way being a quite undisguised blue-stocking. It is greatly to be feared that she will be more hindrance than help when it comes to launching the girls into the world. Left to her, they are likely to end unmarried, as she is, and writing letters to professors of chemistry and other such extraordinary people. I ask, how can steel gauze be of interest to any rationally minded woman?'

Amusement gleamed in Lucius's eyes. 'You

are referring to Professor Davy's discovery that double *wire* gauze can be used in miners' lamps to retard flame and so greatly lessen the risk of fire in coal-mines. It must, I think, be of interest to miners' wives.'

'Among whom Hermione does not number!' snapped the countess. 'What Mawdsham's girls will need is a mother capable of seeing them safely fired into society when the time comes!'

A more lavish desert than usual being then set on the table, the countess waited only for the servants to withdraw before taking up the subject of marriage with a different object in view.

'Well, Emmington, the New Year is only a week away — a year in which you pass your twenty-ninth birthday. As much as Mawdsham, you should be giving thought to the succession. Death has taken heavy toll of this family in late years. It would be a relief and a comfort to me to see a healthy new generation established before I am removed to a higher realm.'

Champagne had accompanied each of the three removes and enough had flowed through their glasses to mellow them all. Though drifting in a pleasant haze, Kezia was aware that Lord Emmington pushed his chair back from the table as though seeking the shadows. With mocking gravity, he asked, 'You're sure of your place then, Countess?'

For a moment the dowager did not catch the point, then, with a short laugh, she shot back, 'Not enough to lay my gelt on, but more sure than you of yours, I venture to guess! My point, however, is not to be side-stepped. There is a grievous possibility of the line becoming extinct if you do not father an heir.'

Something shadowed the green eyes before his lordship looked down at the glass he was slowly turning between his fingers. Softly, he asked, 'But why are you so certain I am not married?'

The dowager was shocked into unbreathing rigidity. Vividly, she recalled the possibilities Lady Holford had presented to her notice. An Egyptian wife? More than one? Shaken, she asked, 'Do you now tell me you are?'

Kezia found herself awaiting his answer quite as intently as the dowager.

At last, flatly, he said, 'No.'

Glancing from one to the other, Kezia wondered if the old lady realized how equivocal that answer was. Had he meant no, he wasn't married, or, no, he did not intend to tell her?

The dowager, her head less clear than usual, chose the answer she preferred.

'Then why delay?' she asked. 'It cannot be for fear of losing your freedom. Men please themselves as much after marriage as before . . . change is the bride's portion. And you may look where you please. Only, I beg you, choose better than did my son and nephew — one marrying a bigot and the other a harpy!'

The shadows the earl had sought were not deep enough to hide his closed expression. The dowager had small hope of being reassured, Kezia thought. His eyes were hidden behind his black lashes and unaware of what she did, Kezia let her gaze slide over the fine-boned face and linger on the mouth that had once taken hers so unkindly. For a moment she seemed to feel that ruthless pressure again, and she wondered dreamily, what it would be like to be kissed in a different way. With warmth and liking? By that same mouth? Unconsciously, her own softened, her lips parting a little as though to receive the imagined kiss . . .

In that unwary moment her gaze lifted again to find the green blaze of his lordship's stare now fixed on her. Under his enigmatic smile she blushed deeply.

'Well, Miss Aston,' he said, 'what opinion have you of the married state? Would you expect a husband to continue exactly in the fashion of his bachelor days?'

With champagne valour, Kezia disowned her blush and arched quizzical brows at him. 'I can present no considered opinion of the case, sir, though I may suppose that what I would expect of a husband would depend very much on his behaviour as a bachelor.'

It was what she thought of marriage that most interested Lucius. Given the suspected irregularity of her situation, did she look on wedded bliss with some solid citizen — however dull — as the highest good? Or could she be tempted by a glittering alternative?

'Some thoughts on matrimony you must have,' he urged. 'It is the natural goal of all young women.'

'A goal reached *naturally* by as many men as women, sir.'

His eyes glinted at her. 'Yes, very neat, Miss Aston, but no proper answer. Tell me plainly, are you in favour of the married state, ready and willing to submit to the changes marriage would impose?'

She gave a small laugh that was almost a hiccup. 'I must presume such a willingness if I have married willingly, because change would be inevitable. My name, my home, my way of life, all would be different.'

'The wonder is so many brides brave so

much!' Cynicism clipped his words.

The dowager forgotten, Kezia finished her champagne with a flourish and laughed at him across the empty glass. 'The wonder is all in their reason for doing so.'

'They love the men they marry, you mean? I wonder how many do . . . ?' The cynicism was heavier now. 'In Egypt, marriages are contracts made between parents, sometimes when one, sometimes when both of the contracted pair are still in the cradle. Such marriages are made to strengthen the family and rightly so. It is not so different here: marriages are frequently made to enhance fortune and status.'

'The participants have my pity! Such a cold-blooded arrangement would not do for me!' Suddenly serious, her eyes were luminous with indignation. 'Marriage without love must be a wretched, joyless state!'

He captured her gaze, his eyes narrowed and intent. 'Love? It has been centuries under discussion, yet I doubt if two people could be found to agree either on its true nature or its positive existence. *Joy* is a different matter and not necessarily found in marriage. But, you, Miss Aston, plan to fall in love, do you?'

There was a hardness in his tone that robbed their exchange of the jesting quality that had permitted her to soar a little. A glance towards the dowager showed her that the old lady was dozing. When she looked back at the earl, she found him waiting with his black eyebrows tilted demandingly.

Hoping to recover the lighter mood, she said with a slightly breathless laugh, 'I plan nothing, sir. I am simply the means by which you have avoided discussion of your own position.'

He acknowledged the truth of that with a laugh and half-denied it with a shake of his head. Leaning further back in his chair, he stared at her through half-closed eyes. There was wisdom, he thought, in a society that shrouded its women in veils. In Egypt, never could Miss Aston have been seen as she now was, a delight to the eye in her second-best evening gown, a warm flush on her cheeks, candlelight magically lighting her hair, glimmering in her eyes, gilding her creamy skin — and presenting a potent temptation that knew nothing of the desire it provoked! At that moment he wanted nothing so much as he wanted to lift her out of her chair and kiss the provoking smile off her lips ... kiss her into some understanding of the reality of passion and ravish her delectable body with a pleasure that would show her the romantic love she hoped for was no more than an insipid, girlish dream.

Marriage, and some shadowy knowledge of what had passed between the other two, was in the dowager's mind as she surfaced from her brief nap. With acid dismissiveness she interposed, 'Miss Aston means to remain a spinster all her life, but an earldom does not hang on her marriage as it does on yours, Emmington. There are many pretty and eligible young women at no great distance whom you have yet to meet. The Dymont girls are both charming young women and the elder is thought to be something of a beauty. I have it in mind, too, that their cousin, Lady Delia Brandon, is to come to them in the New Year. Now there is a young woman who might well please you! Only a small fortune, but an ancient line, pretty-behaved, and with considerable style.'

She snickered a laugh in her throat, throwing him a look not untouched with malice. 'You might find yourself called on to exert yourself to please *her*, though. Word has it that she has refused both the Marquis of Claverhill *and* young Perle-Langford who, they say, is rich enough to buy the City.'

Brought back to the dowager's point of interest, Lucius frowned. Restraint had its costs in physical discomfort and a huge unsettling impatience. More curtly than Kezia had heard him speak to the old lady before, he said, 'May we have done with the subject of marriage for tonight, Countess?'

He stretched a hand towards the bottle in its icy nest. 'Allow me to pour you a little more of M'sieur Moet's excellent wine.'

12

In recent years it had become customary for Harry, his aunt, Mrs Robby, and the elderly, widowed rector to eat their Christmas dinner at Old Hall. Lord Emmington would allow no alteration to the arrangement and a carriage was sent at the usual time to bring the three guests to the house.

The Reverend Dorling was a pleasant, intelligent man, two years past seventy, perfectly at ease with his world and an easy conversationalist. Mrs Robby, sister to Harry's mother, was a neat little woman in her early fifties, with a plain face, a quiet manner and a dry wit. Liking them both, Kezia looked forward to a pleasant evening.

The meal was nearly at an end when Kezia, her head bent to attend something the rector said to her, whispered a quick reply, giving him a mischievous glance under her lashes and making him laugh delightedly.

Witnessing the exchange, the dowager felt a sharp pang of the old grief. *Just so* had Charlotte looked — Charlotte, the dear and darling girl who had once lit her days with joy . . . Little as Miss Aston resembled Charlotte, occasionally an expression of hers would so exactly catch something of Charlotte's as to pierce her determination to ignore the fact that this was Charlotte's child. Miss Aston offended simply by *being*.

Lucius, too, caught the moment, but the fascination he saw in Miss Aston was all her own. The impatience he had felt the previous evening was still with him and for his own peace he knew that the sooner he could deliver himself from Miss Aston's spell the better.

Some time later the party divided, the earl joining the three older people to play whist while Harry and Kezia settled to a game of piquet.

Lucius, partnering Mrs Robby, played well until halfway through the second game when he became aware that play at the other table had stopped. Miss Aston, he saw, was unwrapping tissue from a small packet. His ears reached for what Harry was saying.

'It is nothing great, but I hope very much that you will like it.'

From the slim, white vellum-covered box she had uncovered, Kezia took an ivory fan and flicked it open. As exquisitely worked as fine lace, it showed figures of legend in a setting of gardens and pagoda houses. In the centre, her initials were gracefully entwined on a needle-fine, pierced oval panel.

She looked up. 'Oh, Harry! It is the most lovely thing! I don't know how to thank you.'

'Your pleasure is all the thanks I want.' He smiled at her with a warmth he had not allowed her to see before.

Kezia's own gaze fell and she said a little huskily, 'My gift for you is very ordinary — just a book. I asked Sopworth to pass it to you when you leave because I could not be sure of being able to do so myself.'

'Then I will give you my first thanks now.' He hesitated, then said wryly, 'Our rides have become sadly rare. I have found myself wishing Lord Emmington were a less early riser.' He hesitated again before adding, 'How I wish we could be private . . . that I could say what it is not possible for me to say here and now.'

Though the last words did not reach Lucius's ears, Harry's expression spoke clearly enough and his lordship was shaken to realize how stupidly blind he had been. Harry — attractive, intelligent and free to marry where he chose — was not to be underrated as a rival. However unreal or transient the state of 'being in love' was, Miss Aston had declared a positive interest in it — and Harry was patently in love!

Lucius's scowling gaze switched to the bone of contention. She was *his* — pledged without covenant — but still *his*! The certainty of it was embedded in his mind. Harry could go hang! As for Miss Aston, sitting there so innocently . . . he had made some progress with her lately, fretted by impatience but knowing that *el agela min esh Shaitan* — haste is from the Devil.

His partner's slightly pained voice recalled his attention. 'It is your play, my lord.'

Turning from Harry's ardent look, Kezia had encountered one of such savage anger from Lord Emmington she was startled. It was a look she remembered from another occasion — one so hard, so dark, so nearly cruel, she shivered. What could she possibly have done to deserve it?

She was still puzzling over it while preparing for bed that night, but because his lordship's behaviour towards her during the rest of the evening had been pleasantly courteous she concluded that she had merely strayed into its path. She was reminded, however, that behind the urbane presence he generally presented was a different, even dangerous, 'other self'.

More important, though, than Lord Emmington's peculiarities was what Harry had revealed of his feelings for her.

145

She had been wrong, she realized, to attach so little importance to what the dowager had said on the score of Harry's interest for his words tonight had hinted at a proposal. If Harry did propose, how would she answer him? In the past, she had indulged in daydreams as bright and insubstantial as any other girl's, her one certainty that she could marry only for love. The question now was, did she love Harry?

Ready for bed, she stood staring into the diminishing glow of her fire. Harry, she was sure, would make the best of husbands; kind, considerate, companionable, loyal . . . Her knowledge of men was not large, but she thought it unlikely she would soon meet another man possessing more admirable qualities. Was that appreciation the sum of love? She had thought love would come with glorious certainty, unmistakable as a cloudless summer sunrise. Perhaps, after all, it simply stole in very quietly . . .

★ ★ ★

Melissa Holford came on Boxing Day, attended by Miss Flemming, her one-time governess now translated into dresser and chaperone. Six weeks in the company of her godmother had made their mark and she presented a charming picture of a fashionable young lady. The velvet redingote she wore exactly matched the blue of her eyes and her huge quilted muff was of the same material. Her black curls were now modishly cropped and supported a jaunty hussar's cap in gold grosgrain with a cockade of blue jay feathers. She had never lacked confidence but its evidence was now more refined; but not, as Kezia observed, to the point of removing the promise of mischief in the young girl's bright eyes.

For a week Melissa went in awe of his lordship, but when her natural exuberance finally surfaced and appeared to be tolerated, she was soon at ease with him and ready to test her acquired stock of fashionable slang on everyone.

The dowager viewed their promising accord with complacence, more than ready to be gratified if a second lady of her own family became Countess of Emmington. Charlotte's disaster, however, was enough to keep her from even hinting as much to the girl. She saw nothing inconsistent between that restraint and her fixed resolve that Miss Aston should marry Harry Osborne. What mattered most to her was that Emmington should marry *soon* and beget an heir. Melissa's presence in the house allowed her to invite all the neighbourhood's most eligible young women under the guise of providing entertainment for her great-niece. Their mamas could be depended on to recognize the valuable opportunity presented.

The young ladies came, dressed beneath their outdoor wraps in the airiest of silks and muslins though winter winds moaned in the trees and bellowed down the chimneys. Kezia watched the parade of nymphs and Graces with amused curiosity, wondering who among them was most likely to catch his lordship's interest. The dowager, she remembered, had particularly recommended to his notice the elder Dymont sister and her cousin, Lady Delia Brandon. Miss Dymont, she thought, had a fairy-tale prettiness rather than beauty. Eighteen years old, her figure was petite, her eyes large, remarkably long-lashed and softly blue, while her complexion had a clear, porcelain delicacy which was set off by the palest, silkiest blonde hair Kezia ever had seen. Additionally, nature not art, had arranged for it to break into delicate tendrils around a sweetly shaped face. Dark beauties were in high fashion just now, but this appeared to matter not at all to the young male guests who pressed eager attentions on this vision of loveliness.

Lady Delia was very different. At twenty-six, she was the eldest of the young ladies and the tallest. Her dark hair clouded about a pale intelligent face which drew its charm chiefly from the contradiction of an expression of quiet gravity and the twinkling humour which lay banked in her grey-blue eyes.

As the dowager had said, the young woman had style and was very pretty-behaved. Seeking flaws in this paragon, Kezia could find none: Lady Delia could not even be detected showing the dowager's companion a shade less courtesy than she showed her fellow guests — a failing from which the fellow-guests were not all exempt. Lady Delia might well be the one to interest the Earl of Emmington.

It seemed she was wrong. It was Miss Dymont who drew the Earl of Emmington's gaze most often, and it was soon evident to Kezia that Miss Dymont had been marvellously well coached to succeed in the marriage mart. A biddable girl, clearly she had accepted as a first principle that men were superior creatures and women helpless without their physical and moral support. Her faith in this belief radiated from her, but a cautious mama had not left her defenceless: less in evidence, but held with equal certainty, was Miss Dymont's conviction that only a girl lacking in all propriety would disoblige her family by encouraging the advances of a *poor* man, however superior.

It was a disappointment to Kezia that it was to this tame butterfly that Lord Emmington appeared most drawn, but supposed that Miss Dymont was as close to the subjugated women of Egypt as was likely to be found in England. For how long, she wondered, could a man like Lucius Sellon — sharply intelligent and moved by strange passions — live happily with a girl like Miss Dymont? Reminding herself then, that he wasn't looking for happiness in marriage, she decided that Miss Dymont would probably suit him very well.

It was Melissa's friendliness towards Kezia, her unthinking expectation that the other girl would be included in whatever pleasure was planned, that alerted the dowager to the need to place stronger emphasis on the difference between the Countess of Emmington's great-niece and that same lady's *companion*. Tedious occupations were easily found to prevent Kezia's participation in the young people's amusements and her attendance on the dowager became unnecessary when Melissa and the dowager were guests elsewhere.

The pettiness of it depressed Kezia. If ever she had had any small hope of winning her great-grandmother's affection, it slipped from her now and she began to look towards the end of her stay at Emmington with impatience. Even Harry had given her reason for disappointment. She had seen nothing of him since Christmas. It seemed as though he was avoiding her — perhaps embarrassed by having been led by wine and the occasion to hint more than he had intended.

A fine, mild morning towards the end of January found a mixed party of young men and women assembled at Old Hall to enjoy a late breakfast to be followed by games.

Among them were three of the Dymont family: Miss Dymont, her shy, 16-year-old younger sister, Penelope, and their brother, Valentine, who was twenty. Breakfast over, the company removed to the Green Saloon, named for its delicately tinted walls, and blessed with a fireplace at each end of its forty-foot length. It was a cheerful room, its floor laid with Shirvan carpets, French seventeenth-century needlework decorating the Flemish settees and chairs, and two fine Coromandel cabinets prominent among the remaining, very handsome, furniture.

It had already been decided that the first game was to be charades and the audience, the dowager and several mamas who had accompanied their daughters, sat comfortably close to one of the fires. Lord Emmington stood nearby watching with slightly sardonic amusement the energy being expended by the young people in simply dividing themselves into three teams. The numbers being found to be unequal, Melissa, in her usual lively manner, appealed to his lordship.

'My team is short of a member, sir. Will you not join us?'

Lord Emmington made a hurried decision and shook his head. 'You have my sympathy but my person you must do without. To my infinite regret, I am compelled to put duty before pleasure and take leave of you all. I shall not be missed, for I have not the least skill in the thespian art.' He could not resist allowing his gaze to slide round to Kezia who was sitting outside the fireside group mending the lace of one of the dowager's caps.

'Oh, you cannot be so shabby as to abandon us!' Melissa protested. 'Think how disadvantaged we shall be!'

'Alas, go I must! But perhaps Miss Aston would be kind enough to oblige you.' Again, he sent a fleeting glance in Kezia's direction.

'Of course!' Melissa whirled about to appeal to Kezia. 'You will join us, won't you, Miss Aston?'

The dowager's head lifted sharply. 'I regret

it cannot be so. Miss Aston is needed to go upon an errand for me. I was this moment about to ask her to make ready.'

Kezia flushed. This was the most blatant snub she had yet been given and anger sparked in her eyes. As she laid aside her mending, she was aware that Lord Emmington had turned abruptly to the dowager as though about to intervene. Apparently, he thought better of it. Blandly expressionless, he looked back at Melissa.

'I fear you must accept the handicap, though I cannot believe the resourceful team I see assembled around you will find it so. My greatest regret is that I am compelled to miss the performance.'

With equally suave civility he excused himself to the older ladies, bowed to them all and left the room.

13

Mutiny burned in Kezia's heart and mind as she changed into her riding dress for the second time that day. The dowager was making it abundantly clear that she now regarded her companion not as *Miss Aston and no more*, but as *Miss Aston and something less*. She would not allow herself to be further diminished! Yet, she thought frustratedly, what had the dowager done except behave towards her as she might to any companion she employed? The rub lay in knowing that there was a difference.

Sending a message to the stables to ask for Hebe to be again saddled for her use, she was reminded that she was fortunate in having most of the servants respond to the few requests she made with a pleasant readiness — a readiness she attributed to Sopworth's influence. For some reason, he showed her an unfailing courtesy which made her position at Old Hall far more comfortable than it might have been otherwise.

When she reached the stable-yard, however, the mare was not to be seen. Very much in view was a gleamingly new dark-blue curricle, to which was hitched an equally new and gleaming pair of matched bay horses. Cressick stood holding their heads while two underlings and a stableboy made an admiring audience.

Lord Emmington was talking to Ahmed, but as Kezia arrived, he turned and walked towards the curricle. Pausing before he stepped into the vehicle, he looked across at her and said, with a casualness that belied the speed with which he had seized the opportunity the dowager had quite unintentionally given him, 'You, too, are bound for the village, are you not, Miss Aston? If you are not deterred by the thought that I am about to try this outfit for the first time, allow me to drive you there.'

With a wistful look at the handsome equipage, Kezia said, 'Thank you, sir, but I think Hebe may be already saddled and waiting.'

'Well, Hebe can be unsaddled with no great trouble,' he assured her. 'And,' he continued, correctly interpreting the glance she gave her long riding skirt, 'it will be a simple matter to take you up again on my return journey. But perhaps you doubt my ability to drive you safely?'

Hastily repudiating the suggestion, she crossed to the curricle, allowed herself to be handed in and, taking the moleskin rug he offered her, tucked it neatly around herself. The earl joined her, the reins were shaken out and as soon as Cressick stood away, they were off.

Though her mood was lightened by this unexpected pleasure, its edge of rebellion did not quite vanish and she decided that for the short time it would take the horses to reach the village she would be Kezia Aston, a young lady as much entitled to be taken for a drive in Lord Emmington's new curricle as any of the guests left behind at Old Hall.

A pale sun was pouring silver-gilt brightness through the winterbare branches of the chestnuts flanking the Grand Avenue and the air was bracingly cool making her glad of the velvety rug.

While his lordship was preoccupied with taking the measure of his new horses, Kezia amused herself looking about her at a familiar scene viewed from a different vantage point. Suddenly, it occurred to her that his lordship's offer to drive her to Emmington village might have been less unpremeditated than it had appeared . . . a kindness, in fact, intended to offset the dowager's petty unkindness.

Simple benevolence was not something she had associated with Lucius Sellon so far and she slid a cautious glance towards him. The man was such a chameleon it was not easy to make an assured judgement of him: there was the gypsy, the lordly lord, the man who had 'lived as a prince' in Egypt — and possibly as a despot! — and, lately, there was the detached, well-mannered English gentleman. Who among those was the true Lucius Sellon?

She had let her gaze linger a moment too long. His eyes, brilliant as ever, were turned to catch and hold hers.

'Well, Miss Aston?'

She almost faltered out of her own role of a carefree young lady, but taking hold of herself, she answered lightly, 'Indeed, sir, very well. The curricle rides most smoothly.'

His eyes gleamed at her. 'And the bays pull together perfectly, don't they?'

'I think Melissa, or possibly her brother, Jeremy, would describe them as *sweet-goers*,' she told him demurely.

He laughed, turning away to take the horses through the park gates.

Kezia sighed softly for a pleasure so near its end, but then found the curricle turning left along the lane in quite the wrong direction. The small sound she made brought Lord Emmington's head round towards her again.

'Yes, Miss Aston?'

'I must alight here, sir. I am to go to the village.'

He smiled blandly down at her, making no attempt to bring the horses to a halt. 'And so you shall. But quite reprehensibly, I mean to pursue my own interests before attending to the dowager's.' He saw her uncertainty and added with sly humour, 'I have made no real trial of this rig yet and your opinion added to mine will be invaluable.'

She laughed. 'My opinion can have no great weight, I fear. I have never ridden in a curricle before — as I think you may have guessed.'

His brows lifted in mock astonishment. 'You astound me. You spoke so knowledgeably of the smooth way the curricle rode.'

'On the level gravel of the Grand Avenue the greatest ninny might observe as much.'

'I declare I was shockingly misled,' he rallied her, slackening the horses' pace again to turn them out of the main lane into a narrower right-hand one. 'Still, if I cannot make use of you in one way perhaps I can in another. Since I have not yet explored in this direction, you may be my guide.'

'This way there is Emmington Heath and little else,' Kezia said, and then, entering into the spirit of the thing, told him in the portentous manner of a guide conducting a tour, 'The lane upon which we are now entered is noted for its wandering length. It traverses the extensive moor you see before you and is part of the imposing estates belonging to that most noble lord, the Earl of Emmington. Skirting the eastern boundary of the moor, the lane returns to the village of Emmington, serving only those habitations known as Squatters' Row and Lolly's Farm except when the gypsies set up camp in Fox Spinney.'

She gave him a sparkling glance and concluded in her usual voice, 'And that, sir, is the whole sum of my knowledge except to tell you that the farm is entered on your rolls as Low Ley, but to the villagers it is always Lolly's Farm.'

Lucius bowed exaggerated acknowledgement. 'I am indebted to you, Miss Aston.'

Aware that she had lowered her defences a little, he felt a sudden surge of pleasure. Almost, he could recapture the light-heartedness that had been his when he had first discovered the delight to be found in the company of young women. The conventions of Egyptian society had buried that delight deep: Miss Aston brought it abundantly to mind.

Travelling the grassy track, the curricle

lurched them together occasionally and Kezia found herself awakening to the same physical awareness of the man beside her that she had experienced at their first meeting. Caution awoke. Men of Lucius Sellon's rank did not customarily drive lady companions jaunting about the countryside. If they did, it would be assumed that it could only be to the companion's ultimate sorrow. And that might well be so!

Lucius's smile quizzed her. 'Wouldn't you say this is better than playing charades with the children?'

Indeed, it was! Even if all they were doing was playing a charade of their own. 'Children?' she queried. 'Some of the young ladies are older than I am.'

He mimed astonishment. 'Truly. I should never have guessed.'

'Do I appear so stricken in years? So marked by the crow's foot?' Caution forgotten, her eyes bright with sunlight and laughter dared him to agree.

'How you appear I must not, in politeness, say,' he teased, finding it an effort not to drop the reins, sweep her into his arms and kiss her beautiful mouth. The result of which would be to overturn the curricle and throw them both into the abundant gorse, he thought wryly. His impatience to reach

160

his ultimate goal grew by the day: and what other goal could there be but to lead this girl who so bewitched him through the delights of physical love — which he knew, and she would learn, were the only reality between a man and a woman.

Something of his intensity reached out to her like the heat of a too-near flame. The check was a little firmer this time. Turning away to look over the sunlit heath, she moistened dry lips and let the game lapse.

He sensed her nervousness; felt an uprush of something he did not recognize as tenderness. It flashed into his mind that he was stalking her like a beast of prey and his conscience stirred uneasily. But he could afford no pretty illusions. There could be only one end; he would have her; the fury of his desire would burn itself out and his malaise would be cured. With months of celibacy behind him, the wonder was that he had maintained so far the gentle slowness necessary to bring her to want what he wanted.

His gaze focused on a huddle of mouldering hovels they were approaching. Clumsily built of boulders and scavenged wood, thatched with sagging, grass-grown heath and each with one glassless window, they leaned together like drunken old men.

'What is Harry about to have left such ruins to deface the landscape?' Lucius wondered aloud, bringing the curricle to a halt just short of the group.

'Because they are still lived in. See, there's smoke coming from two of the chimneys,' Kezia told him.

'No other Emmington people live in such conditions, surely!'

'They are not Emmington people. Or not in the sense that you employ them, or they pay you rent.'

'They're on Emmington land.'

'Yes, but it is also common land and the villagers have commoners' rights to pasture. The gypsies have the same time-honoured rights when they come to sell horses at the hiring-fair. The dwellings, such as they are, were built under something called squatters' rights.'

'Which are?'

'As far as I know, it is, or was, a right allowing a man to build a dwelling between sunrise and sunset and if by that time smoke could be seen rising from the chimney, the house could remain. The first of those was built nearly a hundred years ago, I'm told. The other three were added gradually. No one lives in the original one now, the back wall collapsed when the roof-beam broke. I think someone keeps a few hens in what remains.'

'The hens deserve better! But how do the occupiers support themselves?'

Kezia shook her head. 'That is something of a mystery, but in any case rather poorly. They are thought to poach and raid the village gardens. They are all related, so I imagine they help each other. The villagers don't approve of them but they go to the old woman called Gammer Mullinger when driven by need. She cures warts and boils and . . . other things.' The 'other things' had never been specified in her hearing.

'How do you know all this?'

'Harry — Mr Osborne told me,' she said.

Harry! He stirred the bays to life again, giving the hovels a last scowl as they passed. 'They'll have to come down,' he said shortly.

Kezia glanced sharply at him. Did he mean to have the squatters evicted? Surely not! Dreadful as the hovels were, they were all the occupants had.

Squatters' Row was a silent quarter of a mile behind them before Kezia put her disquiet into words. 'If you have Mullingers' dwellings pulled down, what will happen to them?'

He looked at her and laughed. 'Still no faith in me, Miss Aston? I promise you that

163

every living thing from Gammer Mullinger down to the last hen, will be out of those dwellings before they are brought down. Does that satisfy you?'

She blushed, recalling the unhappy scene in the library when he first came to Old Hall and she had tried to explain why the dowager had not removed to the Dower House. Doggedly, she asked, 'But where are they to go?'

'I am confident Harry will be able to rehouse them somewhere in the village . . . to their considerably improved comfort and convenience!'

'Oh, but — ' She halted abruptly.

'Don't stop there, Miss Aston. I'm sure you have something very pertinent to say.'

Her lips quivered. 'I think you mean *impertinent*, sir. But what I was about to say was that you might not find the Mullingers happy to leave the common. You see the houses are *theirs*. And they are not liked . . . they are unlikely to find a welcome in Emmington.'

'I see. But how do they bear the squalor they live in here? What, for instance, do they do for water?'

'I believe there is a dipping-pool nearby. But it is understood that they do not see water as a first necessity of life.'

He laughed. 'Well, let us forget the Mullingers and find a more interesting subject for discussion.'

None occurred to them quickly however, but as they reached the summit of a small hill and the widening view made it evident they had reached the highest point of the common, Lucius brought the bays to a stand again. At this time of the year, the moor's chief attractions lay in the formation of the land and the contrasts created by the winter colours of bleached gold grass and the rich chestnut of dead heather. An exception to this was located just below them where Fox Spinney filled the floor of a small coombe and flung up a few graceful outliers of birch and hawthorn. Here the grassy slopes remained green and a few snugly placed gorse bushes already showed a ruffling of sumptuous yellow-gold.

The silence pressing on Kezia, she said with slightly breathless banality, 'It was very pretty here in the autumn.'

When Lucius made no acknowledgement of this remark, she turned to look at him and found him gazing intently at her. Silence tightened around them again, the winter-stark heath faded from their consciousness and they saw only each other.

Without thinking of what he was doing

or of what he meant to do, Lucius looped the reins over the guard rail and brought his hands up to rest on the curves of her shoulders. Through the velvet of her jacket and whatever else she was wearing, he felt the delicacy of her bones. Light as was his hold was on her, it was enough to bring a wild leap of anticipation to his loins by which he was warned that there would be nothing temperate in his actions if he took her in his arms at this moment.

He meant to kiss her, Kezia was sure of it. However blinkered she had been in the past, she saw now, with sharp clarity, that she had always known this moment would come and that she would be willing.

She saw the change happen: saw the thick black lashes veil the glitter in his eyes, heard the indrawn breath. His hands tightened painfully on her shoulders in the moment before he leant nearer to merely touch his lips to her forehead.

'Time to head for the village, I think, Miss Aston,' he said with brittle brightness, dismissing his action as the merest shadow-play of flirtation.

Kezia sat as though turned to stone. Had he suddenly remembered she was only 'the companion' and he the Earl of Emmington? Much that had mattered when he had kissed her in anger! She dredged up her pride. She was not a village innocent eager for the distinction of being kissed by the Earl of Emmington, she told herself furiously. But it did nothing to lessen her sense of having been cheated . . . could not tell whether the tears that pricked her eyes sprang from disappointment, humiliation, or any other emotion.

All she was sure of was that the silly game she had been playing had come to the end it deserved.

14

The pleasure first aroused by her drive with Lord Emmington, appeared to Kezia to have been short-lived compared with the feelings of guilt and anger left in its wake.

She had, she knew, wanted quite desperately that Lucius Sellon should kiss her. Therein lay her guilt. She lived in a world that imposed the belief that well-conducted young women had no such wants before marriage. Her anger was two-fold and contradictory: with herself for wanting his kiss; with Lord Emmington for withholding it. And under all lay a wild panic that she was on the road to falling in love with the man. What could be more foolish than that!

One blessed relief was that Lord Emmington's behaviour remained exactly as it had been before that portentous drive had taken place. Another relief was that no one had informed the dowager of the way her companion had spent the time that was meant to be a corrective to any mistaken ideas she might have as to her status.

In the days that followed, Kezia found her moods fluctuating dangerously. Chafed by her false position at Old Hall, she was increasingly convinced of her unwisdom in coming to it. That she and the countess had rubbed along comfortably for a time had been only because it had suited the countess's convenience. And now, even the comfort of Harry's friendship was failing her.

The weather, too, had changed. A thin fall of snow had been followed by a bitter frost that froze it to a treacherous glaze. Broken limbs were frequently the reward of those compelled to venture out and mere visiting was brought to a halt.

The intense cold put an ache in the dowager's bones, shortening her temper. Over-indulgence in a rich game pie one evening gave her a disturbed night and a sharp reminder of mortality. Having refused her breakfast, a nuncheon of milk soup did nothing to improve her temper and Rudge, Kezia and even Melissa, were made to know it. An afternoon spent sitting by a comfortable fire with Kezia reading aloud Sir Walter Scott's lately published *Guy Mannering* brought some amelioration and half-past five found her very soundly asleep in her chair.

It was the time at which the old lady normally went to her room for the slow process of changing for dinner now set at 6.30. Melissa had already gone to her room, but for a while Kezia hesitated to wake the dowager. A quarter of an hour later, she knew it must be done. Bending over the old lady, she shook her gently by the shoulder.

The dowager was deep in the dearest of dreams: she and Charlotte were to have a picnic nuncheon beside the largest lake and she sat contentedly on a seat in the warm sunshine, waiting for her grand-daughter. The girl's hand on her shoulder took her by surprise. She opened her eyes to see a smiling face and, half dreaming still, she said softly, 'Charlotte . . . there you are, dear girl!'

In the next instant her mind clicked awake. The bitterness of fierce disappointment brought a scowl to her face and she snapped, 'What are you about! Don't crowd me, girl!'

More sensitive than usual to the dowager's waspishness, Kezia's defences were penetrated and she straightened as though slapped.

The dowager, not entirely exempt from knowledge of her own injustice, gathered her wits. Casting about for a genuine grievance, she remembered her discontent over Kezia's refusal to co-operate with her where Harry Osborne was concerned and launched into a different line of attack.

'So little heed you pay to my wishes, miss! Do not think I have forgotten your ingratitude for my care on your behalf! I bestir myself to point out to you Harry Osborne's interest — an opportunity far above your reasonable hopes! — and you do nothing! You may wake one day to find all chances gone and with nothing to keep you from want except you join the sisterhood of the streets. And so I tell you!'

Astonished at the irrelevance of the charge, Kezia returned with more heat than wisdom, 'Be at rest, ma'am. Should Mr Osborne honour me with a proposal, I must decline it. We should not suit.'

She heard herself with surprise. On Christmas Night, she had decided — she had *almost* decided — she would accept an offer from Harry. But that, too, was irrelevant — if Harry had intended to propose marriage, he appeared to have changed his mind.

Several ominous seconds flowed past in which time the dowager gathered furious breath to say, 'Graceless girl! You have not deserved my notice! Wilful . . . headstrong . . . ungrateful! Your father's daughter, without doubt!'

Her father aspersed again! That kind, clever, enchanting father she still mourned. Bitterness lanced through Kezia.

'For what am I ungrateful, ma'am? I came here by your desire. *Why* you wished it, I have never understood! But I should not have come. Indeed, I wish I never had! I — ' The cold dignity with which she had begun fled as angry tears suffocated the words in her throat. Turning, she rushed from the room, jerking the door shut behind her.

She ran blindly and literally into the arms of Lord Emmington who had been about to enter. He steadied her, saw her distress and did not let her go.

'What has happened?'

Emotions out of control, she thrust wildly at him. 'The trouble is that I am my mother's daughter, though it is my father for whom I am blamed!' The words spoken, for a moment she was too absorbed by their truth to realize the unwisdom of having spoken them aloud.

'Difficult charges against which to plead, I can see.'

There was a smile in his voice, but it was the warm sympathy that released her angry tears.

Lucius gathered her close. The small convulsions of the sobs she was trying to stifle vibrated through his own body, generating a deep solicitude for her and a partisan anger against the woman who had caused her distress.

Wrapped in her trouble, Kezia accepted the haven she had found, bowing her head against the convenient shoulder while she fought to regain control. She was unaware of the kiss he ghosted on her hair, had no notion of the depth of pleasure he felt in being able to hold her unresisting in his arms, nor of his growing desire to hold her closer still, to kiss away her trouble, to — Oh, yes, to —

As the storm abated, he said softly, 'Tell me, how does being your mother's daughter offend her ladyship?'

Abruptly Kezia awoke to whose voice asked the thorny question, to whose arms held her. Guilt and guilt again! She moved uneasily within his hold and murmured, 'I should not have said what I did. I beg you will forget it.'

'It might help to share your trouble.'

She shook her bent head. 'I am the wrong person to be the countess's companion. I provoke her because — ' No, that would not do! Hurriedly she amended, 'I provoke her simply by being myself. I should never have come to Old Hall.'

'Don't say that.'

The soft, caressing tone brought her head

up. His face, lean, dark, purposeful, was very close to hers. The nearest candelabra shed just enough light for her to see the intensity of his gaze, almost to feel it press against her skin.

He kissed her then, at first to give comfort, but found such delight in the giving, compassion soon gave place to something more self-seeking and even more rewarding.

Closing her eyes, Kezia yielded her mouth to the gentleness of his, accepting, following, answering with inexpert eagerness a kiss that deepened and deepened until her heart beat wildly and every nerve danced with delight. Mindless and unashamed, all the reproaches she had showered upon herself since the curricle drive washed from her memory. She found no fault with the closeness of her body to his; no fault with the hands that caressed her; no fault with this revealing and marvellous experience.

It was the sound of a servant's footstep on the stone flagging of the ancient floor of the hall, the chink and rattle of a laden tray being carried to the dining-room that slowly, slowly, pierced their absorption and forced them apart. Almost too late to avoid detection, Lucius eased them both into the deeper shadow and shelter of a pillar.

Slowly, Kezia roused from enchantment to

realize the narrowness of their escape. It was all very well for her to let this man into her private thoughts simply as Lucius Sellon — but it was the Earl of Emmington who would have been seen with the dowager's companion locked in his arms — and what a *sauce piquante* that would have provided for the servants' supper-table!

The dining-room door closed on the servant and Lucius exhaled a slow, deep breath. Bending to put a light and final kiss on her lips, he said on a note of satisfaction, 'Well, Miss Aston, *well* . . . ' Then, holding her away from him, suddenly practical, added, 'Go to your room now and I'll have a meal sent up to you. It will give me opportunity to smooth your path with the countess.'

'Oh, but she — '

He touched a finger to her lips. 'No buts. Leave all to me. Go now.'

Watching her slim figure pass out of sight, Lucius knew he had caught her when she was vulnerable. He could not regret it: her response to him had gone beyond an unthinking acceptance of comfort.

He turned his thoughts to the old woman whose tongue and temper had brought it about. He admired her indomitable spirit, but suspected it had been without check long enough to become tyrannical.

The dowager was frowning into the fire when he entered the Lily Room and he saw at a glance that temper had taken toll of her. Reminded that age brought fragility, he softened the manner of his approach.

Having bid her good-evening, he opened with, 'I saw Miss Aston in the hall. She appeared distressed.'

The dowager's frown deepened. 'An obstinate and ungrateful young woman. I am quite out of patience with her!'

'You surprise me. What has she done?'

Too arrogantly confident to feel the need to lie, she was not above selecting which truth and which aspect of it she wished to present.

'It is what she has *not* done! Her disregard of my concern . . . of my advice. Her unwillingness to co-operate in advancing her own interests. Placed as she is, it is quite beyond permission!'

'Oh? How *is* she placed, Countess?'

Her pale gaze jerked back to him. That was a question she did not care to answer. Side-stepping it, she said, 'In no case to refuse an offer of marriage from Harry Osborne! His position here as steward of the Emmington estates is sufficient recommendation for a young woman such as Miss Aston without considering that he has the additional consequence of being nephew to General Sir Hubert Osborne, a baronet and a soldier of distinction. The general has a son, so Harry has no expectations in that direction, but to have attracted the interest of such a man is reason enough for Miss Aston to thank Heaven on her knees! But will she lift a finger to make sure of him? She will not!'

The strength of the jealous alarm that woke in him was surprising, but it had occurred to him that what Miss Aston said to the dowager bent on shaping the girl to her will, and what she might say to Harry, making a proposal with warmth of feeling and his damnable charm of manner, could be very different. Harry was a positive danger. Since Christmas he made it as difficult as possible for his steward and Miss Aston to meet. If more stringent measures were needed, he would take them.

'Have you certain knowledge of Harry's intentions?' he demanded brusquely.

The dowager shook her head. 'No. But you have only to see the way he looks at her to know he wants only a little encouragement.'

'Well, she has the right of choice we must allow,' he said mendaciously.

'A young woman's business in life is to find a husband. Lacking consequence, she marries where she can and thinks herself lucky to do so. Women of more importance oblige their families by marrying where they should. It is the way of the world, as you know and I know. It is time Miss Aston knew it!'

Lucius regarded the iron-willed old woman with sardonic curiosity. 'Was that how it was with you, Countess?'

For a moment she was bereft of words. Memory rushed in of the tears and tantrums with which she had fought long-ago battles. It was nearly seventy years since her beauty and wit had caught the attention of a duke. But her heart had already been given to the mere younger son of an earl. Mighty had been the storms she had conjured up to win the right to marry the Honourable Gerard Sellon. Fate alone had made her a countess through the untimely death of her husband's elder brother. Thrusting the traitorous recollections away, she said testily, 'It is Miss Aston's wilful folly we are discussing.'

'Perhaps Miss Aston feels her income is sufficient to permit her a degree of independence?'

'*An income?*' She stared incredulously at him, then snapped, 'It isn't possible!'

Her tone told him how unwelcome was the idea that her companion was not entirely penniless. Contemptuously, she declared, 'It cannot signify! At best, it can be no more than a pittance she dignifies with the title of income. Enough, merely, to deprive her of common sense.'

So she did not know all there was to know about Miss Aston. He decided to probe a little. 'She is obviously a well-bred young woman. What of her family, Countess?'

Malice sparked in her eyes and her lips thinned. 'She has none prepared to recognize her. An unknown father puts her outside the pale.'

His guess concerning the irregularity of Miss Aston's parentage appeared confirmed. He wished he could shake out of the dowager the details of whatever sorry story she was concealing, but it was plain that the energy that had sustained her so far was at an end. Her pallor had increased and she leant back in her chair with closed eyes. 'To have such discord around me is more than I am able for,' she lamented faintly.

Discord of her own making, Lucius thought; but age and weakness still commanded consideration. With more sympathy than he felt, he said, 'I applaud your concern for Miss Aston's future, Countess, but let the matter rest now. It is an insufficient reason to risk losing her excellent services. Wiser thoughts may yet prevail with her. My present concern is for *you*. Sit where you are for a while longer and I will have a restorative glass of Madeira brought to you.' He moved to tug at a bell-pull as he spoke.

The dowager made no demur. It was pleasant to have better motives attributed to her than she deserved; pleasant to be made to feel that her comfort was a matter of importance to Emmington. She needed time, too, to decide how to mend matters with the girl. Obviously, there was a point beyond which Miss Aston could not be pushed; as obviously, she could not be allowed to leave Old Hall on her own whim. It occurred to her that it was several weeks since Harry had been seen at Old Hall. That must be remedied and something done to promote his interest in her companion.

When the wine had been brought, Lucius took leave of her. He waited until the footman who had followed him out of the room had closed the door, then said to the man, 'See that a message is sent to Mr Osborne immediately, Merrett. Say that I will see him in the Cabinet at eight o'clock tomorrow morning.'

15

Harry emerged from his meeting with the earl
next morning with his belief in his lordship's
freedom from caprice considerably shaken.
More troubling was the feeling that their
hitherto easy relationship had changed. It
brought sharply to his notice that he had not
entered Old Hall since Christmas: a period
already distinguished by his inability ever to
find himself alone with Kezia.

He had accepted as inevitable that extra
work would descend on his shoulders with
the coming of a new earl; equally, he
accepted that he and Kezia were fixed in
spheres which made them subject to the
commands of others and so could not order
their comings and goings as they chose. What
he found strange was that lately, Kezia had
become as inaccessible as though she lived a
hundred miles away. He did not guess the
reason, but now that he was in the house
he decided to make use of opportunity.

It was a gift of fortune that Betty Bassett
should emerge from one of the old hidden
stairways just then and agree very willingly
to carry a message to Miss Aston.

★ ★ ★

The small room to which Kezia came in response to that message had once been a writing parlour, but being placed on a chilly northeast corner and further doomed by an incurably faulty chimney, it had fallen into disuse. Its tall narrow window gloomed out on a view that took in only a plain strip of grass before being lost in the blackness of an ancient yew-tree. In the dim grey light, even the room's furniture now looked forlornly unwanted.

Harry stood facing the door when Kezia entered, his face too shadowed for her to read his expression. His choice of meeting place puzzled her, hinting at a need for secrecy which prompted her to close the door behind her.

Harry was already regretting his choice of location. Its single virtue lay in the unlikeliness of anyone coming to it. With a wan smile, he said, 'I have thought I was never to see you again. Now that I do, you are likely to take a chill from it.'

Why she felt a shyness with him that she had never felt before, Kezia did not know. Harry saw it was so and groaned inwardly. Too much time had passed and the early hour and dreary surroundings were all too unpropitious for his purpose. Unable to draw back, pushed into unusual gracelessness, he blurted, 'I had to see you before I go!'

'Go?' She was startled.

'Yes.' For once, a sense of grievance echoed in his voice. 'I must go again over a large part of the journey Lord Emmington and I made in November. There is no necessity for it that I can see. Before I go, I must arrange for Squatters' Row to be pulled down.' He saw her arrested look and said, 'Oh, they are to be rehoused! On the common and with a well dug for their use. As if that were not sufficiently unprofitable, no rents are to be required of them. If his lordship looks for gratitude from the Mullingers, or even willing co-operation in anything done for them, he is likely to be sadly disappointed.'

Puzzled by such an unusual flow of complaints from Harry, Kezia said lamely, 'I'm sorry.'

And what a fine, sour opening to a proposal he'd made! Harry thought despairingly. Where had their old comfortable relationship gone? Baldly, desperately, he said, 'I love you, Kezia!'

So completely had she dismissed expectation of a proposal from Harry, she was utterly unprepared. She had come to meet him with her mind clouded by thought that had nothing to do with Harry and everything to do with Lucius Sellon. Dismayed, she was able to say only, *'Oh, Harry!'*

But Harry now found his voice. From his heart, with a sincerity that pierced her through, he said again, 'I love you, Kezia. I can draw no grand pictures of what I am, or what I have to offer, for both are known to you. But if you could find enough in what there is to be my wife, there is nothing in this world that could make me happier, and I would leave nothing undone that would give you happiness.' He caught one of her hands in his and carrying it to his lips pressed a loving, anxious kiss on her fingers.

Kezia could not hide her dismay. Coming after a night made sleepless by see-sawing wishes and fears, longings and self-reproach, she knew with miserable certainty that whatever her future was to be, it did not lie with Harry. She would never know how she would have answered him if he had spoken sooner, but with sad conviction, she knew that *now* it was too late.

And this was still Harry whose feelings she cared about deeply; Harry, whom she must answer with all the kindness and honesty he deserved though knowing she could not hope to soften the bleak truth. Gently, she said,

'Harry, you honour me in every way. I truly have the greatest regard for you, but I . . . I cannot marry you.'

He had not been sure of her, yet, because his hope of success had been high, the hurt and shock of her refusal was great. She saw it in his eyes, heard it in his voice when he said, 'I hoped so much . . . thought — ' He closed his eyes momentarily; opened them to throw a swift, disconsolate glance around. 'This wretched room . . . this isn't where or how I wanted — ' He broke off, recognizing the futility of the words. Releasing her hand, he said with a twisted smile, 'We may still be friends, I hope.'

She nodded, tears stinging her eyes. And then they were interrupted by the one person who knew where they were.

They had missed the knock on the door, but they turned as it opened to reveal Betty Bassett, red-checked, wide-eyed and over-full with the feast of this morning's interest. She dipped a curtsy. 'Sorry, miss, sir, but there's a Frenchie come and no one to understand him properly and Mr Sopworth's sending everywhere for Mr Osborne to come and speak to him. So I thought as I'd better let you know.'

Harry made a sound in his throat close to a bitter laugh, then walked to the door.

Looking back, he said, 'Will you allow me to hope?'

Though she felt his hurt as if it were her own, she dared not weaken. Shaking her head, she said, 'I'm sorry . . . so sorry! But it would not be wise.'

Left alone, the coldness of the place seeming to press even closer about her, and she shivered. She blamed herself for having allowed Harry to grow fond to the point of proposing, only to disappoint him. He had deserved better of her. But she had not understood her own feelings. Still did not, beyond being deeply aware that Harry — dear as he was — had no power to wake her senses to exquisite life as they had been woken by Lucius Sellon.

Late into the night, she had lived and relived the magic of those moments when Lucius Sellon's hands and lips had opened the door on the world of physical sensation, when her skin had discovered a new sensitivity to touch and her mouth had grown greedy for the pleasure it was being given. In the first blind, absorbed moment when she had collided with Lucius and his arms had closed about her, her quiescence had been innocent. But from the moment she had looked up and read his clear intent, she had been his willing partner, and through it, had been changed forever. Yet, with the afterglow of delight still lying richly along every nerve, still filled with a deep longing to do again what had been done, she had made herself listen to cold reason's voice.

Reason had pointed to the fact that had the Earl of Emmington kissed any of the young ladies who came to Old Hall as he had kissed *her* an immediate offer of marriage would be expected. Miss Aston, without fortune or family, could have no such expectation. What Miss Aston had rashly invited was an offer of *carte blanche*; or, even worse because more humiliating, being left to discover that what had been so momentous to her had been nothing more than a few moments' entertainment to him.

So what did she want? An affair leading to her own inevitable ruin? Hallie, within the limits of her own virgin state, had made her a little less ignorant than most girls. She had been told it was a false persuasion that women did not feel desire; that for women, as for men, desire could exist separately from love. But, Hallie had impressed on her, love had its greatest power when desire was an inseparable part of it. What did she feel for Lucius Sellon? She recognized that her mind turned to him in endless fascination, knew now that her body sang to his touch — but was that *love*? Surely love attached itself to qualities. What qualities in the Earl of Emmington, that man of many guises, called to her? Perhaps she was merely 'in love', that lesser, less enduring state of loving without reason, of half creating the object of one's devotion.

What was unbearable was to know that if she had met Lucius in different circumstances things would be very different. Once again, she had been a fool and the falseness of her position at Old Hall was becoming impossibly vexatious. If her parents had married, she, as the granddaughter and great-granddaughter of two noble families would not be altogether beneath Lucius Sellon's consideration as a wife.

She had always prided herself on her good sense but none came to her aid now: weakly, she told herself that how Lord Emmington behaved towards her today would have some bearing on what she ultimately decided to do.

Harry's proposal, she thought sadly as she left the room, could hardly have been more mistimed.

16

The Frenchman, a courier, heralded the arrival of two be-shawled, robed and turbanned Egyptians. Melissa, halfway down the main stairway, was privileged to witness this later event.

Having relayed the interesting news to her great-aunt and Kezia, she was in hourly expectation of meeting these exotics, but the day passed and nothing was seen of Lord Emmington or his visitors. The ladies dined alone and though the Egyptians were known to be spending the night at Old Hall, their curiosity remained unsatisfied and by daylight the next day, the Egyptians had gone.

Kezia, however, had an advantage not enjoyed by Melissa and the dowager. When she had retired to her bedroom the previous evening, she had found Betty Bassett kneeling by the fire, ostensibly sweeping up ash. Scrambling to her feet, she burst into excited speech as soon as Kezia entered.

'Oh, miss, what a day it's been with them two foreign gentlemen in their fancy rig! And such a carry-on at dinner-time as you'd never believe! I declare John footman will take a month to recover. Him seeing his lordship kissing them both like they was ladies when they come, was nothing to what he saw later. 'Tis no wonder, he says, that Ahmed don't eat with the rest of us if he goes on in the same unaccountable way. But it was Ahmed, himself, what told us that gentlemen don't eat with the ladies in Egypt — which is a queer enough start for anything!'

A gasp for breath and she plunged on: 'Anyway, dinner for they two and his lordship was ordered to be served in the small red salon in the east wing. First though, a whole pile of cushions was to be taken in because they wasn't to sit to table but on the floor! But it was when Ahmed showed John footman and Will what they was to do before his lordship and his guests ate anything that they was struck like ducks in thunder. They and Ahmed was each of them to carry in a jug, a basin and a towel and then pour water into the basins slow-like while the gentlemen washed their faces and hands, swilled out their mouths and even sniffed water up their noses. It was all such a raree show as you never did see! And why it wasn't all done in their rooms like Christians, I don't know!'

Kezia smiled as Betty was forced to a

halt again. 'Lord Emmington's guests are probably not Christians but Mohammedans, Betty. Things are done differently in their country.'

'Does that mean they're heathens, Miss?' Betty's eyes grew rounder.

'No, not heathens. They have different customs and a different way of worshipping God, that's all.'

'Well, they does a whole lot of other things different, too! They didn't use no knives nor forks, only spoons for the puddings. John and Will had to wait outside the room to fetch and carry like, but when the door stood open once or twice, they could see even his lordship putting one of his hands in the dishes and eating like that. What's more, they all passed bits to each other in their fingers. If that's what their religion tells 'em to do, it's queerer than what they Shakers do over to Bagman's Hollow. And John said things wasn't so friendly between them all the time. It sounded to him like there was a sizeable argument going on one time.'

Kezia dismissed the girl at this point, feeling a little guilty for having allowed her to run on so far. But gossip in the servants' hall was inevitable and Betty, as the youngest and newest maid, would be allowed very small say, however much her tongue itched for exercise.

Tired but unready for sleep, she sat for a while by the fire. The day had dragged. What had passed between her and Harry had laid a weight of depression on her already troubled spirit and she had gone to her first meeting with the dowager that morning caring very little about what might ensue. the old lady's airy dismissal of the previous evening's discord as a mere bagatelle, had surprised her but she had accepted it with indifference.

And then, staring at Kezia, her expression fierce with inward struggle, the dowager had wrenched out, 'Do not think me unaware that you are, in your way, a very good sort of young woman.'

Even that commendation, qualified but extraordinary, had hardly breached Kezia's preoccupation with wondering how Lucius Sellon would behave towards her when next they met. But the Egyptians' coming had meant there had been no meeting: instead another night had come with all her questions unanswered.

★ ★ ★

Soon after the door had closed on his departing visitors, the earl rode out on

Moorsi. A rumour that he now had a visit to Egypt in view set Melissa and the dowager in competition to air their dissatisfactions. This was only ended by the arrival of the Duke of Mawdsham and his sister.

'Well, you see we are come, Countess, just as soon as the horses could be safely allowed on the road,' the duke said in his usual easy manner. 'We must be thankful that with so little snow fallen we have not now to face such floods as we had last year.'

Kezia regarded Lady Hermione with interest, remembering that this woman had been her mother's close girlhood friend. She was a small woman, elegantly gowned in deep amethyst-coloured *mousseline de laine*, over which she wore a sable pelisse somewhat adrift on her shoulders. Even her pale-grey, high-crowned hat trimmed with puffed gauze was slightly askew as though she had dressed in a hurry and whisked herself out of her maid's hands too soon. There was a strong likeness between the brother and sister, but Hermione's face was thinner, sharper, with more reserve in its expression. For all that, it was a likeable face, Kezia thought, its best feature being the dark-brown eyes lit by a lively intelligence. She was older than the duke, about forty, the age Kezia's mother would have been had she lived. It was surprising she had remained single: even if she had lacked personal attractions, her rank and the fortune she must be supposed to have, would have guaranteed her being sought after.

When introduced, Kezia received a brief searching look, a small smile and a nod. How would they have met if it were known that she was Lady Charlotte Sellon's daughter, Kezia wondered.

Conversation among them ranged more widely than usual since Lady Hermione did not scruple to introduce such unconventional topics as the acute distress in some parts of England and the problem of the common soldiers returning from the wars against Napoleon, many of them wounded and little or no provision made for them.

'Poor fellows,' said the duke. 'Heroes all, not long ago. Now thought a nuisance and a public danger because some are driven to poach to keep alive.'

'I cannot think you would welcome them in your coverts, Charles,' the dowager observed dryly.

'True. But I wouldn't grudge a bird to a hungry man. And this new rule — seven years' transportation for a single offence — too much. Not right!'

'The Gierneys' gamekeeper could never be

convinced of that!' the countess shot back.

'Are the Gierneys still in Madeira? My head man told me only recently their keeper is a fanatic liable to shoot the rector's cow should she put her head over the wrong fence. Too free a hand too long!'

'Some say the man's mad. But until the Gierneys return, what can be done?' The dowager shrugged aside the subject, turned to Lady Hermione and, a subtle edge to her voice, said, 'My London correspondents tell me your favourite poet creates worse scandal than ever, Hermione, difficult though that is to believe!'

'You are speaking of Byron, I suppose?' Lady Hermione's glance was cool. 'Few marriages can be such total mismatches as was his with Anne Milbanke. What meeting-ground could ever be found between his generous mind and spirit and her narrowness? Given his intelligence, it is the greatest wonder to me that he yielded to her yearning to bring him under her reforming zeal!'

The dowager's eyes glinted. 'An impossible task, certainly, if she thought to reform a rake of such magnitude!'

'I suspect her gaze was fixed on the magnitude of her triumph should she succeed,' Lady Hermione returned.

'What I cannot like,' the duke put in, 'is

Lady Byron removing to Scotland with their month-old infant and refusing to return. It has hit George hard. And still to write him affectionate letters while posting north as though all were well! Dishonest! Perhaps, though, she submitted to family pressure. The Milbankes will have found him expensive but can hardly claim surprise.'

'If that were all!' The dowager snorted a derisive laugh. 'It is what *else* is laid to his charge that has set London in ferment — or so I am informed.'

'Ferment from a yeast of spite supplied by Caro Lamb? Since when has society placed reliance on anything emanating from that irresponsible quarter?' Hermione countered coolly. 'But how easy it is, as Swift says, to 'Convey a libel in a frown, And wink a reputation down'.'

The duke nodded agreement. 'Damned by mere accusation! Until I'm told there is irrefutable evidence of inc — ' His recollecting gaze touched Melissa and Kezia and he amended his sentence to . . . 'of infamy, I shall not think differently of him.'

Bravo! thought Kezia. Whatever the truth was regarding George Gordon, Lord Byron, she admired the Delarives' championship of their friend. But what roused her curiosity was her feeling that the malice underlying the dowager's remarks was directed less at Byron than at Lady Hermione.

Tactfully, the duke turned the conversation to Melissa's approaching come-out and after a moment or two, leaving that to be discussed by the others, he moved his chair a little nearer to Kezia and said quietly, 'So, we meet again, Miss Aston. How do you go on? It must be pleasant for you to have a companion close to your own age in the house,'

His speaking as though she and Melissa were equals surprised Kezia, but she accepted it as an instance of the duke's charming manners. She found him very easy to talk to, his slightly staccato delivery adding to the amusement of the way he sometimes aired his private opinions. Their rapport, however, soon attracted the dowager's notice. It was then Kezia discovered that Charles Delarive's democracy was not a cover for weakness as, with firm courtesy, he resisted all efforts made by the old lady to draw him from her companion's side.

Before the brother and sister left, Lady Hermione extended an invitation to the Old Hall party to dine at Staneflete Castle the following day, but learning that Lord Emmington might be absent, she amended the invitation to those able to come.

Saying goodbye to Melissa, the duke gave voice to one of his asides, remarking as he turned away, 'Engaging little handful . . . '

Dinner that evening was twice put back in hope of the earl's coming but the meal was an hour past and they were all again in the Lily drawing-room before he appeared. He looked, Kezia thought, both tired and moody. After a brief apology for his absence, he told the dowager abruptly, 'I leave for Egypt early tomorrow. The sea journey will take ten days — longer if we meet adverse weather. An overland journey and a stay of a day or two means I cannot look to return much under five weeks. Harry Osborne will remain here in my absence since it is inadvisable that both he and I should be absent at the same time.'

The dowager exclaimed and questioned, endeavouring without success to discover the purpose of his journey, and then marvelling at his going at all.

The moment she paused, Melissa cried brightly, 'Sir, I have a quarrel to discuss with you! I hold it most unkind that you kept your interesting visitors entirely to yourself.'

The dowager snorted indignation at this presumption, but before she could speak, Lucius, turning a darkly sardonic look on the young girl, asked, 'You converse easily in Egyptian, do you, miss?'

'Oh!' Melissa grimaced. 'Still, just to look, you know.' She gave him a saucy smile.

'My guests would have thought it a great impertinence. Women do not raise their eyes to men in Egypt, nor do they speak unless spoken to.'

'Good heavens! How unnatural! I should not care for it.'

'If you were born there, you would know no difference.'

'I doubt that would reconcile me!'

'I doubt it, too.'

He was turning away when she said, 'Well, having been deprived of one treat, may I beg another in its place? Will you give a dancing-party — a ball — as soon as you return? Very soon after, you know, I am to go London for the Season, and it would be a splendid chance for me to show off the steps I have been practising before I go.' She dimpled prettily at him. '*Do* say yes, Lucius.'

So much was too much for the dowager and she rapped out, 'That is freedom abused, miss! It is beyond the mark for you to address the Earl of Emmington with such familiarity!'

'I invited Melissa to use my name, Countess,' Lucius intervened. 'We may consider ourselves cousins by marriage, I suppose. As for the ball . . . I imagine that in the past the dancers of the neighbourhood have looked to Old Hall to provide for them occasionally. So we will think of it as a possibility.' For all the dry indifference with which he spoke, it was clear that Melissa was likely to have her wish.

The dowager flashed a hopeful glance between the two. The chit had a saucy charm; something might come of it.

'Oh, famous!' Melissa swept Lucius a curtsy and blew him a kiss as she rose. 'You will hurry back, won't you? Five weeks is a prodigious long time to wait.' Without waiting for an answer, she spread her skirts and, twirling round, declared, 'But I shall use them to practise my steps and amaze everyone with my grace and proficiency.'

'You might practise for a little modesty at the same time,' the dowager observed dourly.

Kezia, reknotting the ravelled fringe of a silk shawl she had been given to repair, let the work rest in her lap as she watched this small pantomime and wrestled with a searing bitterness. Not once since he entered the room had Lucius Sellon looked towards her. That he was preoccupied — and not pleasurably — was plain; even so, he had spared some attention for Melissa. Miss Aston was unremembered.

The dowager's voice cut across her unhappy reflections. 'For the second time, Miss Aston, will you be good enough to bring my lorgnette from my room? I cannot think how you have failed to notice I am without it.'

Laying aside the shawl, Kezia walked out into the hall. She was aware of a faint tremble along her nerves that comes from a sleepless night as she started up the stairs. She had reached the eighth tread when a voice behind her called harshly, *'Miss Aston!'*

The sudden, explosive sound startled her and turning too suddenly, she was thrown off balance. The foot supporting most of her weight was not fully on the tread and her ankle twisted painfully. She made a wild grab for the banister, missed and fell, striking her head on the newel post as she reached the bottom.

She came back to half-awareness to find Lord Emmington's arm supporting her shoulders and Melissa, not quite in focus, peering anxiously down at her while the dowager stood a disapproving presence in the background.

'She's not badly hurt, is she?' Melissa

asked with concern.

Answering for herself, Kezia said faintly, 'No. In a minute . . . in a minute . . . '

The hall blurred and swam around her as she tried to sit up and only determination and help from both Melissa and his lordship allowed her to stand. When she tried to put weight on her left foot, however, it gave way and it was her helpers' support alone that saved her from falling again.

Resignedly, the dowager said, 'John footman had better carry her to her room where she may rest awhile. Bassett can attend her.'

Before she had finished speaking, Lord Emmington had lifted Kezia into his arms. 'No need for John. I'll take Miss Aston up. And I suspect she will need to rest more than a while.' He nodded at Melissa. 'Go ahead and ring for Bassett.'

What a tiresome creature he must think her, Kezia thought, gritting her teeth against the pain of movement. But the accident had been his fault! It was his peremptory call that had brought it about. What had he wanted? She looked up at him. Still preoccupied, he now looked grim, too. She closed her eyes.

He laid her on her bed with gentle care but spoke brusquely, saying, 'I need to look at your ankle to make sure it is a sprain and no worse.'

Without waiting for her acquiescence, he turned back the hem of her gown and ran firm but gentle fingers over the swelling joint. 'A bad sprain almost certainly, but the apothecary shall decide. Meanwhile, cold compresses, rest, and no running around after . . . no running around for any reason.'

Oddly, his expression now appeared to be one of barely concealed satisfaction. As though, Kezia thought incredulously, he's actually pleased my ankle is sprained.

'Your foot will bear no use for some time,' he continued. 'In particular, there can be no riding until recovery is certain. Three or four weeks — No. Let there be no riding before my return.'

'Oh, it cannot take so long! Hebe — '

'There are grooms in plenty to exercise Hebe. So may Melissa. It will allow the livery hack she uses so occasionally to return to eat its head off in its own stables instead of mine.'

He shot a gleaming look at Melissa on the other side of the bed. 'You may thus practise your riding in addition to your dancing, which will enable you to display your prowess in the Row as well as in the ballroom when you go to London. I leave you, too, with the responsibility of seeing that Miss Aston complies with my instructions, so keep it all in mind, young lady, if you hope for a ball when I return.'

Melissa bobbed a saucy curtsy. 'As you have spoken, so shall it be, oh master!'

Goaded by suspicion that there was some devious purpose behind the earl's commands, Kezia said sharply, 'You called me just before I fell.' Belatedly, she added '*sir*', which weighed the word under with a tangle of nuances.

'So I did,' he agreed smoothly. 'But your accident changes everything.' Her accident was surely godsent to ensure that Miss Aston and Harry would find it far from easy to be private together in his absence.

The singular complacency she sensed in him, the lack of apology for having startled her, infuriated Kezia. Diverse emotions possessed her. She felt ridiculously weak and weepy while longing to be upstanding on two sound feet and able to stamp one of them.

Nodding down at her, Lord Emmington said, 'I leave you in Melissa's hands. Both of you, I trust, will attend strictly to my wishes.'

A small bow and he was gone.

17

A bad sprain and a nasty bump, the apothecary had pronounced, and advised Kezia to spend at least two days in bed and not to expect to put her foot to the ground for eight more.

A morning of Melissa's zealous ministrations, a lingering headache and an uncomfortable ankle made Kezia glad to be alone in the afternoon while the younger girl exercised Hebe. She was physically more at ease after a short sleep but then found herself with too much freedom to think about the awkwardness of the situation between herself and Lord Emmington and the difficulties that might lie ahead.

She was listlessly watching a lively breeze frisking with the sunlit treetops visible through her window, when Melissa came in to show off her choice of toilette for dining at Staneflete Castle that evening.

Kezia gave generous approval to the overdress of white embroidered Indian muslin on a gown of hyacinth-blue sarsenet with a demi-train. A pearl-sewn blue ribbon threaded through the girl's black curls supported a dashing little cockade of curled white feathers and completed an altogether charming picture, which for some reason accelerated Kezia's descent into depression when Melissa left her.

Departing in daylight, the visiting pair returned in bright moonlight. Candle-glow beneath Kezia's door was sufficient invitation to Melissa to knock and enter.

'You don't mind, do you?' she said. 'I'm not in the least tired and Miss Flemming is no fun to talk to.'

Kezia laid aside the book she was reading with a smile and Melissa, seating herself on the end of the bed, announced airily, 'Now that I have seen Staneflete, nothing less than a castle will do for me! How many young, handsome, unmarried dukes with such desirable abodes are there to choose among, do you think?'

Kezia laughed and shook her head. 'Very few, I imagine.'

'Oh, well — he need not be so *very* handsome,' Melissa conceded. Perhaps there are castles owned by lesser gentlemen? I would accept even a plain *mister* if he could endow me with the right establishment!' Laughing at her own nonsense, she rattled on about keeps and gatehouses, moats, triple portcullises, and the delight of having both a minstrels' gallery and an *oubliette.*

It had not occurred to Melissa, Kezia noticed with amusement, that she might possibly acquire a castle by marriage with a widower in his thirties.

Turning at last from a vision of reigning triumphantly over such splendours, Melissa said, 'It was a quite splendid evening. I do wish you had been there. We sat down twenty to dinner. A young cousin of the duke was there. He and his friend both as fine as peacocks in their regimentals but sad to say, they leave tomorrow. All the Dymonts were there. They came last and the duke — having first said all that was proper — then said in that odd way of his, 'Handsome family . . . Poor Scroffy!' 'Scroffy', Great-aunt Emmington told me, was the late Mr Dymont's nickname. It seems he died about four years ago. Of course, everyone pretended not to have heard what the duke said, but Valentine caught my eye and winked.'

A moment's frowning thought and then she asked, half seriously, 'Why are men so captivated by yellow hair? They stare at Miss Dymont so, whenever they think themselves unobserved. She was my opposite at table and though her eyes are blue, not brown, their expression was exactly that of the young heifers when they gaze at one over a gate. How terrible if I fall in love with a castle but have to compete for its owner with someone like *her!* I cannot change my hair, but do you think that if I cultivate the art of looking so, it would be enough?' Widening her eyes, she parodied a look of bovine simplicity. Then, with a laugh, stretched and stood up.

'I expect I've talked you to weariness, but before I go I must tell you how particularly the duke enquired after you. He was most concerned to hear of your accident, but when I said I had been charged with your care, he said he was sure you could not be in better hands. What do you think of that?'

'That he is a kind and gentlemanly man, astonishingly lacking in self-consequence.'

'And dukes don't have to be, do they? Gentlemanly, I mean. Great-aunt said that most indulge themselves far above the common. Do you suppose the same licence extends to duchesses?'

Not waiting for a reply, she said goodnight and whisked herself out of the room.

★ ★ ★

To the dowager's astonishment, a basket of fruit for Miss Aston was sent from the Staneflete progression houses next day, with enquiries as to how she went on.

'A most unnecessary attention,' the dowager told Melissa when the servant had gone. 'Miss Aston is not ill, merely incapacitated — to *my* inconvenience! But the Delarives are quite beyond knowing what is appropriate.'

It was a week before Kezia was first carried downstairs by John footman and was able, with the aid of two walking sticks, to limp with painful slowness between rooms. With the weather so much improved, there was again an influx of young visitors to Old Hall, though with the earl absent, the dowager showed less interest in their coming. What surprised Kezia was how rapidly Melissa's interest in riding advanced, even to the extent of rising earlier than had been her custom.

Having declared his intention of looking after the Old Hall ladies in the earl's absence, the duke became the most faithful of their visitors, sometimes bringing his sister with him. Lady Hermione was with him on the occasion he called soon after Kezia's first coming downstairs.

It was on this occasion that the duke glanced around the Lily Room with a look of great content and remarked, 'How like old times it is to be sitting here. I could have been only just breeched when first I entered this room.' Smilingly, he turned to his sister. 'You, Hermione, must have spent quite half your days here as a girl, such close friends as you were with Lady Charlotte.'

His sister's frown and small shake of the head warned him he trod dangerous ground. Looking a little conscious, he added hastily, 'And now it is Miss Melissa's turn to be young and looking forward to what the future may bring.'

This small by-play, set Kezia wondering if Lady Hermione's friendship with her mother was at the bottom of the antagonism the dowager sometimes showed towards the duke's sister.

Four weeks after her fall, Kezia's ankle had recovered to the point where she was able to take her first long walk through the park. Unable to find Melissa, she went alone while the dowager was taking her nap.

She had walked the mile to the gates at the entrance to the Grand Avenue and was about to turn back when her attention was caught by a small, metal plaque newly attached to the high wall of the Gierney estate on the opposite side of the lane. Passing through the small judas-gate, she crossed over to read with a chill of aversion:

Take heed that poachers entering these grounds will be shot on sight and questioned afterwards if practicable.
Signed: Murdoch M'Glaisch
Head Gamekeeper to Sir Fredrick Gierney

Turning from this grim message, she found the Duke of Mawdsham approaching on his handsome grey hunter.

'Well met, Miss Aston,' he called, dismounting. 'How very pleasing to see you so much recovered! But afoot a full mile from the house . . . Should you have come so far alone?'

Kezia assured him of her complete recovery and indicated the plaque. 'Have you seen this, your Grace? It makes most disturbing reading knowing it is issued by a man reputed to be zealous in his duties to the point of unbalance. And how many of those to whom it is directed are able to read?'

Having scanned the plaque, the duke said soberly, 'Poaching can be a serious matter for landowners, especially the smaller ones. Gangs of ruffians sometimes strip whole coverts and don't scruple to give the keepers cruel treatment. Some have even been crippled by them. But this notice threatens murder. Is there no one to keep the man in bounds?'

'There is only the Gierneys' steward, but he is old and known to be afraid of the keeper.'

After a moment's thought, the duke said, 'Sir Joshua Rowland is your district justice of the peace, is he not? I'll see what a word in his ear can do.'

Turning their backs on the grisly warning, they found the Old Hall lodge-keeper already opening a leaf of the gates for the duke and his mount to pass through. The duke chose not to remount but continued to walk beside Kezia, leading his horse, and chatting in his easy way. Presently he said, 'With the earl's return drawing near, Miss Melissa's ball is first topic with all the young people of the neighbourhood. Your ankle being mended, you will be looking forward to it as much as any.'

Though Melissa spoke of Kezia's presence at the ball as a settled thing, the dowager had remained silent on the point. With this in mind, Kezia responded only with a smile ... a smile that charmed the duke into thoughtful silence for several moments.

At the house, Kezia left Sopworth to conduct the duke to the countess and went upstairs to change her shoes and pelisse. When she came down it was to find Melissa also present and the duke saying, ' . . . and the snowdrops, though so late this year, are now in full flood through the woods and Hermione longs to show them off.' He nodded smiling at Kezia as she seated herself, adding, 'And this time Miss Aston cannot be excused from joining us.'

The dowager's brows twitched disapproval of her companion's inclusion in the invitation just extended but could not immediately think of a way to frustrate it.

The weather continued kind and the party that assembled on one of the terraces of the castle two days later to make the proposed walk into the woods was small enough to be considered intimate. Besides the duke and his sister, there were the duke's daughters, their governess, Melissa and Kezia. The dowager elected to remain by the fire with a glass of Tokay and chat to an elderly widowed cousin of the duke who was his pensioner and also, at present, his guest.

The woods the walking party entered had been planted with care to appear as if the trees had arrived entirely by Nature's choice. Under mostly bare branches, the snowdrops glimmered in satiny drifts, thickest along the banks of a wandering stream. The two little girls, the Ladies Louise and Isabel, aged eight and six, walked sedately by their governess's side at first, but taking courage from the informality of the occasion, very soon danced ahead to point out anything they thought might be of interest to the rest. The duke, walking between Kezia and Melissa, smiled indulgently at their liveliness.

The snowdrops having been given their full measure of admiration, the party strolled back to the castle for an agreeably unceremonious nuncheon. When the Old Hall ladies were ready to start on their return journey, the duke's daughters presented each of them with a small basket trimmed with ivy and filled with the snowy-white, greenscalloped flowers they had come to see. Even the dowager, mellowed more by Tokay than snowdrops, allowed that it had been a tolerably well-managed event.

The sun had set when they reached Old Hall, but the sky was light still, fading in the west from sapphire to a pale and lovely green that foretold a frosty night. Following the dowager and Melissa into the house, Kezia came to a sudden halt just inside the door.

Waiting for them at the foot of the stairs, three days under the five weeks he had conjectured his journey would take, was the Earl of Emmington.

And with him, all her remembered problems . . .

18

Light from a nearby candelabra showed the weariness of hard travel in his lordship's face, but even weariness could not diminish the power and authority of his presence. There was, too, a taut, burnished look about him, the look of a man committed — even dangerously committed — to a fixed end.

Keeping to the shadows, Kezia examined his appearance with passionate attention to detail until, with dismay, she realized she had been waiting for his return every minute of his absence; realized that against all reason, she loved him.

How, she wondered desperately, was she to keep the resolves she had made with such brave determination during the dull days of his absence? The dowager and Melissa were welcoming him in their different ways but she remained where she was, held by an almost superstitious dread of taking even one step forward towards the uncertain future.

Over the heads of the other two women, Lord Emmington's gaze sought and captured hers, holding it with a determination that set an inner tocsin clanging fresh alarm.

Lucius's purpose was indeed fixed on Miss Aston and now he was a man in a hurry. His brain seethed with plans and with the need to bring them to fulfilment soon. Just the sight of her made him long to cross the hall to sweep her into his arms and kiss her with a fervour that would make her cry mercy. Hemmed in by the dowager and Melissa, all he could do was incline his head towards her green-gowned shape and say coolly, 'I am pleased to see you are recovered from your fall, Miss Aston.'

★ ★ ★

Estate business and social obligations occupied most of the earl's time during the next two days but did not prevent his noticing that Miss Aston seemed always to be pinned as closely as a shadow to either the dowager or Melissa. He dismissed the idea that she might be avoiding him, unable to think of any reason why she should. His patience was wearing thin by the afternoon of the third day when he saw her enter the library and followed her in.

It was a graceful room, added to the house at the time of the dowager's marriage to the fifth earl. Kezia was standing by one of several tall windows, a book already

216

in her hands and her head bent over it. Noiselessly closing the door, Lucius stood renewing his delight in her slender grace, in the curve of her neck into the slope of her shoulders, the swell of her breasts under the blue kerseymere gown. What was it in her shape, colour, style, that dulled for him the attractions of other women? What was her special quality that roused and focused such an intense desire that he was hamstrung by his fear of driving her from him by the force of that desire? Until he possessed her it seemed to him he could not again be wholly in possession of himself.

As though drawn by the fixity of his gaze, Kezia turned, her eyes widening into wariness as he walked towards her.

Expecting welcome, Lucius was unprepared to see an almost fierce guarded stillness take possession of her. Himself driven by imperatives, it had not occurred to him that the intervening hours, days, weeks might have weighed heavily on her. He had thought they needed only to be alone and for him to take her in his arms again to find her lips yielding to his as sweetly as before.

Thrown off course, he said with brittle lightness, 'It seems Melissa has been true to her instructions and earned her ball.

Have you been as faithful in obedience, Miss Aston?'

It was the lightness that set the seal on Kezia's resistance. She could only hope his lordship would accept in a gentlemanly way her intention to bury deep all memory of the kisses they had exchanged.

'I have not ridden in your absence, sir,' she told him austerely.

'And since my return — have you begun again?'

Kezia shook her head, not troubling to explain that she would be riding at this moment if Cressick had not told her that Melissa had already taken Hebe out.

Lucius could think of only one reason for the change in her: *Harry!* He clamped down hard on the surge of jealous fury that swept through him and attempted diplomacy. Glancing through the window to where daffodils nodded yellow-tipped buds, he said with a coaxing smile, 'It's just the day for a drive in a curricle, wouldn't you say?'

'Your bays would welcome an outing, no doubt.'

'And would not you?'

What she would welcome above all was the right to walk into his arms and relive the happiness she had found there before. A remarkably short-lived happiness, she reminded herself. She would be foolish indeed to think she could ever be more than a passing amusement to him. She managed a small shrug of indifference, saying, 'The countess will rise from her nap soon and will want me to read to her.' She made a small movement of the book in her hand.

Her pretence was too successful. His smile died and he said in a hard voice, 'Oh, come, Miss Aston! So cool! What has been done between us cannot be quite forgot.'

That slew her hope of bringing to a quiet end the situation between them she had so recklessly helped to create. Now it must be done more positively.

She met his gaze squarely. 'No, My Lord. I behaved stupidly in a moment of weakness and I can only appeal to your generosity and ask you to forget what happened. I was at fault, but please believe I am not given to such . . . such — ' She faltered into silence under his inimical glare.

'Loose behaviour?' he snarled sarcastically, smarting under the inference that her response to him had been an aberration. He took a threatening step nearer. 'And now you are all virtue! But if I kiss you again, my dear Miss Aston, will you remain virtuous?'

'*Oh, no! Please don't!*' The words were

a breathless whisper and she raised a hand between them as though he had threatened to strike her. 'Before, I was willing. Now I am n-not.'

Words and action fed his anger. He had wanted to woo her gently, charm her through a courtship delightful to them both, even like Zeus with Danae, shower her with gold . . . but he had been robbed of time. If he could have offered her marriage . . .

Marriage? Even at this moment the thought had power to startle him. Never before had he thought of marriage in the context of securing a particular woman for his bed. That he had done so now showed him the depth of his obsession. It was beyond serious consideration, of course; marriage was a dynastic matter. Perhaps, though, Miss Aston was playing some devious game, was less unwilling than she claimed. He reached out and pulled her close. She was trembling deeply and looking into her eyes he saw only panic. His anger vanished. Raising a hand to her cheek, he stroked it gently.

'Don't look at me so! I mean you no harm.' He slackened his hold on her and bent to set the softest of kisses on her brow. 'You are my *sahabe makbūl*.'

Kezia stared up at him, confused by his sudden change of mood. His words woke an echo in her mind. In a drained voice she said, 'You have said that to me before, but I do not know its meaning.'

'The words translate as *accepted friend.*' He did not explain that what they expressed could vary from being a formal courtesy to having, for lovers, the deepest significance. Holding her gently now, he discovered that though he still refused belief in romantic love, she had unsealed a spring of tenderness in him he had not known existed.

More afraid of his kindness than his temper, Kezia's panic returned. She must not weaken, she told herself, but had not found the strength to withdraw from his hold when the door opened and Sopworth entered.

'The rector has called on parish business, my lord. Connected with the Mullingers, I believe. He is in the small parlour. I thought you would wish to see him.'

There was no hint in the major-domo's voice or expression that he saw anything unusual in Lord Emmington and Miss Aston standing linked by his hands on her arms; no least indication that he had seen Lord Emmington follow Miss Aston into the library and observing with what care he closed the door, had waited only to decide what particular excuse he would use to interrupt.

The rector's timely arrival had supplied the excuse he had been seeking. He stood holding open the door as though he did not doubt for a moment his lordship would walk through.

Within an ace of telling Sopworth to go to the devil and take the rector with him, Lucius stood immobile for several seconds. Then, taking his hands from Kezia's arms, he said with quiet emphasis, 'You will, I hope, consider me always your accepted friend, Miss Aston.'

Whatever Sopworth made of that no flicker of it disturbed his urbanity as the earl strode past him.

★ ★ ★

That evening, waiting in the Lily Room for dinner to be announced, Melissa decided that the time had come for Lucius to attend to her interests.

Curtsying deeply to him, she said, 'Sir, you see Miss Aston standing very firmly on her two feet and Hebe's fitness is witness to all the exercise I have given her. Now I claim my just reward.' She was too impetuous to maintain the grand manner and abandoned it to beg, 'Oh, Lucius, do say I may have my ball and soon! It has been an age of waiting for your return!'

Teasingly, Lucius allowed her to wait until an edge of apprehension began to show. Then, laughing, he told her, 'Very well, brat. Consult with your great-aunt and decide the day between you.'

'Oh, Lucius, *thank you!*' Blowing him a kiss, Melissa darted to the writing-desk and, taking up a sheet of paper, handed it to him.

'Great-aunt Emmington and I drew up a guest-list and Kezia has written it over and over. We could start sending out invitations tomorrow.' Looking archly at him, she added, 'Lady Delia and Miss Dymont are to be invited, of course.'

'Of course,' he agreed blandly, passing the list back to her. 'And judging by your list's length, you have not forgotten anyone living within fifty miles of us.' Not even Harry Osborne, he had noticed. Well, if Harry was not kept fully occupied with duty dances, he was sure he could find other ways of preventing his steward from pleasing himself in the matter of partners.

Two weeks were named by the dowager as the least time necessary for invitations to be sent, replies received and all the preparations completed. She herself must have a new gown, she announced with the solemnity of a royal proclamation.

Kezia was developing a skill amounting to cunning in contriving not to be alone with Lord Emmington. *Sahabe makbül* might translate as *accepted friend* — but how did *accepted friend* translate in Lord Emmington's mind? She had little doubt that to him it meant the same as *petite amie* . . . little friend . . . mistress? Married or not, her parents had lived as a married couple. That was not how it would be if she was so foolish as to put herself in the hands of Lord Emmington: it would simply advance her from being *scandal's daughter* to *scandal's self*.

Lucius, having no key to her thoughts, imposed restraint on himself and sought by quiet courtesy to wipe from Miss Aston's mind his last lapse and restore himself to favour.

With the day of the ball decided, the dowager sent to the nearest warehouse for samples of material and informed her *modiste*, Madame Barquin, a French refugee who had settled in Reigate, that her services would soon be needed.

The warehouseman was quick to deliver his samples and, with Melissa's exuberant help, spent a delightful afternoon changing her mind before fixing on a handsome bronze satin to be trimmed with deep violet velvet.

Melissa, draped in a quite unsuitable crimson damask, was still admiring the effect in a pier glass when Kezia began to fold away the rejected pieces.

'It is a great pity I don't stand in need of a ball-gown,' Melissa repined. 'But I have not yet worn any of the three that Godmother Lorrimer had made for me. They are all beyond everything delightful I do not know how I am ever to decide which to wear first.'

Lucius, walking in at this moment, said drily, 'Why not wear them all.'

Melissa spun round to face him, her eyes dancing. 'And remove them one by one! How that would set the neighbourhood all about! Shall I do it?'

The dowager looked up from the sheaf of patterns she was now studying. 'Only if you want never to attend another ball, miss! And I should consider it a favour if your frenzy of interest could be abated a little.'

Melissa bobbed a token curtsy. 'I beg your pardon, Great-aunt, but it is the first ball given especially for me.' She turned impulsively to Kezia. 'What colour is your ball-gown, Kezia? It would not do for us to clash.'

'I have none that may strictly be called so,' Kezia told her with a rueful smile.

'It will not signify,' the dowager interposed.

'Any of Miss Aston's evening gowns will serve since she will be present solely as my assistant. She can have no thought of dancing.'

Because the dowager had not previously corrected Melissa's assumption of Kezia's presence as a guest at the ball, Kezia had begun to consider how she could furbish up her rose and white muslin to pass for a ball-gown. This late unkindness cut deep, but schooling herself not to show it, she continued about her task as though she had not heard.

Melissa however, prepared for battle. 'Oh, but Great-aunt — ' she began indignantly when another voice, heavy with irony, cut across hers.

'Do not tease, Countess, when so serious a matter is under consideration. It is more than ladies' delicate nerves can be expected to bear.'

The dowager's head jerked up again. 'Indeed, I do not jest! At my age, the burden of such entertainment as we contemplate is not easily carried. Who more proper to be my aide than my companion?'

And who more determined than you to keep that companion from all pleasure! thought Lucius grimly.

'Naturally Miss Aston is your first choice,' he agreed smoothly. 'But I am certain you will not wish to keep her from an uncommon pleasure. Remember, too, it is Melissa's ball and she wishes Miss Aston to be a guest. Rather than disappoint either young lady, why not make use of the dragoness Melissa brought with her? She has been at Old Hall long enough now to acquaint herself with the general run of things and there is always Sopworth to be applied to if she finds herself in difficulty.'

So much effort on Miss Aston's behalf made the dowager stare, but she dismissed suspicion in favour of believing Emmington's object was to please Melissa. Irritating as was that young woman's unsuitable cordiality towards Miss Aston, it must end soon when Melissa went to London. With no intention of adopting Emmington's suggestion, she said stiffly: 'Miss Aston will have a better notion of her duty than to resign it to another on the mere hope of dancing perhaps once or twice in an evening.'

That was intended to depress pretension and flood her with guilt, Kezia understood, but refusing to be a willing martyr, she remained deaf.

A hint of steel in his voice, Lucius said, 'I do not doubt Miss Aston thinks just as she ought, but an occasional holiday from duty is a refreshment to the spirit. I'm sure you remember the pleasure you once had in dancing, Countess.'

'There is no parallel!' the countess snapped. 'Miss Aston would be wise to consider whether she would be entirely comfortable in the company we are to entertain.'

That piece of spite put her in Lucius's hands. 'Ah! Now I understand you. You are thinking Miss Aston will not have time to acquire a suitable gown. But with a battalion of sewing-women supporting the labours of your *modiste*, I am sure another gown can be furnished without too many candles being burned late into the night. The cost shall be a charge on the estate in recognition of all Miss Aston has done and, no doubt, will yet do, towards the ball's success. I leave it to your good offices to arrange, Countess. It is fortunate we still have the warehouseman's samples, so Melissa may now have the pleasure of helping to find something to Miss Aston's taste. There you see — all difficulties are done away with.'

Though his lordship was smiling, something in his expression warned the dowager she would be wise not to offer further argument. Nor was she given opportunity to do so. With a nod for the incensed old woman, but without even a glance in Kezia's direction, Lord Emmington left the room.

19

Eight days before the ball, Harry received a note delivered by hand. Having read it, he at once carried it to Lord Emmington.

'My presence at Tumbry Hill is most urgently sought, as you see, sir. I am puzzled; no reason is given and I do not recognize the hand, but everything about it suggests great haste. I suppose my uncle, Sir Hubert, to be ill and his son out of reach.' Frowning down at the note in his lordship's hand, he added, 'I confess myself to be very much disquieted by the note's brevity and the haste to deliver it. I owe much to my uncle — not least the expense of my education — and I should like, with your permission, to set out for Kent at once.'

Lucius's permission was given willingly and was accompanied by generous offers of help. By noon, Harry was on his way.

At the same hour, a note of a different nature was handed to the dowager. The day being chilly, she was making a slow perambulation of the painted gallery in company with Kezia and Melissa. The gallery was long, running the full width of the wing. Eight large windows in the west wall made it light, and the charming fresco of animals, both real and legendary, following each other in endless succession through jungle grasses on the remainder, gave it interest.

Having read the message with the aid of her lorgnette, the dowager exclaimed pettishly, 'Are we really expected to be eager to travel to Staneflete again so soon! As if I am not perfectly familiar with the Mandersby rooms, or have ever expressed the least wish to see Staneflete's dungeons.'

Melissa's interest was immediate. 'Are we invited to view them? Oh, how famous of the duke to arrange it so soon!'

'Is this by your contriving, miss? How did that come about, may I ask?' the dowager demanded.

'It was when the duke was last here. I remarked what a fine thing it was to have dungeons and an oubliette. The duke said he thought his ancestors had derived more satisfaction from them than he did. Then he asked Kezia if she was interested in dungeons and she said 'not above the ordinary' — which I thought remarkably tame of her! — though she did say that any place as steeped in history as a castle generally is, must fascinate. The duke then told us the story of the Mandersby rooms. He said that in Queen Elizabeth's day — '

'Spare me the rest! I have known the tale these sixty years,' interrupted the dowager.

'But are we to go? Will it be soon? You won't — *you could not!* — say no!' Melissa entreated.

'I shall leave it to Emmington to decide,' said the countess uncooperatively.

'Oh, he will not be so poor-spirited as to decline!' Melissa declared as much in hope as certainty.

'We shall see.'

Melissa's trust in his lordship being validated, on the appointed day, the Old Hall party set out for Staneflete Castle an hour before noon. Miss Aston having been named in the invitation and Emmington unable to see her inclusion as ineligible, the dowager was obliged to contain her own feelings.

A number of other guests were before them at the castle, including Mrs Dymont with her three children, her niece, Lady Delia, and two couples who, between them, had brought three bachelor sons, a prodigality much appreciated by the younger ladies.

Half an hour was allowed for those who did not know each other to become acquainted before the company sat down to a generous collation. Lord Emmington, Kezia noticed, spent the greater part of that time improving his acquaintance with Lady Delia.

Elegantly carved beams braced the dining-room ceiling and the severity of its stone walls was mitigated by trophies of arms and the chase and a number of portraits, the largest of which was of Queen Elizabeth at her most dauntingly imperious.

The meal had scarcely begun when a newcomer was shown into the room by a young footman who, having imperfectly heard his name and not recognizing him, had assumed he was a late guest.

Kezia, seated between Valentine Dymont and the duke's elderly cousin, Mrs Bentham-Tracy, was aware of the old lady's sharp intake of breath and felt the sudden stillness in the room. Looking up from her dish of scallops in a Dutch sauce, she saw the entrant had halted just inside the door, his expression showing the uncertainty of someone who had not expected to find the duke in company. Unlike the young footman, Kezia had seen too many representations of that handsome and famous face not to recognize him immediately. He was already turning away as though to leave the room, but the duke, quickly on his feet, reached his side in an instant and took his arm to turn him about.

'My dear fellow, how pleased I am to see you! You will join us, of course.' He nodded to a footman to set another place, leading his latest guest forward as he did so, and shaking his head at something said to him in a low voice. Unusually, there was a look of challenge in the duke's dark eyes as his gaze passed round those seated at his table.

'You have some acquaintance here,' he said to the man at his side, 'but there are others — Ah, yes.' His attention settled on Lucius. 'Allow me to introduce you to the Earl of Emmington . . . Lord Emmington, I have the honour to present my friend, Lord Byron.'

There was an unbreathing hush as everyone waited for the earl's response. Lucius rose and turned slightly to meet the poet's fixed gaze. A moment passed before Byron bowed. While the head of tight auburn curls was bent, Lucius flicked a sardonically aware glance at the duke. But when Byron straightened, Lucius's own bow made courteous acceptance of the introduction.

Though there were some grave faces and tight lips, the highest ranking notables of the neighbourhood having signalled acceptance, none of the company chose to follow Lady

Jersey's example of a few nights ago and walk out of the room.

Byron took the place prepared for him between Lady Delia and Lady Hermione with an appearance of ease that Kezia suspected must have cost him something. The position placed him at a slight angle across the table from her and though she was careful to keep her own gaze away, she was aware that others were less scrupulous and subjected him to avid, and not always covert, stares. He appeared well acquainted with the two ladies flanking him and maintained an easy flow of conversation with them as though oblivious of being an object of vulgar interest.

Soon after the meal, those who did not know the castle, mostly the younger people, set off on a tour of its special interests, Lady Hermione acting as guide, the duke remaining with those guests who chose not to go. This left only the duke, Lord Byron and one other gentleman to entertain the older ladies, for which reason Lucius abandoned his first intention and remained also.

The dungeons, deep, dark, and coldly dank, elicited all the shudders of horror to be expected from the young ladies and all the gruesome and pleasurable interest of the gentlemen — and Melissa. The *oubliette*, a black and almost airless hole opening in the floor of the lowest dungeon, answered her every expectation and she turned from it with a deep sigh of satisfaction.

As the party began the long upward trail to the Mandersby rooms, Lady Hermione related its history. Kezia, having heard it recently, fell towards the rear of the group as they climbed yet another curving stone stairway. It was now that she became aware of a limping step behind her and, looking round, glimpsed Lord Byron at a turn in the stairs.

As they continued up, Lady Hermione's clear voice floated back to her saying, ' . . . it was at the time of the Babington plot, of course, and Sir Ralph Mandersby being of the Catholic persuasion. Following his arrest, he was given into the charge of the then Earl of Mawdsham — the dukedom not yet having been conferred on us — and the earl was placed under threat of losing his own freedom should Sir Ralph escape. They were both young men, and for all they were prisoner and jailer, a strong bond of friendship was formed between them. Two years later, however, the earl was ordered to put Sir Ralph to the question.'

'You mean to *torture* him!' protested an indignant young voice. 'After two years! Whatever for?'

'The constant fear of assassination made Queen Elizabeth extremely nervous,' Lady Hermione replied, 'and unfortunately for Sir Ralph, he was cousin to Anthony Babington. However it was, it was now suspected he might have information not extracted from anyone else. The earl could not for his own safety ignore the order. First, he asked Sir Ralph on his word of honour as a gentleman and a friend, to say if he knew, or had ever known, anything concerning either plot or plotters. Sir Ralph vowed he had not and had met his cousin only twice in his life. The earl then arranged for various grisly instruments to be applied to his friend's person but without inflicting the least pain. Afterwards, he wrote to Elizabeth assuring her that though thumbscrew, boot and rack had all been employed, Sir Ralph had not wavered from his claim to have known nothing and to have been a loyal subject of Her Majesty always. Six months later, Sir Ralph was exiled to Holland, where, sadly, he remained until he died.'

Arriving at a heavy oak door high in the east wing of the castle, Lady Hermione produced a large iron key with which to unlock it, explaining, 'It has become a family tradition to keep these rooms exactly as they were left more than two hundred years ago.

236

Little though this part of the castle is now used, we lock them to ensure that nothing is disturbed.'

Eagerly, everyone crowded in as she pushed the door wide. The first of the four rooms was the largest, its furniture indicating it had been both dining and sitting-room. The centrally placed table was covered with a bullion-fringed tapestry cloth and bore a silver candelabrum in which were three half-burned wax candles, brown and shrunken with age. A crimson rug covered much of the blackened oak flooring and two comfortable chairs flanked the open stone fireplace.

Looking round with interest, Kezia saw that much had been done to ease the wretchedness of imprisonment. A rack of clay pipes hung on the fireplace wall under a shelf holding a painted wooden tobacco canister, a tinder box and a pot of spills. A side table set against another wall held a chess set, a box of playing cards and dice, an inkstand with two quill pens, several books and a silver-gilt tankard.

Each room opened into the next. The second was a bed-chamber with tapestries on the wall and a postered bed hung with faded amber silk. On the embroidered bedcover lay a lace-trimmed linen shirt, perhaps left behind in the bustle of departure. An iron brazier stood in a corner and a carved chest at the bed's foot. The two remaining rooms were furnished more simply, one for the use of Sir Ralph's personal servant and the other containing no more than a prie-dieu and a table holding a silver crucifix.

There was little to interest the majority in this room and Kezia, entering last, found herself alone there almost at once. Taking up a small leather-bound missal lying on the shelf of the prie dieu, she turned the brittle pages carefully and came upon a slip of vellum which perhaps had been used as a bookmark. On this, written in the flowing, curlicued hand the Elizabethans favoured, she read words vaguely familiar to her: *Forego your dream, poor fool of love.*

If the prisoner had written them, of whom had he been thinking, she wondered. His wife? The girl he hoped to marry? Had he, like herself, expected love to bring joy and discovered its pain? And what had it meant to the young man, Ralph Mandersby, to find himself entangled in the web of dangerous politics? To have his life torn apart; to be shut up in these rooms knowing the horrid end of his cousin and his friends? Knowing, too, that his own life hung on the whim of an all-powerful queen made tyrannous by her own danger. Kezia shivered and, waking from her musing, carefully replaced the book.

Walking back through the servant's room, she realized she could hear nothing of the other guests and quickened her pace in alarm, remembering that the outer door was kept locked. There was no one to be seen anywhere and when she reached the oak door the ring-handle turned uselessly in her hand. She beat on the thick oak timbers with urgent fists, but produced little sound and drew no response from anyone beyond the door. What sound she made, though, was enough to penetrate the gloomy absorption of the man who, hidden by the bed-hangings, had been staring out of the bedroom window. He limped into the outer room.

Turning, Kezia saw him with surprise and between a frown and a laugh, flung at him, 'They have locked the door on us and gone, my lord!'

Without answering, with hardly a glance, Byron went past her to try the handle for himself. His impatient fist made a little more noise than had hers but was no more effective. The face he then showed her was dark with suspicion and as malevolent as any that might have been shown by one of the heroic villains or villainous heroes of whom he wrote.

'Is this by *your* arrangement, madam?' he demanded, low-voiced and venomous. 'If so, be warned you may have reason to rue it! I've had my fill of women and their schemes . . . am in just the mood to make the next suffer for the rest!'

Until that moment, the particularity of who was her fellow captive had not sunk in. Now, bereft of words, Kezia stared mutely into the fine and furious blue-grey eyes until a swelling sense of indignation gave her voice and she was able to return, 'Being as much a victim of mischance as you, my lord, I do not find those words easy to forgive!'

'What women find hard to forgive is being found out!' he sneered bitterly. Then, dropping his voice to a softer, more frightening savagery, added, 'Well, here we are, and what your reputation is, I neither know nor care. In the unlikely chance of your not knowing mine, I tell you that whatever I do now, nothing can sink it lower.' He moved a step or two nearer, his smile jeering and ugly. 'Having left yourself no room to retreat, I fear you are about to discover you have embarked on a rasher enterprise than perhaps you bargained for, my dear.'

His wicked look forced home on Kezia that

her danger was real. This was a man goaded past endurance; one who, like a wounded animal, would strike at anyone who came within reach. His fame and infamy had blazed too fiercely for knowledge of it not to have reached everywhere with any means of communication. Women, she knew, had pursued him relentlessly, creating more than half the scandal attaching to him. But hot-blooded violence was part of his inheritance; his father had been both a man of passion and a callous philanderer with the nickname of 'Mad Jack'; the great-uncle from whom he had inherited his title had been known as 'the Wicked Lord' and had killed a friend in a duel following a drunken brawl.

With raging mischief staring at her from the present Lord Byron's eyes, her heart began a frightened drumming.

20

Clutching at courage, Kezia said with desperate calmness, 'You are offering to kill the slain, sir. Am I to learn that poets are no more just, no more generous than the rest of humanity?'

Byron checked. His eyes still hard and suspicious as he stared at her, there was slightly less virulence in his tone, when he said, 'A dagger-thrust between the ribs, madam! Be sure I have no relish for being lumped with the rest of humanity at this particular time.'

'My thrust was no sharper than your unflattering suspicion, sir. I speak no less than the truth when I say I had no hand in arranging our joint imprisonment.'

After a moment, his gaze less angry, he conceded, 'I begin to think myself mistaken.'

'I begin to be relieved.'

That brought a twisted smile to his beautifully shaped mouth. 'You have my apology, Miss — ? Were we introduced? I regret your name does not come to mind.'

'My name is Aston. I am the Dowager Countess of Emmington's companion.'

He bowed. 'Miss Aston . . . '

Relieved, her heart slowed to a more normal beat and she nodded towards the window. 'Could we make ourselves heard from there, do you think?'

They crossed together to look out through the narrow, mullioned panes of hazy glass. All that could be seen below was a neglected-looking courtyard bounded on one side by the building they were in and by the ruins of old fortifications on two others. The remaining boundary was made by the wall between courtyard and parkland. Windows in the other rooms all had the same view, except the tiny chapel which looked out on the Norman keep set on a mound and surrounded by a dry moat. Grazing sheep were the only living creatures to be seen.

Returning with Byron to the chief room, Kezia sensed his withdrawal into contemplation of his personal problems rather than their present plight and with no wish to be shut up with a man sunk in melancholia, she said with a liveliness she could not feel, 'All that is left to us, my lord, is the hope that we are missed before Lady Hermione next invites visitors to view these rooms.'

He was gracious enough to rouse himself to match her lightness. 'If that fails, we must console ourselves with thinking how prodigiously our cadavers will add to the general interest!'

'Sir, what greater comfort can we ask!' she mocked.

She had his whole attention again. 'Madam, you are a balm to the spirit and an astonishment. Does the dowager know what a treasure she houses? Perhaps, after all, I shall have one pleasant memory of womenkind to take out of England.'

'You go abroad?'

'It is possible — probable even. And soon.' He stared into distance as if he sought to see what his future would be. Returning his gaze to her, he said bitterly, 'I am lied out of life in this cold-hearted country. And when what has been sworn to be undying love yields without resistance to vengeful pressure — ' He abandoned that to say through his teeth, 'The hypocrisy of my virtuous judges sickens me! There must be a better breed to be found elsewhere.'

After a moment, Kezia offered quietly, 'I think you have not been altogether fortunate in your friends.'

He gave her an odd look. 'Oh, in my *friends* I have been more fortunate than I deserve. What has been disastrous to me is not always to have recognized my foes. And though I have myself created much of my misfortune, worse deeds have been imputed to me than I am capable of performing and by two beings who know it well enough!' Taking a halting step or two away from her, he stood in thought for a moment, then shrugged and said, 'Well, if I go, I shall leave little behind that I value, take few memories of real happiness with me.'

He had opened matters too delicate for her to venture into and she turned from them to ask, 'What of your poetry? Shall you continue to write?'

'That is another matter entirely. Write I must and shall! Perhaps my poetry will fare better in my country's memory than I am like to do.'

In the hope of changing the direction of his thoughts altogether, Kezia said quizzingly, 'The company below are unflatteringly slow in missing us, my lord, shall we pass time with a game of cards? Piquet, perhaps?'

His assent was more polite than enthusiastic, but bringing the box of cards to the table he asked, 'Are you a gambler, Miss Aston? What do we play for? Vowels?'

'No. Spills.' Kezia added the pot to the table. 'There are no great number, so we must limit our stakes.'

Something gleamed in his eyes. He gave her a long look, his gaze lingering on her mouth. 'I can think of other things we might play for . . . '

She understood him, felt his charm, saw how effortlessly he could fascinate. Though her colour rose a little, she gave him back a look of sparkling comprehension and said, 'Spills are more easily managed though, and we must hope our game will be short.'

Laughing, he bowed. 'That will be your hope — mine will be otherwise.'

By the time their third game was drawing to an end, Kezia was finding it difficult to sustain conversation. It had been a grey day and the clouds had thickened to bring an early dusk that filled the corners of the room with cold shadows. She shivered and could no longer hide her worry. 'They are very slow in coming! How long have we been imprisoned?'

Byron glanced at his fob-watch. It was later even than he had thought. Understanding her anxiety, he answered evasively, 'A little more than an hour, perhaps. I have not previously noted the time.'

It was much longer than an hour, Kezia was sure. Certainly long enough for her reputation to be ruined. It would be the same whoever was the man with whom she had been shut up: Byron's notoriety would merely add an extra zest to the scandalmongers' enjoyment.

Watching her, Byron said understandingly, 'Do not despair, Miss Aston, the day may yet be saved. Though you must think it the most damnable bad luck to have been incarcerated with the most infamous rake of the day.'

Conjuring up a smile, Kezia said gallantly, 'I make no complaint on that score, sir. It would make small difference to my situation if my co-prisoner were the Archbishop of Canterbury.' She ghosted a laugh. 'Indeed, it is possible that His Grace would be more concerned for his own reputation than for mine.'

'You have a valiant heart, madam. I hope it will always receive the generous treatment it deserves.' Reaching across the table for her hand, Byron kissed her fingers lightly. With the impulsive kindness of which his friends were so much aware, he said, 'Your position . . . the dowager. If you meet with overmuch trouble, consider coming away with me. I make the offer with no intention of insulting you, shabby as the proposition may appear to you. Unfortunately, I can make none better. But desperate ills need desperate remedies and I think we might find ourselves the best of good companions.'

It was odd to find herself regarding his offer with amused gratitude. She bowed acknowledgement. 'Thank you, my lord. I appreciate the generous spirit in which your offer is made. I am not without a refuge though. I have a friend and guardian who will welcome me at any time.'

He continued to look at her, smiling a little, but a sombre look in his eyes. 'The more I learn of you, the more I come to wish it might be otherwise. I should like to persuade you to join me.'

She shook her head, saying quietly, 'It would not do, you know.' Then to turn the conversation, she looked down at the cards and said, 'But you have been inattentive to your game, I see. This one I must surely win.'

They were laughing, their easy comradeship plainly visible, when the key at last turned in the lock and two people came quickly into the room.

Lady Hermione, slightly in advance and wearing an expression of lively concern, said at once, 'Miss Aston! Lord Byron! What can I say? How could I be so remiss as to lock the door on you! We thought you, my lord, had sought solitude somewhere. But because the party divided to follow various pursuits, your absence, Miss Aston, was not realized until Lord Emmington — ' She made a small gesture towards the man behind her, leaving the sentence unfinished, saying instead, 'Can you possibly forgive me for such carelessness? How it happened, I cannot think, for I was assured no one was left behind.'

Rising from their seats, Byron and Kezia made civil disclaimers, Kezia unhappily conscious of something dark and condemnatory emanating from Lord Emmington.

'Is there a frenzy of speculation below?' Byron asked.

'Fortunately, no. But — ' Lady Hermione hesitated, glancing at Kezia. 'I think it would be best that you do not reappear together . . . '

'I suggest,' said Lord Emmington's voice at its coldest, 'that if Lord Byron can reach the garden unobserved but makes his re-emergence from there noticeable, it would serve. Some other ploy to cover Miss Aston's absence from among the guests might then be found.'

'Of course!' Hermione agreed quickly. 'Let me think . . . If I put it about that Miss Aston was suffering a headache and I persuaded her to lie down — Yes, that is it! She lay down and fell into a sleep from which I have just awakened her. Perhaps you, Lord Emmington, would descend first, knowing nothing of missing guests, of course. But if you station yourself close to the window in the King James's parlour, you could draw attention to Lord Byron's return to the house. You, Byron, must be sure to walk between the gazebo and the house which will put you in Lord Emmington's view. That should meet the circumstances, but we must lose no more time. People are beginning to think of returning to their homes.'

The plan accepted, Byron turned to Kezia. With a bow, he said, 'I must thank you, Miss Aston, for the pleasure of your company which, for me, made our imprisonment end too soon. Though you cannot want it, I could wish it about to begin again.'

If she had not heard Lucius Sellon's angry mutter, had not seen the ominous way his eyes narrowed, Kezia would not have responded as recklessly as she did. Tilting her head, she smiled brilliantly at Byron, sketched the gayest of curtsies and said, 'I thank you, sir. In the circumstances — thinking of Canterbury — I own myself to have been fortunate.'

Byron laughed, Lord Emmington growled, and Lady Hermione, who had been gathering up playing-cards from the table, straightened abruptly and spilled most of them back on to the cloth.

'I'll go below and play my part,' Lord Emmington announced curtly and turning, went from the room. He was followed almost immediately by Byron.

A very silent Lady Hermione accompanied Kezia along two passages and down three flights of stairs before rousing herself to say, 'I cannot apologize sufficiently for having placed you in such an awkward situation, Miss Aston. It must have caused you great anxiety, though I am sure you came to no actual harm.' She glanced briefly at Kezia. 'Byron has been our friend these several years. We are aware of his reputation but we know him only as a man of great talent, wide sympathies and unusual generosity. Accused as he is of many things, nowhere among them is the charge of having forced himself on a woman.'

Remembering Lord Byron's first threats to herself, Kezia's smile was a little wry, but she said, 'I have nothing of which to complain, Lady Hermione. It was foolish of me to linger so long in the furthest room. I was looking at Sir Ralph's missal and thinking how terrible it must have been for him to be shut away for three years with the threat of a barbarous execution hanging over him. Lord Byron had his own preoccupations and was gazing out of a window in the bedroom. We discovered each other's presence at the time we realized the rest had gone from the suite.'

They had come now to King James's parlour, a cosy wainscotted room, warmed by a generous fire. Lady Hermione led the way to the dowager, saying a little more loudly than was necessary, 'Here is Miss Aston restored to you, Countess. She had been suffering from the headache and I persuaded her to lie down in the music room where no one would disturb her. She was so peacefully asleep when I returned, I was sorry for the need to waken her.'

'Miss Aston is privileged to have had such attentions shown her,' the dowager said acidly with a darkling look at Kezia.

The level of chatter in the room was at that pitch when last-minute conversations are being hurried through before the move to the door begins. And now Lord Emmington, turning from the window, said in the direction of the duke who stood at a short distance from him talking to Mrs Dymont, 'Lord Byron is returning from a stroll in the gardens, I see.'

If the duke was surprised to be given notice of the fact, he did not show it, merely nodding and saying, 'Poor fellow! He can have small desire for company, so much malice as he has met with lately.' He was silent a moment, and then in one of his asides, added, 'I could wish his common

252

sense equalled his humanity . . . '

Walking across to the dowager, Lucius's glance swept unseeing past Kezia. 'Have you had a sufficiency of poet for today, Countess? Shall we go before he comes back among us?' he asked.

'Indeed, yes. Miss Aston, be good enough to inform my great-niece we are leaving.'

The earl returned as he had come, on horseback. In the dowager's chaise there was silence during the first mile. Kezia's feelings were divided between hurt and anger at Lucius Sellon's assumption that she was deserving of contempt. What reason had he to be so ready to believe the worst of her? So much for being his lordship's 'accepted friend'! Friendship with him appeared to rest on insecure foundations! Though she curled a mental lip at his opinions, the hurt did not lessen nor her thoughts become less occupied with the man who had inflicted it.

The dowager, having thoroughly reviewed her reasons for having lost three games of bezique in a row, then remembered she had another cause for annoyance.

'You did not inform me you had the headache, Miss Aston,' she observed acrimoniously.

Kezia roused herself to say, 'There was no opportunity, ma'am.'

'You are not about to become subject to disability, I trust. Recently, there was your ankle and on an earlier occasion you suffered some other disorder. I do not complain of what is unavoidable, but you cannot have recollected that had I wanted you while you were sleeping, I should not have known where you were to be found.'

'I apologize, ma'am, but it was not quite in my hands to do other than I did. I agree it was fortunate you did not need me.'

The dowager frowned over the last remark uncertain how she should take it. Before she had decided, Melissa came to life, saying brightly, 'Was it not a famous thing to have Lord Byron walk in on us like that? 'Mad, bad and dangerous to know,' as Lady Caroline Lamb has informed the world! And *quite* as handsome as anyone has said! Mr Dymont told me no lady is allowed to call him by his baptismal name of George, though men may do so. How odd that is! But I do wish he had been more to be seen. I wanted to tell him how much I enjoyed *The Prisoner of Chillon*, but I found no opportunity until the last minute before we left. And *then* he looked so dauntingly at me, I lost all courage and walked on by.' She laughed without much dismay at her rout.

The dowager sniffed. 'You should never

have been in his company at all. It was beyond everything that Mawdsham should have allowed him to remain among us. One can only be thankful that the man himself appeared to recognize how unwelcome was his presence and took himself off for much of the time. I marvelled, too, at Lady Delia showing such forbearance at his being seated next to her at table. Indeed, there was little that was pleasing in any of it, save only seeing Emmington at last paying Lady Delia the attention she deserves.'

Kezia was thankful to reach Old Hall, yearning, despite the early hour, for the day to end and to be alone.

Sopworth met them at the door of the house and with the privilege of his position, asked if her ladyship and Miss Melissa had enjoyed their day.

Entering behind them, Kezia found her arm firmly grasped and a minatory voice rasping in her ear, 'Be good enough to come with me, Miss Aston. I have a few words to say to you.'

21

Propelled through the nearest door, Kezia found herself in the ante-room leading to the Grand Salon. Small and intimate, two walls were hung with richly coloured Hungarian silk-and-wool needlework and a deep blue and gold *gros point* rug covered most of the floor. Three comfortable chairs and a cabinet of curios was all its furnishings and a pale amber hanging candle-lamp provided light.

Standing face to face in the centre of the room, Lucius and Kezia were aware of nothing but the storm of their own feelings. Kezia's anger was not for the ache of her arm where his lordship had recently gripped it but for the insulting manner in which he had compelled her to enter the room. It was not the first time he had treated her so, she thought throbbingly, glaring into the eyes glaring at her.

His voice thick with the press of an anger that had waited too long for expression, Lucius said, 'Had you much trouble in contriving this afternoon's enterprise? Was it greed for adventure that thrust you along the route of a harlot eager to engage with the greatest lecher of the age?'

Kezia could find none of the moderation with which she had answered Lord Byron's initial assumption. Her voice low and pulsing, she threw back at him, 'Your supposition is as offensive and as wrong as when Lord Byron made it. Though he expressed himself less crudely.'

The fever in his brain allowed him no pause in which to fully comprehend what she said before he demanded, 'Do you tell me it was not so?'

'I tell you nothing! It is plain I should waste my breath.' And then, like a careful insult, she added, 'My Lord.'

His look flayed her. 'One thing you *will* tell me, madam, is just what is proposed between you and that rake-hell in Canterbury!'

It took her several seconds to make the connection. When she did, a wild, unhappy laughter almost choked her. 'What need to tell you, my lord? Are you not certain you know? What discomfort you must have suffered in being joined with Lady Hermione in shielding me from public disgrace!'

She triumphed in having reached the end of that unconciliatory speech without suffocating on the way. Triumph faltered when she saw its effect reflected in his lordship's expression. Feeling sick, she gasped for air, but clung fiercely to her determination not to give ground before his attack.

The words he snaked back at her hissed like a whip about her ears. 'Insolence does you no service, madam. I'll have the truth from you yet!'

Love and hate melding into bitterness, she flung out, 'But will you recognize it? What's truth to a hanging judge?'

The silence that followed was dreadful to her. She had pushed him too far and for one terrible moment she thought he would strike her. As much as his fury bewildered her, so did her own passionate response to it. Bleak with despair, she heard his goaded mutter, 'If it is carnal adventure you seek, I can supply all and more of your need!'

And then his arms were tight around her and his lips on hers again, as savagely inexorable as the first time. But because she had since found delight in his arms, it was cruelly harder to endure with apparent indifference. At the point when she knew she could hold out no longer, he wrenched himself away.

'We'll leave it at that for the present!' he told her harshly, and raking open the door, left her with the first slow tears beginning to slide down her cold cheeks.

★ ★ ★

Acceptances of invitations to the ball had poured in at an enthusiastic rate matched only by Melissa's interest in each and every one as it arrived. But as the great day drew nearer, this interest suffered a strange eclipse. Sunk in her own wretchedness, Kezia failed to notice it at first, but almost as soon as she did, Melissa supplied a clue to her discontent.

Sitting with Kezia over the breakfast cups, she said naïvely, 'Only a day or two more before the ball now. What a poor thing it will be if Mr Osborne does not return in time for it. You don't suppose he will forget the date?'

Kezia was startled. Was Harry the reason for Melissa's late dedication to exercising Hebe? During Lord Emmington's absence, Harry had been free to ride at what hour he chose. If they had ridden together, had five weeks of occasional meetings been enough for Melissa to form a romantic attachment? She could not doubt it and was at once concerned for the girl. Such a romance was doomed to disappointment: Baroness

259

Holford would see to that! But what of Harry? Was he on the way to returning Melissa's regard? What a tangle it all was . . .

★ ★ ★

The dowager had decided that her Brussels' lace fan was the only fan she wished to carry with her handsome new gown. It was tiresome to discover then that one of the mother-of-pearl guards and three sticks had detached from the pivot head. Kezia must at once go with it to the man in the village skilled in the repair of such things.

A green and golden day under the warmest sun the spring had yet provided made Kezia choose to walk rather than ride. The small but daunting chance of encountering Lord Emmington in the park persuaded her to follow the most secluded footpaths and go out by one of the estate gates left unlocked in daytime for the convenience of the workers.

In the lane, the grass was freshly green between the ruts and the air sweet with an indefinable scent. Kezia walked in a quiet dream until the discharge of a gun somewhere near at hand behind the high Gierney wall made her jump convulsively. In daylight and at this season the probability was that the keeper or one of his men was out after vermin, but it was a disagreeably forceful reminder of the ominous warnings still attached to the Gierney walls.

Her errand accomplished, she returned by the same route, walking briskly, conscious that the dowager would soon be waking from her nap. *The dowager.* Rarely now, did she think of the old lady as her great-grandmother. The six months at Old Hall still demanded of her loomed darkly ahead. She had come to it with a degree of light-hearted optimism she remembered. That had vanished. She was unsettled, unhappy . . . and the blame for that did not all belong to the dowager.

Only Old Hall itself had neither failed nor disappointed her. She loved the house which seemed to accept her feeling of belonging; seemed, too, to speak to her of its past in a murmur just beyond the ear's reach, hinting of occupants not long gone from its rooms. Walking the ancient cloistered passage, she had amused herself sometimes with the thought that if she came again in the silence of midnight, she might even catch some last trembling resonance of the monks' chanting.

But neither Old Hall nor pride could hold her here in the unquiet state to which Lucius Sellon had reduced her. Even ignominious flight was preferable to remaining spellbound and helplessly spinning like a web-wrapped fly.

Forego your dream, poor fool of love . . .
The words were echoing in her mind as she re-entered the park through the same close-boarded gate by which she had left and shut it carefully behind her. As her hand came away from the latch, she saw the stain on her lavender glove and with a shiver of revulsion, recognized it as blood — blood that was still wet. While she was trying to strip off the clinging kid she heard a child's wailing cry. It was cut off abruptly, as though a hand had been clamped to the mouth that uttered it. Five yards from the gate, the path bent in between a tangle of guelder rose and sweetbrier: the wail had come from just beyond.

A child hurt? But why that sudden stifling of its cry? Breath suspended, she stood a moment, waiting for some other sound to reach her, a primitive sense of danger skittering along her nerves and prickling her scalp. Somewhere just out of sight, she was sure, someone else held their breath and waited, too.

Attempting to rationalize, she told herself it could only be children at play where they should not be; perhaps a painful scratch and an older child's hasty hand cutting off the give-away cry. In any case, there was a child in distress. She walked forward.

Beyond the short run of bushes, a clearing opened where bluebells and stitchwort graced the soft woodland grasses and the birch-tree boles shone bright silver in the sunlight. It was odd, she thought, that the charm of the scene should register in her mind even as she took in the man sitting slumped against a tree at the path's edge, one arm clasped about a small child and the hand of the other still laid across its mouth. Hatless, unshaven, filthy, his coat was a soldier's red. Beside him, something feathered lay tangled in a fowler's net, an unsheathed knife resting across it.

The man made no move, simply stared at her with wary, bloodshot eyes. It was then she noticed the spreading patch of blood seeping through the once-white cloth of his breeches from a wound in his left thigh.

Before she could speak, the gate she had closed behind her slammed open, there was a rush of movement and a voice twanged in accents of such jagged dissonance she barely distinguished the words: 'Stand aside, Mee-stress, while I finish ma wor-rk!'

A swift backward glance showed her a man in the unmistakable garb of a keeper holding at the ready a twin-barrelled shotgun unlike any she had seen before. Above it, his narrow, long-jawed face looked as though adzed from granite, but his blazing, zealot's gaze was fixed beyond her on the man sitting against the tree.

M'Glaisch! Everything about him proclaimed his identity and his intention. She span round fully now, raising a futile hand, exclaiming on a choking gasp, *'Don't!'*

Pale, almost colourless eyes gleamed at her with manic purpose. 'I'm in ma rights, woman, so get ye out of ma way!'

He was beyond the reach of argument or appeal, she saw, and still facing him she stepped back, keeping herself between him and the pair behind her. In the same moment, the soldier, as certain of M'Glaisch's intention as Kezia, thrust the child away from him. It tripped and fell but was up in a second. Too young to understand, it yet caught the threat pulsing on the air and rushed back to cling to the only safety it knew.

With horror rising in a sick tide, Kezia tried again with all the desperate authority she could command to stop the unstoppable. 'Turn that gun aside. You will not do murder here, sir! You should not even be an Old Hall land.'

'If you'll no move, ye bee-som, ye'll tak' the consequences.' M'Glaisch's upper lip lifted in a mad-dog snarl and setting his cheek to the gun's stock, he aligned its sights.

22

Distance could not disguise the identity of the blue-gowned, beige-pelissed figure Lucius saw emerge from among shrubs to cross a short open space towards woodland. He had been staring moodily through one of the library windows reviewing, as too often he had done, his last encounter with Miss Aston, tasting again the bitter aloes of regret.

'*A hanging judge . . .* ' The words chafed him.

Entering the Mandersby Rooms with Lady Hermione, his suspicion had all been directed at Byron. It was the laughing ease between the imprisoned pair that redirected his suspicion. And then had come Byron's compliments, Miss Aston's sparkling response topped by her reference to *Canterbury!* Byron had studied at Trinity, knew the town, yet, when he had accused her of having made an assignation her surprise had looked like innocence. So had her proud refusal to defend herself; the contemptuous way she had thrown his suspicions back at him; scorned his judgement. But the jealous tyrant that ruled his mind and heart could not concede the possibility of error. He was still sure of nothing except the humiliating fact that given positive proof of her wantonness, he would want her no less, would remain as helplessly in thrall to her.

He had spent the morning looking over a pretty little stone manor-house with a small but profitable estate soon to come on the market. At a discreet seven miles distance from Old Hall, it had the additional advantage of convenience. More immediately he needed to deal with what lay between Miss Aston and himself. He had not changed out of his riding gear since his return and making a decision, he headed again for the stables.

The dowager had been eloquent on the subject of her fan that morning and he guessed Kezia's errand had to do with its repair. He could not be sure she would come back by the way she had gone, but he thought it likely she would. He dawdled Moorsi along, heading for the only gate in this direction, allowing time for Miss Aston's mission to be completed. Reaching the footpath through the band of boundary trees, he was forced to an even slower pace.

He was nearing the gate when a man's voice scraped rawly against his ears, the words unintelligible. But as Moorsi walked on, he saw ahead between the leafless poles of the trees, as brightly lit as a stage, a chillingly explicit tableau. In one frantic moment of comprehension, he rammed his heels into Moorsi's sides, sending the stallion hurtling towards the gamekeeper. The horse's shoulder struck the man at almost the exact second the gun was discharged.

Vaulting from the saddle as M'Glaisch went sprawling, Lucius snatched up the gun and cracked its stock against the now hatless ginger head the moment the gamekeeper attempted to rise.

Only then, with cold dread, did he turn to look at Kezia. To see her still on her feet was a relief almost as painful as his dread had been. Dropping the gun, he closed the distance between them first pulling her into a feverish embrace and then holding her away to scan her face with scalding anxiety.

Her eyes gazed at him blankly. Anger for the danger she had courted and fresh alarm surged together through him. He was unaware of shaking her until from under her hair, close to her temple, a small streamer of blood flicked out across her cheek and he found her slight weight hanging entirely on his hands.

His first horrified thought was that she

was dead on her feet and he gathered her back into his arms as though to snatch her away from death itself. Laying his mouth on the unconscious softness of hers, he accepted what he had long denied: what he felt for this woman was love and he loved her beyond life itself.

Kezia's last moment of full awareness had vanished in a roaring confusion of violent sound, blurred movement and the scorching slam of something invisible against her head. But it was the shaking Lucius had given her that snapped her last tenuous hold on consciousness, spinning her out into a cold black void. She drifted back slowly in a quiet dream of warmth and safety in which loving lips moved like a benediction on hers. Yet, disturbing this lovely peace, she could hear, far-off, an agonized voice murmur over and over, *'My love . . . my love . . . my love . . .'*

The dream faded as, slowly, she came back to reality. No lips now cherished hers, no voice grieved and the arms holding her did so, it seemed, only to keep her from falling.

The practicalities of the situation had forced themselves on Lucius. He had shifted his hold to push back her hair and trace the weal left by the single stray pellet that

269

had struck her. A fraction closer, a slight difference of angle and it could have killed her.

The shock he had been given was not easily forgivable. As life flowed back into her, his first encouraging words were a stony, 'You were luckier than you deserve!'

Trying to draw together the loose threads of memory, Kezia was only vaguely aware of what he said. The gamekeeper, she saw, lay unmoving and the soldier sat as before with the child hugged close. The long years of war had made nearly everyone familiar with military uniforms, and she recognized now that the man's short-tailed red coat, white pantaloons and black gaiters were the regimentals of the Royal Engineers.

M'Glaisch stirred, moaned and lay still, but it was enough to prod Lucius into action. Guiding Kezia to an ancient tree stump, he settled her on it and pressed a clean handkerchief into her hand with which to mop up the small trickle of blood that still flowed from her wound. Picking up the shot-gun, he turned to the soldier. With a nod at the man's damaged leg, he asked, 'What happened?'

Lines drawn by pain made the man look older than he was, but the thick, dark pelt of his hair and the muscled leanness of his body suggested he was little older than Lucius himself. He pointed his chin at the gamekeeper. 'Him. He caught me with a bird over yonder. With the bantling here, I was in no case to offer fight. But that black-hearted hellhound shot me just the same. Only luck got us away. We lay hid what seemed an eternity, but I'd reckoned without his determination to finish me. He was waiting still when I moved.'

Pain nipped him and he wiped sweat from his lip with an impatient hand. 'My leg wouldn't hold for far I soon knew, and I thought to hide again in here. But I fell and Lettie let out a wail that brought the butcher in on us. Your good lady coming in ahead of him did no more than delay what the end would have been hadn't you arrived. I reckon he'd have done for us all three but for that!'

'The man's insane. You'd have done better to have tried my coverts first. My keepers are less bloodthirsty,' Lucius told him sardonically.

The soldier gleamed a wry smile. 'Chance decided.'

'And the rest of your story?'

The man twitched a shoulder. 'Same as a'many others. I was with Old Nosey from Almeida through to Salamanca. A musket

271

ball in the shoulder kept me out awhile but I was back after right up to Waterloo and into Paris.' Pride in his soldiering faded and his face hardened. 'I took my pay and come home to find my wife dead of another man's brat and this one, my own sure enough, scarce alive in her granfer's house. I wasted time and money looking for the sneaking cur who'd — ' He shook his head wearily. 'What's that to you? Lettie and me came a fair piece today, and we was both hungry. I was trying for something to put in our bellies. And that were it.'

'Where are you headed?'

'To see if my sister'll give a care to Lettie. She married a carrier out to Hayward's Heath. They've never managed more than the one bairn, so — ' He shrugged again and said with bitterness, 'Last year I was half a hero; this, I'm naught but a damned landloper . . . What's there for such as I? It'll take another war to give me back a value — yet show me a piece of engineery all to hell and see if I can't make it run!'

'Your name?'

'Randall. Tom. Sergeant that was.' His dark eyes searched Lucius's face, anxiety shadowing his own. 'What's to happen?'

'You'll be transported — '

Shock leeched what was left of colour in

his skin. His clutch on the child tightened and he snarled across Lucius's words, 'God damn you all! Me to Botany and Lettie to slow death in the work'us!'

'*Enough!* The word was ill-chosen. I meant only that since you can't walk you'll have transport to where your wound can be given attention. I judge the account settled for whatever you have in that net. When you're out of danger of bleeding to death, we'll talk again.'

M'Glaisch had hauled himself up to sit with his head between his hands. He showed no interest in what was happening around him even when Lucius went to take a few cartridges from the pocket of his velveteen jacket.

The gun reloaded, Lucius handed it to the soldier. 'As I told you, the man's deranged. I trust you not to take revenge while I'm away. However, should he prove a genuine threat to you and the child, you'll do what you must.'

Randall nodded. 'The blow you give his sconce'll keep him moon-minded awhile yet, I reckon.'

Returning to Kezia, Lucius asked, 'How do you feel?'

She shadowed a smile. 'Alive, I think.'

He held out his hands and when she took

273

them, pulled her gently to her feet, surveying her dourly. 'No longer bleeding. Come then, Moorsi can take us back to the house.'

'I can walk.'

He did not trouble to argue. He simply gathered her into his arms, set her firmly on Moorsi's withers and swung himself up into the saddle, every movement quick and spare.

As though, Kezia thought, he had wasted enough time on her.

'*Missus!*'

Both their heads turned to Randall.

'It was a desperate rash thing you did, ma'am, and brave past question. Could I ever do as much for you, I would.'

A little colour warmed Kezia's wan cheeks as she smiled acknowledgement. Under the ear that was resting against Lord Emmington's chest, she heard the amplification of a grunt. And then Moorsi was moving in a slow easy walk out of the clearing.

23

The dowager heard of the day's doings from Emmington himself, and received it characteristically. 'Why Miss Aston should be so foolhardy as to interpose her person between that of a poacher and a madman with a gun, I cannot think! Did it not occur to her that when the Bedlamite had despatched *her* he would then do what he had always intended? I have no patience with such *opéra bouffe!*'

Lucius kept what sympathy he had with her view to himself and pointed out that a child had been involved and Miss Aston's action had delayed the would-be murderer long enough to permit his own timely entrance on the scene.

This, the countess thought worthy of no more than a grunt. She had every intention of presenting Miss Aston with an impressive jobation but, to her own surprise, the girl's pale face moved her to order her companion to retire instantly to bed.

Rising at her usual hour next morning, Kezia removed the apothecary's dressing from her head, arranged her hair to conceal what she could of the damage done to her scalp and went downstairs to breakfast. Having persuaded Melissa that soreness and a slight headache was all she now suffered, she hoped for peace. It was not given her.

News of the adventure had spread and messages, enquiries and callers arrived at Old Hall in a steady stream. The hero of the hour was, quite naturally, the earl, who had had the foresight to have business at a distance from Emmington. Miss Aston had some interest for the neighbourhood as witness to what had happened and being able to assure callers that the earl was not lying mortally wounded after defying the guns of a mad soldier and a madder gamekeeper.

The dowager's goodwill towards her companion ended when the duke and his sister arrived and proved to be in possession of a fairly accurate account of events having met the earl on their way. They brought with them a basket of hothouse fruit for Miss Aston and set the dowager wondering if Hermione was aware of Kezia's true identity — an idea peculiarly unwelcome.

The duke approached Kezia as soon as he was free of obligatory courtesies. 'What were you about, Miss Aston, to place yourself in such peril?' he asked, gazing at her with genuine concern. 'Your friends must all wish that never again will you give them such cause for alarm.'

'I hope never again to be in such a position as to find it unavoidable, your Grace,' she twinkled back at him.

He shook his head at her, 'You make light of it. But what might have happened — what *would* have happened — if Lord Emmington had not been at hand, does not bear contemplation.'

'All's well that ends well, sir,' she smiled, and anxious to turn from the subject asked, 'How are your small daughters?'

'Well enough . . . well, indeed.' For once he dismissed a subject of which, normally, he never wearied. 'Lord Emmington told us that M'Glaisch has been committed to a house for the insane, his brain having given way entirely. One would not wish such an end on any man, yet must we all feel a little safer for his absence. But now I learn Lord Emmington has taken on the wounded poacher as mechanician. It is to be hoped — ' Swiftly he abandoned what might have sounded like criticism. 'Staneflete has not yet imported machinery, so I have no understanding of what is necessary for its upkeep — I imagine few do.'

A new influx of callers allowed the duke no more time with her, and Kezia herself was again in demand to answer questions she had answered a number of times already and to think enviously of Lord Emmington who had managed to escape the furore.

* * *

It was late in the day, the last before the ball, when Kezia, with Melissa in close attendance, found herself free to go to Madame Barquin for a final fitting of her ball-gown.

Studying the result in the large mirror on the sewing-room wall, she was startled into appreciation of the difference it made to be dressed by someone with Madame Barquin's highly professional artistry. Made on a foundation of palest turquoise satin, the overgown was of white silk tiffany embroidered in silver with delicate trails of ivy. Its style reflected the present revival of the Tudor fashion, the brief bodice dipping to a point, its wide-set puffed sleeves slashed to show puckered satin and the deeply curving neck of the gown outlined by a narrow, upstanding ruff of stiffened lace. Movement set light glimmering along the silver threads like gleams of moonlight in clear water.

Impulsively, Kezia turned to the gown's creator, saying in her pretty French, 'Thank you, *madame*. I have never before worn anything half so beautiful.'

'You'll outshine us all!' declared Melissa without envy. 'I should have asked *madame* to make me another gown, too.'

Creating a gown for Miss Aston's delightful figure had been a pleasure to the modiste that had been enhanced by finding her client patient, courteous and willing to speak a charming, if not faultless, French. She grudged none of the extra trouble she had taken though it was for someone of no importance. Or was she? It was far from usual for a lady's companion to have the services of an expensive modiste made available to her. What was even more intriguing was the fact that — having been told the cost of Miss Aston's gown was to be presented as a bill to the estate — Miss Aston had insisted on paying for it herself well in advance of completion.

With a smile, Madame Barquin told Kezia now, 'A beautiful figure is of great assistance to the creation of a beautiful gown.'

Kezia, casting a last, surprised glance towards the looking-glass, blushed a little and said, 'Thank you again, *madame*.'

'Will you permit me to suggest . . . ? Wear only a simple pearl necklace for ornament, and for your hair, just the strand of white and silver ivy leaves one of my assistants is preparing for you.'

'How very thoughtful of you. It will be my pleasure to follow your advice.' Kezia did not say she had no pearls to wear.

A slight sound behind them made all three turn. The dowager stood leaning on her stick in the doorway, on her face an oddly wounded look. It was gone in a moment. A shutter dropped and without a word, she walked away.

★ ★ ★

Early in her young life, Melissa's buoyant spirit had learned to bounce back from collisions with her overbearing mother, her incompatible sister, and the governess for whom she had little respect. Along the way, she had learned the art of getting her own way in difficult circumstances. Discovering that Kezia had no pearls to wear and having none yet among her own trinkets, she set about securing what her friend lacked. She knew instinctively that a direct appeal to the countess was unlikely to succeed and so chose a circuitous route to her object.

Assured of Kezia's absence from the drawing-room for a time, she seized the opportunity to say with a bright assumption of the earl and countess's interest, 'I have fixed on my peach charmeuse gown for the ball tomorrow, and with it I shall wear the three piece rose-quartz set Papa gave me for my last birthday. It will be just the thing. It is a great pity though that I have not yet been given the pearl necklet promised me by Mama.'

'You think the rose-quartz set insufficient by itself?' Lucius quizzed her.

Melissa shook her head. 'No. It is just that I should have liked to have lent the pearls to Kezia, for she has none and Madame Barquin told her they were the only thing to wear with her new gown.' She turned to the dowager with smiling innocence. 'Great-aunt, I recollect you wore pearls recently. Could you not lend them to Kezia?'

The dowager regarded her with haughty disfavour. 'I have nothing at all suitable to be lent to Miss Aston. I am astonished you should suppose it!'

Lucius's eyes slanted towards her, gleamed and were hidden. 'Something might be found among the family heirlooms to accommodate her,' he told Melissa. He stood up. 'Come with me, brat, and we will see what we can find.'

They were gone from the room before the dowager could voice a protest. When they returned, the earl carried an impressive rope of pearls with a long, pear-shaped central drop and an ornate clasp. With a gasp of indignation, the countess declared repressively, 'Those are the *Wardlow* pearls! Brought into the family by the heiress Anne Wardlow at the time of the Restoration.'

'Does it matter?'

'Of course it matters! Sellon jewellery to be hung about the neck of — ' She stopped short, then said inimically, 'No one could fail to recognize them!'

'What of that?'

'It will be thought — ' She glared at him. 'Many things will be thought and more said! None of it to Miss Aston's credit.'

'I fear we found nothing less opulent,' he told her, a small, unkind smile turning his lips.

The countess closed her eyes momentarily, then opened them and said stonily, 'I will look among my ornaments and see if there is not something more suitable.'

'It is to be hoped you succeed, otherwise I fear it must be this.' Voice and expression were equally bland now. Turning, he held out the necklace to Melissa. 'Here, child, take it in charge in case it is needed.'

★ ★ ★

It was a lifelong habit of the dowager to be always ready to receive guests long before they were due. On the evening of the ball, she came downstairs on Rudge's arm, looking her stately best in *grande toilette*. In her reticule lay the simple necklace of beautifully matched pearls Melissa had so tiresomely remembered. It had yet to be offered to Kezia who had preceded her downstairs in order to put the finishing touches to the flowers on the dining-room table.

Ensconced in her usual place in the Lily Room, the dowager was at leisure to consider again her annoyance at being coerced into doing what she did not choose to do — an infrequent occurrence in her long life. It was not just that a valuable ornament was to be worn by someone of inferior status, what lay at the heart of her resentment was that it was *Miss Aston* who was to wear it.

Thinking of this, hostility was still actively lighting the dowager's eyes as she watched her companion walk towards her. It was an added affront that the girl looked as might any born to this house and trained to elegance. The dowager's hands clenched. What right had this . . . this *nobody* to disturb her so! Disturb her as she had done yesterday when — seeing her in the sewing-room mirror — she had been so forcibly reminded of Charlotte in her first ball-gown more than twenty years ago.

As Kezia drew near, she said sharply, 'Stop there: Stand by the candelabrum. I wish to see your gown.' That bought her a moment's respite, but the pearls had still to be given. Grudgingly, she said, 'Madame Barquin has done well. The gown becomes you.' Her gaze dropped to the gold chain around Kezia's neck.

'I gave that trinket you wear to your mother on her twelfth birthday. Is it all you have of hers? Have you no pearls?'

'No, ma'am,' Kezia said indifferently, more occupied with the dowager's slip of the tongue: not Charlotte but *your mother*. For the first time.

'There were pearls among the ornaments Charlotte carried away with her and young though she was, not all the pieces were to be despised. One can only suppose — ' She broke off. Now was not the time for sour observations, but how difficult it was to be pleasant to the girl! Opening the gold-netted reticule lying on her lap, she took out the pearl necklace. 'This is more suited to your gown. Wear it in place of the chain.'

Kezia gave the pearls one flaring glance before saying, 'Thank you, ma'am, but I do not need it. My chain will do very well.'

To have what she did not want to lend so positively rejected, shook the dowager. It was not to be borne and she snapped back, 'Don't be foolish. Take it at once! It is yours to keep.' And that she had never intended to say.

Held in the brightness of candle and firelight, the creamy lustre of the pearls seemed to Kezia to gleam at her with all the remembered evil of Lady Holford's warning to Lord Emmington regarding the availability of the dowager's jewellery to her companion. She said coolly, 'You are very kind. But I do not wish to have it, ma'am.'

'Do not wish to have it — how can you say so! It is worth a small fortune.'

'What I say is true, ma'am. Though I am grateful for your thought.'

'Are you, indeed! I offer you a valuable ornament to complement your gown and you shrink from it with an appearance of abhorrence! Perhaps you will have the goodness to explain yourself, for you are quite beyond my understanding!'

Kezia regarded her steadily. 'I cannot accept it because from the Countess of Emmington to her companion it is too valuable a gift.'

A dull flush crept up into the dowager's cheeks. Silence filled the room to overflowing and it was at that moment that Lucius walked in.

His glance swung between them. What he saw, taken with the charged atmosphere, gave him so clear an understanding of what was happening he hardly needed the dowager's brittle words, 'Miss Aston finds herself unable to accept this bauble from me. Perhaps you will be more successful in overcoming her reservations.'

In the short time since Lord Emmington had ridden back with her on Moorsi after the shooting, Kezia had seen almost nothing of him. She had made occasion to try to thank him for saving her life and an awkward business it had been. His lordship had brushed aside her words, muttered something in Egyptian and, when she had asked for a translation, had smiled crookedly at her and said, 'What I said doesn't matter, but were you an Egyptian, what I should expect you to say is, *My life is yours!*'

The crooked smile had leant still more towards irony as he waited for her to follow that lead. But she had not. There was something of the same look on his face now as he turned to her holding the necklace.

'Will you really not wear the pearls?'

Wary of his closeness and the softness of

appeal in his voice, she said sparely, 'It is too great a gift, sir.'

So the dowager had progressed to offering a gift, and had had it rejected! He let the pearls swing gently from his fingers. 'I must tell you it was Melissa who promoted the idea that this was the necessary finish to your toilette. She will be greatly disappointed if you do not wear it. To please her, could you not bend a little . . . and so please us all?'

She yielded suddenly, chiefly because it was harder to continue to argue without sounding churlish. Bowing her head, she unclasped the gold chain.

'Allow me.'

Before the words reached her brain, he had stepped behind her and looped the pearls about her neck. She felt his breath warm on her skin, the light touch of his fingers, was conscious of the intimacy of his action. And wanted with despairing weakness to turn into his arms and find again some part of the rapturous dream her swimming senses had created after the gamekeeper's pellet had struck her.

Lucius had his own temptations to fight: the temptation to let his hands stray over the pale, delicate flesh of her shoulders; to put his lips to her neck between the necklace and the bright, soft curls . . . He walked round to stand in front of her again, saying in a voice a little strained, a little off-key, 'Now, Miss Aston, are the pearls such a weighty burden to bear?'

She hung between saying truthfully, yes, they were, and finding a less graceless answer. Filling the pause, he said very softly, '*Pretty lady* . . . ' and her heart contracted.

She stared helplessly at him, one frantic thought in her mind, I cannot — must not — love him! Somehow she dragged her gaze away at last and stepping to one side, curtsied to the dowager, saying woodenly, 'Thank you, ma'am, for the pearls.'

It was hardly an expression of gratitude commensurate with the value of the gift but it was the best she could do.

Voices sounded beyond the door; it opened and Melissa came in with the earliest of the guests.

24

The Grand Salon was Old Hall's ballroom, a gracious white and gold room with many mirrors and elegant crystal chandeliers. Entering it, Kezia felt herself a prey to doubts: perhaps the dowager was right and she would feel out of place — or be *made* to feel so. In a status-conscious society, the knowledge that she was only the dowager's companion would outweigh her being indistinguishable from the other guests. What an ineffectual Cinderella she would be if no one asked her to dance!

That worry, at least, was quickly dispelled. As soon as the musicians began to tune for the first dance, Valentine Dymont had asked her to partner him.

As the highest ranked gentleman present, the Duke of Mawdsham led Melissa out to head the opening cotillion with Lady Hermione and the Earl of Emmington immediately behind them.

Twenty years old, Valentine was a pleasant young man and a competent dancer with a cheerful flow of conversation. Other partners followed and before long Kezia found the music, the flowers, the colour and the gaiety of the many dancers under the shimmering golden light of many candles, working the same magic for her as for the rest. If, occasionally, she became aware of being disapprovingly scrutinized by some of the older women, she was by then able to shrug it off.

Melissa had her own source of special pleasure. News of Harry Osborne's return had reached the house shortly before the ball began. Kezia hoped she was the only one to know why Melissa so frequently scanned the crowd: hoped, too, as time passed and Harry did not come, that she was the only one to realize why the girl's high spirits diminished.

Supper was over and the second half of the evening well begun before Kezia found herself sitting out a dance. Earlier, she had seen Lord Emmington dancing with Miss Dymont — an enchanting picture in blush pink *peau de soie* and fragile lace. His lordship had been listening to his partner's chatter with an expression of polite, if rather wooden, interest. That he was bored, she had guessed and rather ignobly thought that if only she were present as the acknowledged great-granddaughter of the dowager countess with no bar to being partnered by the Earl of

Emmington, she could surely provoke him to a greater show of animation. And that, she told herself, is merest vanity!

He was dancing with Lady Delia now and without showing the least evidence of being bored. Lady Delia's gown of heavy, cream-coloured silk flowed sensuously about her tall, graceful figure. Her clouding dark hair was charmingly dressed and everything about her proclaimed the young woman of impressive pedigree and impeccable breeding. They made a well-matched pair and Kezia, watching the two dark heads incline towards each other the better to converse felt the plunge of jealousy's sharp talons.

A quiet voice at her side said, 'Kezia . . . '

She looked up to see Harry. 'How good to see you back,' she said with smiling welcome. 'But are you not too tired for all this?'

'I came only to present myself to his lordship. I shall not stay.' He gazed down at her very soberly. 'You look . . . very well.'

It was not her health he referred to, she knew, and her colour rose a little. She looked down at the fan she held; an unfortunate move because it was the pretty ivory one Harry had given her.

Harry's glance followed hers and memory brought a wry twist to his mouth.

Hurriedly recollecting the urgency with

which he had been called away, Kezia said, 'I trust you found your uncle on the road to recovery. That is, if he was ill, as you thought.'

Harry's expression grew more sombre. 'It was not my uncle who was ill, it was my cousin. His funeral took place before I even reached Tumbry Hill.'

'Oh, Harry! I'm so sorry.'

'It never occurred to me it might be Nick who was sick. My own age and always so full of life! I cannot quite believe it even now.'

Kezia indicated the vacant chair beside her and he sat down, but immediately half rose, saying, 'But I am not fit company, must not spoil your enjoyment.'

She laid a hand on his arm. 'If you care to talk about it, don't go. I am sorry for your sadness. Were you close friends?'

He sank back into the chair. 'Always. Particularly so while at school and university. But what is so hard to bear is that I gain so much by Nick's death. I am heir to the baronetcy now and my uncle has made me heir to his personal fortune. My ambitions are as great as the next man's, but I have never wanted advancement at such cost! I could forego it without thought if it would bring Nick back!'

'Poor Harry! It is hard to have good

fortune come by ill means. But you cannot reproach yourself for that.'

'No,' Harry agreed and was silent. And then with a touch of cynicism unusual in him, he added, 'In time, no doubt, I shall accustom myself to the idea and consider only its advantages. First though, I must accept that my life has changed. Losing Nick has been a tremendous blow to my uncle and he is anxious for me to join him as soon as possible. Tumbry Hill bears no comparison with the Old Hall estates but it is large enough to miss Nick's good management. The general wants me to take it in charge within the year and begin to look on it as my own. He also wishes me to marry soon . . . hopes to see his grandchildren.'

He glanced obliquely at her, hesitating, then said with a dogged purposefulness, 'This once more, Kezia, and then I will not trouble you again. Is there hope for me? You know me too well, I think, to suppose I have told you of my improved prospects with any expectation that they will weigh with you.'

'I know you well enough to wish my feelings allowed me to say 'yes', Harry,' Kezia said softly, with deep sincerity. 'But though I love, honour and admire you as a dear friend — beyond that I am not able to go.'

He absorbed that in silence, staring out over the dancers. When at last he turned back to her, he said quietly, 'Do not look so unhappy, my dear. Though I am sorry with all my heart, in the same way as one day I shall adjust to Fortune's crooked favour, I shall adjust to not winning you. I am not a man to stay single all my life. One day I shall marry and perhaps be at least content.' He reached for one of her hands and turning it in his, kissed her palm. Folding her fingers over it, he managed a small smile. 'There, that is the last of Harry Osborne, the lover. What remains — will always remain — is Harry Osborne your true friend.' With that he rose, bowed and walked away.

Through a swim of tears, Kezia watched him go towards the nearest door. Before he reached it, he was intercepted by a small figure in a peach *charmeuse* gown; there was a brief colloquy with a great deal of emphasis on Melissa's part and then, the two came back into the room.

The dance that had been in progress had finished and Kezia was still sitting where Harry had left her when Miss Flemming came and took the chair he had vacated.

Dismissed from attendance on the dowager with some disparaging words, Melissa's former governess was in a resentful mood.

Waiting upon the dowager countess in place of Miss Aston, she had hoped — expected — to impress her ladyship with her superior efficiency but had succeeded only in irritating her.

Kezia welcomed her with a greater show of pleasure than she felt. In the beginning, she had been sympathetic towards the woman, understanding how relegation to her present duties must chafe her. And because she did not dine with the family but alone in her room, Kezia suspected she lived in a limbo of loneliness and boredom. Her own willingness to be friendly had been dampened by Miss Flemming's constant air of superiority and her fondness for lecturing anyone within reach.

A festive occasion did not deter Miss Flemming from doing so now. Beginning with a dissertation on the futility of worldly pleasures, she progressed to some pointed remarks on the unwisdom of attempting to move out of one's station in life.

Only half attending, Kezia found herself wondering how it was the impish Melissa and her governess had not succeeded in driving each other insane. She had reached the point of considering ways of releasing herself from this trial of patience when a shadow fell across them and a recognizable voice said. 'Miss Aston, may I have the honour?'

Kezia looked up to see the Duke of Mawdsham smiling down at her. Though astonished to be so unconventionally distinguished, she rose to take the offered arm. A glimpse of Miss Flemming's outraged expression as she did so made her lips twitch and put laughter in her eyes.

As they walked to take their places, Mawdsham said, 'Am I allowed to ask what it is that has amused you?'

Dismissing her first impulse to return a polite evasion, Kezia met his gaze frankly and twinkled back at him, 'I had just been given some well-intentioned advice on the imprudence of stepping out of my place, your Grace, and then you made it . . . quite unavoidable.'

'You are never out of place, Miss Aston. Your style is above criticism in everything you do.'

From another man it might have sounded facile or fulsome, but he said it with such quiet sincerity she was momentarily shaken.

But the duke was not a fool. As they joined one of the sets, his glance swept the nearer groups of eager-eyed chaperones. 'Have I, in pursuit of my own pleasure, made difficulties for you?'

Inevitably, they were the centre of attention. Kezia tilted her chin and gave him a serene smile. 'None that can possibly give me a moment's concern,' she told him.

Mawdsham nodded approval. 'That's the ticket! You know you are quite the most well-judging young lady of my acquaintance.'

The different figures of the lively dance that began just then fragmented their conversation, but once, when they came to a temporary halt, Mawdsham turned to her to say with enthusiasm, 'How pleasant all this is! I should have heeded Hermione and come back into the world sooner.'

It was not until he had returned her to her seat beside Miss Flemming and had formally thanked her that, turning away, he made one of his disconcerting asides, saying, 'Everything that is most pleasing . . . '

Life had dealt Miss Flemming too many disappointments for her to watch with equanimity Miss Aston — surely no higher in the scheme of things than herself! — not only dancing with a duke but in easy conversation with him. A burning envy launched her into speech.

'As one who for some time has had the conduct of young ladies in her charge, permit me to counsel you to greater discretion, Miss Aston. You cannot be unaware of the notice you have drawn to yourself in dancing with the Duke of Mawdsham. In such positions as you and I occupy the first necessity is to keep one's behaviour beyond reproach at all times. *Never* should one put oneself forward so as to be in the way of dancing with gentlemen of high rank — especially when young ladies of birth have not been accorded that privilege.'

So ridiculous a statement made Kezia stare. With a small laugh, she said, 'Your remarks, Miss Flemming, would be more properly addressed to gentlemen of high rank whose privilege it is to extend invitations to dance. I cannot think of anything more likely to occasion remark than to be seen refusing to dance with the Duke of Mawdsham!'

Miss Flemming flushed an unbecoming red and snapped angrily, 'I speak entirely for your own good. A proper sense of delicacy might have suggested to you the impropriety of your dancing at all in company such as this!'

But eyes more jealous even than Miss Flemming's had watched the duke and Kezia dancing.

Lucius had faithfully fulfilled every duty of the courteous host, but his attention had rarely been long removed from Kezia. It was to have been *his* privilege to distinguish Miss

Aston by dancing with her. It had been more than intention, it had been a promise to himself that here in the romantic setting of the ball he would begin laying out the golden apples of temptation; would woo her with every charm and inducement he could offer.

He had fixed on the dance just finished to open his campaign but had been detained by Mrs Dymont just long enough for Mawdsham to reach Miss Aston first. Thwarted and furious, he had watched them take their places, his resentment growing like an evil weed as he saw their smiling ease with each other. By the end of the dance his brain was on fire. Dance with her he would! Though *now*, he knew, it would not be distinction he was conferring on her but notoriety. With savage unreason, he told himself that if Miss Aston chose to throw out lures to Mawdsham she deserved to bear whatever consequences came to her.

So it was that before Kezia could respond to Miss Flemming's last remark, another male voice said harshly, 'Allow me the pleasure of the next dance, Miss Aston.'

She looked up into the cold glitter of unfriendly eyes and to find a hand extended imperatively towards her. With her heart in her satin slippers, she realized how rash had been her claim that no difficulties would trouble her following her dance with the duke.

For here — though heaven knew for what reason! — was unmistakable nemesis!

25

Whether she took the despotic hand held out to her or not, Kezia knew scandal could not be averted. Everyone within range was staring at them and who among the avid observers could fail to think that this was an angry lover bent on quarrelling with his mistress? For a moment her courage failed, but one glance at the ruthless face staring down at her warned her that refusal might bring worse upon her.

Why he should do this to her, she could not understand. The see-saw of his behaviour towards her was utterly bewildering. Gathering her courage, she stood up: whatever happened, she would not give him the satisfaction of seeing her cringe.

The hand that clamped on hers was feverishly hot against her own cold flesh and the pace at which she was forced to walk to the dancefloor was barely decorous. She heard the introductory bars the musicians were playing with disbelief: the dance was to be the waltz for which Melissa had so perseveringly pleaded; a dance still considered by many to be nothing better than a German romp impossible to perform with propriety. She and Melissa had practised the steps together, though with very little hope of the dance being permitted. Facing her grim-faced partner, she wondered with a kind of humorous despair if he knew the steps.

She might have known he would! Just as she might have known how strongly his proximity would tug at her senses. The strength of her physical awareness of him always took her by surprise . . . his essential maleness, the deep impression he made of a dangerous power held leashed but straining. And it helped her not at all.

Yet, when the dance began, despite their tension, the lilting flow of the music carried them along in effortless co-ordination. To be in such physical harmony with her executioner was an added refinement of torture to Kezia, who could think of no crime she had committed to warrant such a wicked punishment.

As the full, scalding tide of jealousy ebbed a little, Lucius began to measure the havoc he had wreaked. Even allowing for the dance being a waltz, there were fewer other couples dancing than might be expected and the greedy gaze of the watchers was an offence. Under all, he had known what he was doing, but as though possessed of a devil, he had thrust forward on his first furious intention. Always, where the girl in his arms was concerned, reason vanished in the smoking heat of feeling. Where now was the skilful courtship by which he had planned to captivate her? And where was the pleasure in dancing with her that he had promised himself?

Quietly savage, he said, 'You smiled at your last partner, Miss Aston. Surely you can smile a little now.'

Bleakly, Kezia returned, 'You ask too much, sir.'

'Matters will not be improved if we appear to be at odds.'

So he knew just what havoc he was creating! Her glance scorched him. 'Whether I smile or not will make no difference to *your* reputation, my lord. Mine you have put beyond help.'

He knew it as well as she did and swung her with such angry suddenness out of another couple's path she stumbled.

They were close to the edge of the dancing space and in the moment before she regained her balance Kezia found herself held in the dark-eyed, coolly measuring gaze of Lady Hermione. She flushed painfully, then paled again. She could imagine what the woman was thinking. But what was one among so many?

Sweeping her inexorably on, his lordship demanded, 'Are reproaches all you can offer me?'

'What else? Would you prefer me to dissolve in tears? Perhaps you will tell me why I am pilloried in this way?'

Guilt and the knowledge that there was no way of redressing the situation into which he had plunged them pushed him into replying with furious unreason, 'If you don't know why, you should!'

Both were silent after that.

Interminable as the dance seemed to Kezia, someone shortened it by sending a message to the musicians to bring it to a close. Walking blindly beside her partner afterwards, Kezia was late in realizing she had been returned to Miss Flemming's company. Miss Flemming was no longer alone for she had seen it as her not unpleasing duty to speed to the card-room to inform the dowager of the entertainment being provided for her guests by the earl and Miss Aston.

A tight-lipped smile rigidly in place, the dowager hissed as the pair reached her, 'What have you been about — '

Cutting across her words, his tone dangerous, Lucius said, 'If you wish for a quarrel here and now, Countess, I am in the mood to oblige you.' And then, his gaze falling on Miss Flemming, all greedy eyes and ears, he turned a whiplash of words on her. 'I trust you are deaf and hereafter will be dumb, madam, because it will be very much in your interest to be so! Remember it! You may go.'

Before the scarlet-faced woman could scuttle away, Kezia laid a detaining hand on her arm and sketched a curtsy to include both earl and dowager. 'I beg you will also excuse me,' she said, and not waiting for assent, pushed Miss Flemming into movement.

It was not easy to walk unhurriedly through the glittering, crowded room as though she was unaware of the stares, the whispers, the sneering smiles following her progress. Absorbed in this and in resisting an unpleasant feeling of nausea, Kezia had not realized she had kept her grip on Miss Flemming until the woman hissed, 'Release my arm at once, Miss Aston. You have no right to make me appear party to your shame!'

Choking back a strong impulse to laugh, Kezia took her hand away and the woman scurried off. The distance to the door seemed greater than ever and her legs were already trembling with strain when she found her path impeded. With difficulty, she focused on the woman's face and recognized Lady Hermione. Suspecting she was about to be publicly slighted, she was surprised that so great a lady should stoop to lead the metaphorical stoning of the outcast. But even a duke's sister was not to be allowed to put her down with ease. Head high, coolly and gravely, she met the other woman's gaze.

To her surprise, her ladyship nodded and smiled. Holding out a hand, she said, 'We meet a little late in the evening, Miss Aston, almost indeed, at the hour of farewells. Shall we combine the ceremonials?'

Astonished, Kezia took the offered hand, remembering only at the last moment to curtsy.

'Will you walk aside with me for a moment? I have something to say . . . to ask you rather.'

Wonderingly, Kezia did so.

Having first gazed penetratingly at her, Lady Hermione said, 'This will seem to you the strangest time to choose for what I am about to say, but I cannot wait longer. Will you tell me, are you Charlotte's daughter?'

The question was so far from anything she might have expected that Kezia was stunned by it.

'My dear, I'm sorry to startle you, but you are . . . must be! From our first meeting, I have felt so drawn — Charlotte was my dearest friend. We were as close as sisters ever could be.'

Kezia came out of her daze slowly to ask, 'How did you guess? I am not very like my mother in looks.'

'In features, no, but there is *something*. Particularly when you smile. And you have her way of moving. But what first opened the door of recognition was when you threw up your head and smiled and curtsied to Byron. You said something about Canterbury and the way it was done was so like Charlotte in mischief, I felt I could not be mistaken! The wonder to me then was only that I had not seen the likeness before.' She blinked away a sudden glisten of tears. 'I have missed your mother so much through the years. As much, almost, as has the countess. What I do not understand is why she is keeping your identity secret.'

'She is afraid of the scandal of my mother's elopement being resurrected.'

'But that was twenty and more years ago! Far more shocking scandals have been outlived by others in that length of time! Unless your father was — But, no! Desperate as Charlotte was to escape the man chosen for her she would never have married someone disreputable.'

'It is the fact that no record of my parents ever having been married that offends the countess.'

'Not married! I do not believe it! Has search been made in Ireland?'

'*Ireland*?'

Hermione nodded. 'Because Charlotte knew that as her confidante I would be relentlessly questioned, she told me nothing beyond her intention to elope — not even your father's name. Particularly that! It was a point of vital importance to her. She must have met the man during her stay in London, but strangely, no one could discover the least clue to who he was. Only a slip of the tongue on Charlotte's part, told me they were going to Ireland. Then, because I knew that much, she told me her lover had relatives there. Something I swore to her I would not reveal.'

Frowning thoughtfully, Kezia said, 'In Putney, where we lived, my parents were known as Mr and Mrs Aston. But I knew — though how I knew I cannot remember — that my father's full name was Aston-Fitzcleve. In the way children come to understand things without being told, I also knew that the second part of his name must never, never, be used. Before I was old enough to ask questions, my parents were dead.'

Lady Hermione stared at her as though stunned. Then, in a shaken voice she said, 'Aston-Fitzcleve! Your father was *Fredrick Aston-Fitzcleve* — the brilliant young serjeant-at-law who drowned seven — no, eight years ago. Of course! The very kind of man for Charlotte! *Who* he was explains so much!' She drew a deep breath and glanced round, saw how many were still watching them and said, 'What an impossible time for such a discussion! We shall have to end it. But tomorrow — oh, most certainly tomorrow! — I will arrange for us to talk at length.'

'But please do not say a word to anyone else yet,' Kezia urged. 'I gave the countess my word that no one would learn of our relationship through me.'

'If that is your wish. But it cannot go on so. What has happened this evening — Well, for the present that must be left.' She glanced round again and making a small gesture with her fan as though indicating something, said, 'Smile a little now, my dear. Let us confound the gossips as much as is possible.' Her gaze slid back to Kezia. 'Yes, that is better. Earlier, you were the victim of the masculine instinct for competition, I think?'

Kezia coloured. 'It was not as it appeared to everyone, ma'am.'

'I had a strong feeling it was not. Hold fast to your courage, be a little patient and you will come about, I promise. We part now, but we shall most certainly meet tomorrow.' She nodded again, smiled and walked away.

The benefit of that astonishing intervention was immediately apparent. The stares and whispers were already of a different kind, and though hard enough to bear, were less destructive.

By the time Kezia reached the door, the musicians had struck up for 'The Queen of Hearts' which was to be the last dance.

Mounting the stairs, Kezia felt dizzied by the events of the evening, but pre-eminent in her mind was her hurt at the wicked cruelty of what Lucius Sellon had done to her. She recalled the contemptuous manner in which he had invited her to dance. *Invited!* There had been no such courtesy offered: everything he had done had been calculated to ensure the worst possible interpretation attaching to his dancing with her immediately after the duke had done so.

The gallery in which her bedroom lay was well lit for most of its length but where it ended in a panelled wall there was no illumination. The wall however, was not as blank as it appeared, its panelling disguising a door that gave on to one of the old, secret, precipitous stairways leading down to the cloister passage. The worn steps were rarely braved by anyone other than Betty Bassett.

Approaching her bedroom, Kezia was too lost in unhappy thought to be aware of this door opening until warned by some sixth sense that she was no longer alone.

As hard-driven now by self-disgust as formerly he had been by jealous rage, Lucius watched Kezia walk towards him. How could he make her understand what he, himself, did not understand? What could he expect from her but loathing? But his need to explain himself was desperate and he moved to intercept her.

She looked at him with fever-bright eyes and her flesh shrank beneath the hand he laid on her arm.

Still he had no words and so resorted to action, gently, insistently, drawing her close enough to slide his hold down to her hands, raising them to his lips to be kissed in an anguish of repentance. When she attempted to pull away, he said urgently, 'For God's sake, don't fear me! How can I *explain*?'

She gazed at him expressionlessly, too weary to fight.

What words could undo the damage he

had done? Drawing her close, he folded her in his arms, set his lips against her brow with a passionate gentleness that begged forgiveness. She remained apathetic, and his mouth moved from brow to temple, from temple to cheek. He was murmuring now in the language she did not understand but which carried the essence of what he said in its tone. Only when his mouth at last came to hers was he silent.

Prisoned at the centre of the spell being woven about her, Kezia told herself she hated him — had every reason to do so. But there was an eloquence in his touch that woke her body to traitorous delight, a magic that subverted her will. Her lips were beginning to answer the lure of his, were doing what was asked of them. And when his hand began to stroke softly over the exposed flesh of her throat, over her shoulders and the topmost swell of her breasts above the low-necked gown, she made no protest . . . made none when his caressing hand slipped the covering from one breast to bare it to his lips.

So occupied, it was a wonder either heard the sudden outflow of voices as a door opened and guests came through into the hall below. It was Melissa's laughing tones that broke Kezia's trance and startled her into movement.

His attention caught at last, Lucius threw an arm about Kezia's waist and urged her towards her bedroom door.

She was innocent enough to think his action protective, that he meant simply to hurry her out of view into her room. With a trembling laugh she slipped from his grasp, whispering, 'You must go. Hurry!'

So certain that her wishes matched his, he was unprepared for her action. When the door closed on her, he stood at a loss, his body a clamouring ache of thwarted desire. Chance alone gave him time to impose some control on his outraged senses when the group ascending the stairs was briefly halted by the hem of a woman's gown being trodden on.

* * *

Standing in the darkness of her room, it was a wonder to Kezia that the room was not lit by her own incandescence she felt so aglow. Every nerve chimed an echo of the sensations Lucius's caresses had evoked and her skin was vibrant still where his hands had cherished and entranced it. No teasing questions entered her dazzled mind and her heart exulted in the memory of his impassioned tenderness.

313

The misery of the evening had dimmed before her recognition that Lucius had been jealous. Having felt its stab herself, she found room for tolerance. The duke's dancing with her had been no more than a part of the endearing eccentricity of a man who did not see his rank as an iron barrier between himself and lesser people. Lucius had seen it as the act of a dangerous rival, had behaved wickedly, but somehow must be forgiven. What was strange was that her own recent behaviour, so contrary to all she had been taught, had not seemed wrong. Her only regret at the moment was for the interruption to their love-making. Her body — drunk with a previously unknown rapture — had wanted something more; felt cheated.

When she had first come upstairs she had felt drained of all energy, all emotion. The languor that possessed her now was different . . . was pleasurable. Not troubling to light the candle, she drew back the curtains and in the pale moonlight, slowly as in a dream, she began to undress.

★ ★ ★

Returning to his duties as host, for the next hour Lucius performed them with outward courtesy and grinding inward impatience.

314

Only when he had spent another hour in his room and judged the household to be asleep did he walk the shadowy galleries back to Kezia's bedroom door.

He had no fear that she would not welcome his coming. It had been a consenting body he had held in his arms earlier and if in those head-long minutes they had not been interrupted, their lovemaking would surely have gone to its natural, inevitable, conclusion. But when at last he stood with his hand on the latch of her door, he paused.

It was late to question what he was about, to discover that love brought responsibilities, opened secret reserves of thoughtfulness. Loving her, he knew he wanted her to have a joyous passage from her virgin state, a passage not fretted by furtiveness and the fear of discovery. Nor, for himself, did he want a mere hasty appeasing of appetite; what he wanted was a slow unwinding of delight, a voyage of discovery. An essential part of her special charm for him was knowing there was so much more to be delighted in than just her delectable body.

In proper order now, like the voice of a prompter from the wings, came the lines he had sought through memory before: *Past reason hunted; and no sooner had, past reason hated . . .*

Past reason.

Too much that he had done in pursuit of her had been past reason. Quietly, he released the latch and returned the way he had come.

26

The household rose late the next day and Kezia was breakfasting alone when Sopworth brought her the message that Lord Emmington wished to see her in the Cabinet Room as soon as was convenient.

As on another occasion, his lordship was standing looking out of the escutcheoned window. There was no mist to hide the view which today had all the sunny sparkle of spring. Here, in the cold embrace of the original building's ancient stone, a fire was still a necessity, but the light of the flames was lost in the morning brightness and, apart from warmth, the fire's chief contribution to the room's pleasantness was a piercingly sweet scent of burning holly and apple-wood.

Tautly aware of how much depended on this meeting, Lucius had been listening for Kezia with an alert and impatient ear. He turned as she reached the doorway and there, caught in a shaft of sunlight, he saw her as he had first seen her on Nob Hill. For a moment he was held silent. Whether or not she was truly beautiful had long ceased to matter to him. What was certain was that she was in his blood, was necessary to him. Smiling, he held out a hand for hers.

Remembering in the uncompromising light of morning, what had passed between them after the ball, there was something of shyness in the way Kezia looked at him, yet she put her hand in his with the confidence of a woman who believes herself to be loved.

He pulled her close and kissed her with lingering pleasure. '*Sahabe makbūl*' he said softly.

' '*Accepted friend*'. It has a cool and distant sound.'

'As I said it, it means *the one dearest to my heart*. No Egyptian can say more.'

'But half your heart is not Egyptian, sir.'

'Are you asking me to say I love you?'

'Do you?'

'Can you doubt it?'

'You told me once you had no belief in love's existence.'

'I have learned differently.'

'Have you?' Her eyes laughed up at him.

He gazed down at her, his eyes fiercely intent now that he was so close to all he desired. On a long sigh, he said, 'You *know*, must know!'

She shook her head, though not altogether in denial.

The silence that followed drew out, waited upon what he knew must be said. In the end, because there was no way it could be changed or softened, it burst from him with muted violence. 'I have to tell you I cannot marry you!'

She had known how ineligible he and all the world must consider a match between them, but astray between accepting its impossibility and a better hope, hearing it said so bluntly was unexpectedly shocking. The alternative was obvious. But if she was to become his mistress, she needed reassurance, needed to be convinced of his continuing love and to have all made right in her own eyes.

Grim with anxiety, Lucius said, 'When I was seventeen, for good reason, my father betrothed me to an Egyptian girl. She was three years old at the time. For all that, the betrothal is binding on me. If I break it, my mother and brothers will be endangered and the girl herself disgraced because no other man will marry her. It was one of her brothers and a member of my mother's family who came here recently to remind me the girl is now at the age for marriage and it should take place soon.'

She could understand the coercion of those circumstances; saw them as more truly compelling than the dictates of society that required him to marry his equal in rank and fortune. But because he had known from the beginning that he was not free, as she had not, it had become still more imperative that she understood just what she meant to him.

Uncertain of her reaction to his explanation, Lucius rushed on in haste and desperation to have it all said and out of the way. 'But it need not — must not — make any difference to us! I have bought a small manor-house, not too far from Old Hall, to be your — to be our home. You will want for nothing. There is nothing I cannot give you, nothing I would not give you!'

A small frown crept into Kezia's eyes and she grew very still. So sure of her as to have bought a house in anticipation! In a small, hollow voice, she said, 'You have made long plans . . . '

He had no idea what was in her mind; saw the plans he had made as sensible foresight, and not perceiving where the danger lay, thought simple truth enough. 'Yes,' he said.

What Kezia saw was calculation, a calculated seduction that had nothing to do with love. He had stopped short, she remembered of even yielding her the word.

He felt some change in her, the beginning

of withdrawal, but would not allow himself to suspect that at this late juncture she might elude him. Hurrying on, he blundered deeper into the mire. 'Only listen. You will never again need to borrow another woman's pearls. Pearls, diamonds, sapphires, I can dress you in them from head to foot.' Pleased with the thought, he laughed. 'You shall outshine the sun, if you choose!'

She said in a light, remote voice that sounded strange in her own ears, 'A Bird of Paradise! I have heard the term but never quite understood it until now. It seems I am to cost you a great deal. Are you sure I am worth so much?'

She had stepped back out of his reach as she spoke and he woke to the possibility of things having gone seriously wrong. He frowned. 'What do you mean — Bird of Paradise?'

'Oh, surely you know the expression! It is, I believe, how gentlemen describe an expensive mistress — a very expensive mistress.'

'That is not how I think of you!'

'Is it not? Isn't it what you have planned for? Planned for some time?' She almost choked on the bitterness of that realization. 'As your mistress I am to dress to fit the part. And then, no doubt, be expected to exhibit myself and your generosity to the world while your unfortunate Egyptian child-bride sits at home. How foolishly naive I have been! How willing to lend myself to your plans I must have appeared. Well, slow as I have been to understand, understand I do now.' Raw with a hurt that even then might have been assuaged if he had said with passionate truth, '*I love you!*', she swept him a mocking curtsy and rose to say, 'Thank you for your offer, sir, but princely as it is, I fear you are not rich enough to buy me!'

Before Lucius could take in how suddenly and completely everything had plunged to disaster, she had gone from the room.

★ ★ ★

The dowager's night had not been a restful one and when she at last came down to the Lily Room she still had not decided which of her several grievances was first in importance.

Fears and dissatisfactions tumbled together through her mind. Just to think of the mischief created last night between Mawdsham, Emmington and Miss Aston was enough to overset anyone's sanity! Charles Delarive had far too little regard for his position, or, for that matter, for that of others! It was only too like him to ignore the claims of well-born young women and choose to dance with a nobody! But because it was like him, it would have been no more than a nine-days' wonder: it was Emmington who had made a scandal of it! Which brought her to the grievous question of whether there was something between Emmington and Miss Aston that she had missed? Missed because, not thinking it possible, she had not looked for it?

And for what reason had Hermione come so dramatically to Miss Aston's rescue? Had it been because she knew the girl was Charlotte's daughter? Had Miss Aston, against her own strict prohibition, told her? *Charlotte's daughter.* A daughter Charlotte should never have had and in whose existence she had never wanted to believe. That being so, why had she ever brought her here?

Never before had she felt so confused, so old, so little able to stifle the stirring of uneasy conscience. Seared into her memory was the quiet dignity with which Miss Aston had rejected the offered pearls and underlined the anomaly of their relationship: ' . . . *from the Countess of Emmington to her companion it is too valuable a gift'*.

Miss Aston was late in coming to make herself of use, but the dowager sent no reminder to her companion. Nor, when

Miss Aston came, did she comment upon the pinkness surrounding her eyes, merely informing her that they would be driving out in the landau in half-an-hour's time.

'Meanwhile,' she was continuing, 'you may continue reading me that new book we began recently — ' when the door opened and his lordship came in.

Her hands clenching on the book she had just taken up, Kezia prayed he was not about to demand another private audience. What would she do if he did? She did not doubt that he was furious at her rejection of his offered *carte blanche*. He had put himself to trouble and expense, buying a manor-house, making plans, sure that in the end he could buy her! Locked into a dark unhappiness, she knew now that having given him her heart and mind, if he had really loved her, it would have been a small thing to have given him her body. *Given it: not sold it!* She sat with her eyes on the book, loathing and loving him together.

'Miss Aston.'

Forced to look up, she saw his expression held all the sustained anger she expected but was startled to find it overlaid by blazing contempt.

A bare step from her, his voice harsh and sneering, he said. 'The visitor you must have watched for with some anxiety waits for you in the library.'

She made no sense of his words and did not at once rise from her chair.

The dowager's head snapped from one to the other. 'Who has come? Whom do you look for, Miss Aston?'

'No one, ma'am. I am expecting no one.' Now she stood up. Obviously, someone waited for her: equally obviously, Lord Emmington had no intention of telling her who it was.

Throwing her a look that chilled her through, Lucius strode back to the door and wrenched it open.

'Do not embarrass Miss Aston with questions just now, Countess' he said. 'She will, I am sure, be only too delighted to tell you her news on her return.'

27

Away from the earl's distracting presence, Kezia remembered Lady Hermione's promised meeting and guessed her visitor's identity. That Miss Aston should have such a visitor must appear singular to his lordship, but to have aroused so much resentment seemed out of character. But when she entered the library she checked in astonishment: it was not the duke's sister who waited for her but the duke himself.

'Your Grace.' Curtsying, she could think only that his call concerned Lady Hermione: certainly, his expression was anxious. He came quickly towards her, taking her hand, saying in a hurried way, 'Miss Aston, so good of you to see me.'

This from the Duke of Mawdsham to Miss Aston must surprise anyone who did not know the man. More surprising to Kezia was the fact that he had retained her hand in his. Her thoughts were already skittering into disorder when he said, 'Did Emmington tell you — Naturally he will have told you why I am here.'

The possibility that then presented

itself to Kezia was so unbelievable as to be embarrassing. She said feebly, 'Lord Emmington told me nothing.'

He looked disconcerted. 'I was sure — Had hoped — More correctly, I should first have spoken to whoever is your proper guardian but your circumstances — It appeared appropriate to open the matter with Lord Emmington.' Finding her unprepared for what he had to say had thrown him out of his stride, made him more anxious. 'I'm a clumsy fellow . . . older, too, by a dozen years and more . . . two children besides — '

He broke off, smiled apologetically, and his nervousness falling from him, spoke warmly as the man he was; with dignity, as the nobleman he also was. 'Allow me, Miss Aston, to tell you how much I have admired you from the time of our first meeting. I thought I should never feel again what I felt for my first wife but I find I was wrong. I have a deep regard for you and if you would consent to marry me, I would do all in my power to make you happy.'

'Your Grace!'

Astonished though she was by the unexpectedness of his proposal and the magnificence of it, as any woman in her position must be who was not simple-minded, she was even more moved by its sincerity. For

327

a moment she could think of nothing more to say and it shot into her mind that it would be no unpleasant fate to become this kind and pleasant duke's duchess and mistress of Staneflete Castle. That apart, it would solve her most pressing problems. But she could not do it. She thought too well of the man to accept all he offered when she could give so little in return. At the same time she was torn between laughter and tears for the sheer perversity of Fate.

'Your Grace,' she began gently at last, 'you do me more honour than I can possibly deserve and I am sorry with all my heart that I cannot say yes to you. I never dreamed — If I have given you the impression that I hoped or expected — '

'No, no. Always acted just as you ought. Too much to hope. Knew it. Come second-hand. No romance in it.'

'Oh, no! Indeed, it is not that. There is an insuperable reason — If I were heart-free I could not want better than to be your wife.'

'Ah! Should have known.' He swallowed painfully. 'Last night . . . I did wonder. No wish to distress you. He's a lucky man. I wish you happy, my dear.' He carried the hand he had continued to hold to his lips before releasing it. 'I'm devilish sorry, you know . . . shall not stay. Won't trouble Emmington again.' He walked to the door, shook his head as he passed through, murmuring again, 'Too much to hope!'

Shaken by her own blindness, Kezia stood where she was for several minutes. She had been sure the duke's singling her out had been no more than manifestations of his kind and courteous nature. Had the earl given her the warning the duke had expected him to give, she might, at least, have been able to prepare a more graceful answer.

A glimpse of the landau passing one of the library windows, reminded her she was expected to join the dowager on a drive and impelled her return to the Lily Room. By now, she hoped, his lordship would have gone about his own affairs.

He had not. Whatever conversation had been under way between him and the dowager was broken off as both turned to stare at her. As though, she thought distractedly, she had suddenly grown a second head. Her return, however, appeared to be all that was wanted to induce his lordship to leave.

Level with her, he paused just long enough to say, 'Let me be the first to congratulate you, Miss Aston. How very satisfied you must be!' before passing on out of the room.

There had been something of the balked tiger in his expression and it took effort to walk on as though bone and muscle had not weakened almost beyond the ability to keep her upright.

'Can it be true? Has Mawdsham really offered for you?' the dowager demanded, her voice spiralling sharply between wonder and disbelief.

'Yes, ma'am.'

'Well, upon my word you aim high! No wonder young Osborne could not interest you.'

Kezia regarded her levelly, her eyes wide and clear. 'I aimed nowhere, Countess. My surprise is as great as yours.'

'If you say so.' The dowager made little attempt to hide her scepticism. 'But some inkling of what was in the wind must have come to you; some ambition budded. Who shall blame you? I confess, though, I never thought you a scheming sort of girl.'

'Nor am I!' Kezia declared, her control slipping a little. 'I had no thought at all of having drawn the duke's notice.'

'Oh, come! Such innocence will not pass. What else could have made Hermione throw her cloak over last night's extraordinary happenings?' She scowled through narrowed eyes at Kezia. 'Unless it was your having revealed to her that you are Charlotte's daughter?'

'No. But she had guessed and last night she asked me to confirm it.'

The dowager grunted, leaned back in her chair and remarked with curling lip, 'So, now you are to be a duchess!'

With a strong sense of having been comprehensively insulted by both the earl and the dowager, Kezia took a small but satisfying pleasure in being able to say, 'No, ma'am.'

'*What!*' The dowager shot upright again. 'You cannot mean — *No, you cannot mean you have refused him! That* is quite beyond belief!'

Riven by her many hurts, Kezia said dangerously, 'Whether I marry the duke or do not seems equally displeasing to you, ma'am. Perhaps my greatest fault lies in having attracted his notice at all.'

The dowager drew ragged breath. 'You forget yourself! Such a tone to me! As a duchess you might enjoy the freedom to speak so, but if, as you tell me, you are to remain as you are, you will do well to keep the limitations of your position in mind.'

Kezia shook her head. 'My position here at Old Hall is no longer endurable. I have found little to make it so at any time.'

Deep under the flat accusing words was a note of passion that reached the dowager's inner ear and prodded intuition to leap the void. With a small gasp, she said, 'You hooked the wrong fish! That's it, isn't it? *Emmington* was the catch you hoped for. Well, you were far out there, miss! He might offer to make you his mistress but never his countess.'

And that was true! Taking a deep breath, Kezia said, 'You make it even clearer to me, ma'am, that it is time for me to go.'

The dowager had not intended to push matters to this end, but it was beyond her to yield. 'Yes,' she agreed. 'It has all been a sad mistake.' She struggled with a guilty awareness of having behaved badly, disturbed to discover that while still not wishing the girl to go, it was not for the old reasons. But it was too soon to make concessions. Miss Aston must first be given time to repent her decision — and her impertinence.

Kezia curtsied. She tried to frame some formal words of farewell, but an aching tightness closed her throat and she left the room without speaking again.

The dowager sat on, her feelings of guilt now laced with a sense of being ill-used. Sopworth coming in to remind her that the landau awaited her pleasure was a welcome interruption. She would take a respite from her problems and be better able to cope with them. Rudge could accompany her in Miss Aston's place.

It was well over an hour before the landau returned. A very subdued Rudge relieved her mistress of her bonnet and sable pelerine before seeing her again comfortably established in the Lily Room. Ten minutes later, Lady Hermione was shown in.

Seated, Hermione said, 'I had intended to call today in the hope of having some private conversation with Miss Aston. It was not until Charles returned to Staneflete I learned he had been before me — and the reason. I must ask you, can she really mean not to have him?'

The dowager's lips thinned. 'Even *Miss Aston* cannot be so rash as to depend on Mawdsham renewing his application, so we may suppose that she does! What beggars belief is that Mawdsham should have offered at all.'

Lady Hermione's dark eyes held her in their quiet gaze for a long moment before she spoke. 'I have known from the beginning how much Charles admired Miss Aston, and though I did not know he had reached the point of proposing to her, I have no fault to find with his choice.'

'Have you not! No fault to find when a man of Mawdsham's rank discounts birth, breeding and fortune?'

Hermione's gaze hardened a little. 'You must know that Charles has no need to look for fortune and Miss Aston herself speaks for the rest. My concern is to know whether she was being merely kind when she told Charles her affections were already engaged?'

'It's true enough,' the countess replied with a snap.

'Is it Emmington? Last night it seemed to me his actions were those of a man in a jealous rage — the rage of a man who had failed to succeed.'

'What Emmington was about last night passed all reason! As to succeeding, he is not the man to stoop to marry a — ' She broke off before the sudden fire in Hermione's eyes.

'Well, Emmington is high indeed, if he thinks the girl *Mawdsham* chooses is beneath his notice,' Hermione said sharply.

'Oh, not beneath his *notice!*'

'You mean that here, under this roof, he has offered to make Charlotte's daughter his mistress? And you do not resent it? I do not understand you, Countess! To have brought her here only to ignore the relationship . . . how could you do it?'

'*Charlotte's daughter, you say!* If her mother wore no ring, what is Miss Aston but the by-blow of a shameful liaison with an unknown man? She has no right to recognition. No claim on me or anyone!'

'What then, have you been about? Punishing her for Charlotte's loss and your unhappiness? Who less to blame than Miss Aston? As to her right to recognition, I tell you with all certainty short of proof, Charlotte was married in Ireland. Knowing her as you did, can you think she would be drawn to any man except one of worth? She was too bright a star!'

Pain had closed the dowager's eyes; angry suspicion snapped them open. 'Ireland, you say! Suddenly you know so much! Yet, at the time, you swore you knew nothing.'

'No, I did not swear to that. The questions I was asked I answered honestly. The one thing I had learned accidentally — their destination — no one asked me if I knew.' She regarded the countess in silence for a moment, then said, 'Even now you seem not to know who was Miss Aston's father. Have you really not troubled to ask her?'

The countess, in mute retreat, gazed past her.

'I found it out only last night and will

tell you. He was Fredrick Aston-Fitzcleve, the serjeant-at-law. Which must also tell you why Charlotte was desperate to keep his identity secret. High in office though he was, with two powerful families ranged against him, the Sellons and the Buckleys, he could have been destroyed. The price Charlotte had to pay for protecting her lover's career was the severing of all former ties.'

Slow tears had begun to creep down the dowager's cheeks. Chokingly, she said, 'What has been so hard to bear has been the thought of Charlotte brought low, perhaps to live in squalor.'

'You know now that it was not so. And Miss Aston has always been evidence against it.'

'Charlotte should have made a brilliant marriage, been the ornament to society she was meant to be.'

'Charlotte made her own choice and, I suspect, was happy with it.' Hermione reached out to lay a hand on one of the thin old hands gripping the chair-arm so tightly. 'Have you not seen how much of Charlotte there is in her daughter?'

Snatching her hand away, the dowager hid behind her handkerchief. 'I am old, Hermione. Old and weary. Charlotte was my consolation for those who failed me.'

It was time to change direction, Lady Hermione decided. 'It was not my intention when I came to say anything about Miss Aston's father until I had spoken to her. I should like to speak with her now, if you will allow.'

'Send for her then, if you will. But I am not able for more today. Before she comes, Rudge shall help me to my room.'

A footman answered the bell's summons and Rudge and Miss Aston were sent for. Before either arrived, Sopworth came into the room. Stiffly correct, he said, 'I have to inform your ladyship that Miss Aston cannot come to you. She left the house nearly an hour ago, taking hand-baggage with her and asking for her trunk to be sent on. She had intended walking to Westerham but I thought it . . . ' he paused just long enough to give his next word significance, '*inappropriate* and I arranged for her to be driven to Reigate where I believe her intention was to take coach for Putney. Before she went she asked me to restore this to your ladyship.' He approached nearer to the dowager and laid a recognizable pearl necklace on the table beside her.

★ ★ ★

Lord Emmington, returning from a punishing ride, entered the room as Sopworth left it. His gaze swept over the two shocked and silent women and came to the wrong conclusion. Having greeted Lady Hermione with remote civility, he said edgily, 'You look less than happy, madam. Is your brother's choice of wife not to your liking?'

Lady Hermione's brows lifted. 'What is not to my liking is that Miss Aston should have refused him and that, between us, she has been made sufficiently unhappy to be driven from this house.'

Into the heavy silence that followed, the dowager put in shakily, 'Someone shall be sent after her.'

Lucius stood as though fixed, his eyes blind, hearing again his last harsh, contemptuous words to Miss Aston, remembering the pale, wounded look with which she had received them. The very intensity of what he felt for her seemed to invite disaster at every turn. In the bleakness of the moment, he told the dowager uncompromisingly, 'No one will be sent after Miss Aston. It appears to me she is much in need of rest from us all . . .'

28

Though Hallie remained what she had always been, briskly loving and dependable, a few days at Miss Halsinger's Academy for Young Gentlewomen was enough for Kezia to realize that too much had changed for her to slip back easily into her old life there.

The greatest change, Kezia suspected, was in herself; she was newly restless and the recent past was too often in her mind for her to shape her future.

Hard to bear were the betraying moments when she found herself filled with longing for the man who thought of her as a purchasable pleasure for his bed. The same man who had so often infuriated and dismayed her and yet always — always — just by taking her in his arms, had the power to wake her senses to vivid life and lap her in enchantment.

Her one specific against the low spirits that these occasions brought was to tell herself that such feelings were a deserved hair-shirt for the pain she had inflicted, albeit unwittingly, on Harry and the duke.

She was absurdly grateful for a letter from Lady Hermione assuring her of her continuing friendship and offering a little more information about her father.

It was never my privilege to meet him, but I remember hearing Fredrick Aston-Fitzcleve spoken of as the most brilliant lawyer of his day and the youngest ever to be appointed serjeant-at-law. There are never more than fifteen of these at any one time and it is their exclusive right to appear as advocates in the Court of Common Pleas. It is, too, from among this small number that judges are appointed. So you see, my dear, you have every reason to be proud of your breeding . . .

In a postscript — a thoughtful warning? — Hermione mentioned that Lord Emmington had gone again to Egypt, it was believed to bring back a bride.

Ten days after her return to Putney, Kezia was in Hallie's study trying to improve her French when Hallie came in, an open letter in her hand.

'Kezia, my dear, I want you to consider a proposal I am about to make but not to think that I am suggesting there is no longer place for you here.'

Kezia waited and Miss Halsinger went on, 'Recently, one of our pupils was called home because her mother had died. Her father, Mr Gibson, writes now to say he wishes to keep Julia at home until after the summer holiday. Besides the infant which so unfortunately cost Mrs Gibson her life, there are two other young children in the nursery, both much distressed by the loss of their mother. The nurse has her hands full with the weakly new infant and the nursemaid is too young to cope alone. Mr Gibson asks if I am able to recommend someone to take the older children in charge until his widowed sister-in-law can come to them in about three months' time.'

Hallie had not been told the full story of Kezia's sudden return from Old Hall, but that it was an unhappy affair of the heart she was certain. The Gibsons' tragedy might well be the means of turning her surrogate daughter's attention away from her own griefs. Briskly, she added, 'I should like to put your name forward for Mr Gibson's consideration, Kezia. Helping this family would, I think, benefit both you and them.'

★ ★ ★

Ten days later, on a late April day of typical sun and showers, the Gibson carriage

341

conveyed Kezia to Overthorpe, a pleasant house set in a small park above the River Mole not far from Dorking in Surrey.

Mrs Thursby, the housekeeper, elderly and comfortable in both figure and manner, welcomed Kezia warmly, though she remarked a little doubtingly as she conducted Kezia to her introduction to Mr Gibson, 'I do not think he is expecting quite such a young person.'

Mr Gibson, however, appeared satisfied with the fact that *someone* had come to the relief of his troubled household. He looked what he was, a youngish country gentleman accustomed to, and generally enjoying, a pleasant, outdoor way of life. As shocked by the loss of his wife as his children were by the loss of their mother, he greeted Kezia with an abstracted air, hoped she would be comfortable, would not find the children too intractable and, Kezia suspected, immediately forgot her.

The first weeks were not easy. Julia, just ten years old, was a slight, dreamy child who grieved quietly and for that reason gave Kezia most concern. Her sister, Florence, at six, was a much more robust child who expressed her bewildered unhappiness in sudden wild bursts of destructive activity, while David, three and a half, repeatedly asked when his mother would return and, dissatisfied with the answers he was given, responded by breaking into noisy crying or fierce tantrums.

Kezia found the days long and full, with a constant need for inventive occupations to be found for the children. Consequently, she had little time for thought in the daytime and slept exhaustedly at night. Discovering that the 'Aunt Daisy' who was to come was a known favourite with the children, Kezia concentrated their attention on this event, persuading each of them to prepare a gift with which to welcome her: Julia was to make and embroider a handkerchief; Florence undertook to stick shells into a pattern on a small box to be used for trinkets and David was to colour a picture of cats. Uneven though it was, a degree of peace began to return to the Gibson nursery.

★ ★ ★

In May, there was a letter from Melissa, redirected from Putney. It bubbled over with the young girl's exuberant spirits: she was now in London, in a breathless whirl of shopping, dress-fittings, more dancing lessons and first social engagements; she had recently shaken hands with the Duke of Wellington, *still the Hero without Compare*, she wrote.

A privilege which will throw my brothers into Envious Despair. On a more serious note, she ended:

> *I have met no one here Superior to the Particular One from whom I had to part when I left Old Hall. I do not doubt you will know Who it is I mean. Him I cannot forget though I fear he has quite forgot me. If only I could be as sure of his Attachment to me as I am of mine to him! I have writ to remind him of the rides we took together when you was laid up with your sprained Ancle and to tell him how much I wish he was here to ride with me in the Row.*
>
> *Yours in Friendship,*
> *Melissa Holford*

So Melissa was still thinking of Harry even in the midst of her present excitements. It concerned Kezia that the young girl might be writing to him without her parents' knowledge and hoped, for both their sakes, it would not lead to trouble.

May was succeeded by a miserably wet June which limited outdoor play for the children, but the beginning of July brought in a spell of beautiful weather which released them to the pleasures of walks and picnics and outdoor games. Aunt Daisy wrote to set a date for her arrival in the last week of the month and Kezia, looking to the future, began to study advertisements in Mr Gibson's newspaper.

Nothing had yet come of these studies when she received a letter from Harry. This, too, had been delayed by going first to Putney. He wrote on behalf of the countess. The old lady had been ill again and her recovery was slower than expected chiefly because she was fretting over the earl's prolonged absence and her own loneliness. She asked as a favour for a visit from Miss Aston as soon as was convenient. If she would signify her agreement and the day and time of her coming, a carriage would be sent to bring her to Old Hall.

As before, Kezia's every inclination was against the visit, but she felt obliged to go. That being so, she arranged to make the call with no loss of time to avoid any risk of an encounter with Lucius Sellon.

* * *

Three days later, the same plain, old, but beautifully kept carriage that had first taken her to Old Hall, carried her back again. Thirteen months lay between the two visits but again — as though to mark the occasion — it was a perfect summer's day.

Memories of those months accompanied her relentlessly all the way. Towards the countess her feelings had withered into something close to indifference, but those towards Lucius Sellon retained all their bitterness. She could not forgive him for thinking she could be bought, or for later thinking she had declined his offer in expectation of a more advantageous one.

Even less could she forgive herself for having laid herself open to being offered such crude inducement to become his mistress. If only he had said, '*I love you . . . cannot do without you . . .* ' Yet deep under the anger and hurt, she knew herself betrayed by other feelings that clung to him with loving, longing obstinacy. If there had been any possibility of meeting him today she could not — *dared not* — have come.

The chestnuts lining the Grand Avenue were in the full dark magnificence of their summer leaf when the carriage turned in beneath them. Between their boles, the sun's rich yellow-gold glinted from the ruffled surfaces of lakes and water-courses, spangled the airy silver plumes tossed high by two fountains and made dramatic contrast with the jetty shadows cast by tree and bush across the lawns. Closer to the house, the various gardens sheltering behind walls of rosy brick or clipped yew, allowed flashing glimpses of brilliant colour through the archways that gave entrance to them. But for Kezia, nothing could exceed the loveliness of the house itself: it looked now, just as it had lived in her mind, as though wrapped in smiling, age-old memories. Gazing at it with gentle valedictory regret, she thought, I shall never see it again.

The door of the house opened as soon as the carriage drew up before the porch and John footman came to let down the carriage steps. She was greeted in the hall by Sopworth with his usual pleasant courtesy. With an apology, he explained that the countess, having passed a very bad night, had fallen into a deep sleep from which it was thought unwise to wake her. If Miss Aston cared to wait in the breakfast parlour which he was sure she would find particularly pleasant at this hour of the day, he would have some refreshment served to her.

Declining anything more substantial than a glass of Tokay and some macaroons, Kezia sat in the sunlit white-panelled room looking out through a window that opened on to one of the green forthrights leading to a distant and graceful little Temple of Flora, gleaming white against the blue, distant haze of the Weald.

Sopworth reappeared as soon as the tray that had been brought to her was removed.

'I regret to say the countess is still sleeping. Rudge tells me that her ladyship was so unsettled she gave her a few drops of laudanum. I hope you will not find a further wait too inconvenient?'

'No, of course not.' Not inconvenient, she thought, but not contributing to her comfort. She glanced towards the window. 'Such a lovely day. Perhaps I will take a last look at the gardens while I wait.'

'Not a *last* look, I trust, Miss Aston,' Sopworth said, surprising her.

She turned to him. 'Oh, yes, I think so. I do not expect to come to Old Hall again.'

'Allow me to say how sorry I should be if that were so.'

Her surprise deepening, Kezia stared at him. Now she recalled the attention with which she had been received today; it had not been of the order a visiting *lady's companion* might expect. Remembered, too, Sopworth's unfailing courtesy towards her in the past. She said slowly, 'You know who I am, don't you, Sopworth? Have always known?'

'That you are Lady Charlotte's daughter? Yes, miss. I have been at Old Hall a long time; since before Lady Charlotte was born. I saw her grow up. There was something about you that brought her into my mind soon after you came here. Then when I saw you wearing the gold chain the countess gave her for her twelfth birthday, I was sure.'

'Has anyone else among the staff guessed?'

'No. If they had, I think they would have been unable to keep from speaking of it.'

Kezia stood up. 'You made the time I spent here much easier than it might have been and I never really thanked you for your kindness. I was always conscious of it. And grateful.' Smiling, she held out her hand.

'What little I was able to do, I did with pleasure.' He shook her hand warmly, bowed and stepping back became again the correct upper servant. 'If you mean to walk in the garden, miss, I will bring you a parasol.'

He was gone only a minute or two before returning with a cream-silk parasol lined and fringed with peach. He held the window wide for her to step over the low sill on to the grass, saying, 'I will send someone to you when the countess is awake. Which direction do you mean to take?'

The forthright with its double borders of limes stretched a daunting length to the temple and rejecting it, she said, 'Oh the West Court garden, I think,' and turned to the right where at a small distance an archway opened in a tall clipped hedge.

Within the yew walls, the air was heavy with the mingled scents of lilies, phlox, roses and clove-pinks banked in glowing mounds against the dark of the hedges. She strolled slowly along the pale sanded paths that wove their winding ways to remembered secret corners, each holding its own special interest with here an ivy-hung arbour, there a rose-embowered marble Bacchus, elsewhere a vast bronze urn spilling over with pale blue violas.

The drowsy warmth turned her footsteps finally in the direction of a small grotto where she knew water trickled over mossy stones into a fern-hung pool. Before she quite reached it, she stopped abruptly. Someone was there before her.

Not for a moment did she doubt who it was: she would know that figure among a thousand! The shock of seeing him drove the blood from her head and for a few fearful seconds she teetered on the edge of dizziness.

Lucius had been staring down into the pool. Now he raised his head, looked at her and smiled.

As her giddiness receded, Kezia's first quivering awareness was of the brilliance and exultation of that smile. He had shown no surprise and his look of triumph could hardly have made it more plain that he thought she had come in search of him.

In an icy passion, she swung about and began to walk away.

29

'*Kezia!*'

The urgency of his tone, his unaccustomed use of her name, startled her and she glanced back. He was looking puzzled, but the smiling confidence had not gone. There was even a hint of laughter in his voice when he spoke again. 'Having come, you surely do not mean to go!' He held out his hand expectantly.

She stared at him in disbelief. Did he suppose her to be suffering a late, coy timidity? Or perhaps pretending it? She said chillingly, 'We can have nothing to say to each other, Lord Emmington. Pray excuse me.'

His smile faded but the puzzled look remained. 'Then, may I ask, why did you come at all?'

She supposed he meant come to Old Hall. 'Because the countess particularly requested it.'

'But in Heaven's name, why now so determined to run away before you hear what I have to say?'

'Because, my lord, you can say nothing

that I would want to hear.'

An edge to his voice now, he snapped, 'I do not understand you!'

The long misery of the past months rose up to taunt her. 'No, I think you never have. I was foolish enough to love you — more foolish to begin to think you loved me. But you are too steeped in the opinions and customs of a barbaric culture. To you a woman is simply a piece of purchasable merchandise. If I have held your interest it can only be because you cannot bear to fail of your purpose! You made plain your contempt for me and I, to my deepest regret, gave you some cause for it.'

He was pale and grim when she had done and asked bitingly, 'And you came to find me to say *this*?'

'I did not come to find you to say anything!' She could not understand why he persisted in thinking she had and to wipe the idea from his mind, she said, 'Believe me, my lord, far from seeking you out, I wish we had never met!'

Trite words, but they made the point. And just to make quite sure he understood and did not suspect that just seeing him filled her with painful longing to be in his arms, she added, 'If I now despise myself for past folly, I despise you more.'

This time he did not call her back when she moved away and Kezia's rapid pace slackened only when she saw John footman coming to tell her the countess was awake. She needed every minute of the time it took to reach the dowager's bedroom to restore herself to even the appearance of composure.

She found the old lady was sitting up in bed, supported by a multitude of pillows. Her face was thinner than Kezia remembered and there was a new darkness under her eyes, but beneath the drooping lids the eyes themselves had lost none of their keenness as they cast an encompassing glance over her visitor.

Waiting in silence until Kezia had drawn near, she then said with her well-remembered tartness, 'So, Miss Aston, we meet again.' Her lips pursed. 'Properly, I suppose, I should now address you as Miss Aston-Fitzcleve, if that is what you are.'

'Miss Aston will do very well, ma'am,' Kezia returned.

'Sit close. I have not the breath to shout.'

It was as though she had never been away, Kezia thought, as she lifted a chair nearer to the bed and sitting down, said, 'I'm sorry to find you unwell, ma'am.'

'One learns to accept the burden of age,' the dowager returned inaccurately.

'Less easy to accept is the behaviour of others. The young so perverse, so lacking in consideration, so indulgent of themselves!'

Uncertain who was considered at fault, Kezia offered no comment.

The dowager's pale eyes stabbed at her. 'This thing between Melissa and Harry Osborne . . . do you know about it?'

Warily, she shook her head.

The dowager grunted. 'It appears the chit has already had an offer from a man of rank and fortune and turned it down out of hand. To her mother's fury, hardly needs to be said. But she crowned her offence by announcing that her heart is pledged to *Harry Osborne!* On which account Lady Holford has favoured *me* with a letter of such insolence as I shall not soon forget!'

'What does Harry say?' Kezia asked cautiously.

'Less than is helpful but all that is proper. He made no disclaimer to the young minx's discredit, but he looked to me a man astounded.'

Her eyes gleamed wickedly. 'The girl's a true Holford! For my guess, she'll out-match her mother and if she doesn't change her mind with her next gown, she'll have him. Amazed I don't doubt young Osborne was, but not horrified. Why should he be?'

She shifted her shoulders a little more deeply into her pillows, reached for a glass of cloudy liquid on the table beside the bed and studied Kezia over the rim of the glass as she sipped.

'Well, it was not just to tell you of that I asked you to come.' She set the glass down again. 'You left Old Hall very suddenly. I did not think you truly meant to go. Or not so soon.'

She sighed reluctance over what more there was to say, grasped the nettle and said, 'I did not deal with you as I should but cannot explain it. Charlotte's going was the cruellest blow! I wanted — *needed* — to hit back at someone and there was only you.' Her look burned on Kezia demanding understanding. 'It is the way I am.'

'It is past. Perhaps if you had been able to find proof of my parents' marriage we should have dealt more comfortably.'

'Hermione Delarive is certain there was a marriage. she has had some correspondence with an acquaintance of your father. He remembers there being a general understanding that there was a wife who was thought to be a sad invalid and so was rarely seen. Now Emmington has the matter in hand and has extended the search to Ireland, perhaps we shall at last arrive at the truth.'

Kezia stilled. 'Lord Emmington? Why should he trouble?'

The dowager gave her a long enigmatic look, before saying drily, 'Have you really no idea? The man returned from Egypt only yesterday and could not wait a decent hour before informing me he wishes to marry you ... *will* marry you if he can and without needing proof of your legitimacy, though the search for it in Ireland was put in hand before he went away.'

Something of her old fierce humour came into her face as she saw Kezia's astonishment. 'To put no gloss on his words, he said were you ten times a bastard he would have you — if you would only have *him!* You are the one, he says, who wants proof. You and the law, because, as your mother's legitimate heir, there are certain inheritances due to you from settlements.'

Kezia, she saw, looked more shocked that flattered, and she demanded acidly, 'Now what's amiss?'

Flatly, Kezia said, 'I don't understand. I was told Lord Emmington went to Egypt for the purpose of bringing back a bride.'

'Had you that from Hermione? Emmington said some wild words in her presence on the day you went from here. For a time I, too, thought that was what he intended. But when he came back, he told me he had gone to settle some troublesome business that had cost him dear but which had been worth every penny expended. Whom he brought back with him was the younger of his two brothers. The boy is to go to school here.'

Painfully, Kezia asked, 'Are you certain he said he wished to marry me?'

'I am not deficient in understanding, miss! But you may hear it from him.' Her puckish humour flared up again. 'Never before has it been given to me to play the go-between, but hearing you were to visit me today, Emmington desired me to limit my enjoyment of your company and send you to him. That is, if you were willing to hear what he has to say. He is waiting for you in the West Court garden.'

Kezia closed her eyes but found no refuge there from despair. It had been a refined cruelty of fate to direct her footsteps to the West Court garden before she had seen the dowager . . . what wonder that Lucius had looked at her with such expectation, had spoken with such confidence! And how different an interpretation could be placed on his question '*And you came to find me to say this?*' With dismal clarity she recalled what she had said in reply. Never, she thought, her despair deepening, did they ever seem to meet in clear understanding of one another. Nor would they — because she could be quite sure Lucius Sellon was not still waiting for her in the West Court garden!

Puzzled by her silence, the dowager prompted impatiently, 'Well, miss, have you nothing to say? It was my belief you had a decided *tendresse* for the man. Don't tell me you are about to turn away a third suitor; they are not as plentiful as trees!' She hm'mpd a laugh. 'Though for you, I will say they have that appearance! Still, having run through a baronet, an earl and a duke in short time, you would be unwise, I think, to depend on a fourth man of rank offering himself.' When Kezia made no immediate response, she added a little testily, 'Emmington believes himself as deep in love as any woman could wish, what more can you want?'

Kezia gazed at her with dull eyes. 'I chanced to go into the West Court garden while you were asleep, ma'am, and met Lord Emmington there. I did not know — There are things between us — He seemed — I thought — ' she made an effort to pull her reeling mind back into control. 'We were fatally at cross-purposes. He thought I had come from you and I thought we were met by chance. I said things — Told him I despised him utterly. Told him that I would not look for him if there were no one else left on earth.'

Surprisingly, the dowager's thin lips quivered. 'To so ruin all! How could you be so foolish!'

'It is wonder to me, ma'am.' With a small bitter laugh, Kezia stood up and took one of the fragile hands lying on the coverlet in hers. 'Do not distress yourself. I will bid you goodbye, Countess, but I leave my good wishes with you. We are unlikely to meet again, I think.'

The hand she was holding turned in hers, clutched at it. 'Do not say so! Now there is better understanding between us . . . Kezia. Granddaughter?' She looked up in stark appeal.

Kezia bent to kiss the withered cheek. 'I cannot promise anything just now, except that I will write. That I will do without fail.'

Outside in the gallery, she stood still, needing time to adjust. Too much had gone awry for any hope of putting things right. The words with which she had scorched Lucius had been said to a man who — so the Countess had said — was *as deep in love as any woman could wish!* Those words scorched her memory now. What man whose pride had been so comprehensively punished, would wish even to see her again?

But she had a choice before she left the house. She could accept what ill-luck and her own destructive words had brought about and slip quietly away to lick her wounds: or she could humble her own pride and do what she had vowed she would never do and go in search of Lord Emmington and offer him the apology he was owed. Whichever course she chose, supposing he would as much as meet her again, the end would be the same: for the rest of her life she must live with the grief of lost love.

She was still flinching from the second choice as she came down the stairs. John footman left the hall as she stepped from the last tread and a moment later Sopworth came to meet her.

'Are you intending to leave now, Miss Aston?' he asked gravely.

She sensed he knew that something unusual was afoot: servants of Sopworth's calibre always did.

She gave him a nervous look, clutched at courage, and said, 'If Lord Emmington is in the house, I should like to see him before I go. If he will allow it, that is.'

His gravity did not lighten. 'Lord Emmington is in the Cabinet. Will you go to him there, or would you prefer me to tell him you wish to see him?'

She understood at once the alternatives he was offering. If Lord Emmington chose to offer her a rebuff, it could be tempered by being delivered through him — or she could meet it head-on.

Nailing her colours to the mast, she smiled sadly at him. 'Thank you, Sopworth. I will go to him.'

He nodded, bowed and left her. With slow steps she walked across the hall and down the ancient flagged passage leading to the cabinet. The door stood ajar. Pushing it open, she entered. Lucius Sellon stood as she had found him once before, staring out of the window into the courtyard beyond.

He turned with slow deliberation, his face as unrevealing as though graven in stone, but the aura he gave off was more formidable than she had ever known it to be.

'I had to come. Had to tell you — ' Her throat closed. She began again. 'To tell you I did not know . . . had not seen the countess when I met you in the West Court garden. We were at cross purposes. I said things . . . cruel things I neither truly meant nor believed. I am here only to say I am sorry.'

Except for a slight tightening of the flesh over the bones of his face, a slight sceptical twist to the severe line of his mouth, she would not have known he heard her. Clearly, she had offended beyond all hope of pardon and it would be useless to ask for it.

She turned away, had reached the door when his voice came snarling after her, 'And that is *all!* Well, by God, it isn't enough!' He moved fast. Before she could step out into the passage his hand was on her shoulder and he had spun her back to face him. He was breathing hard but she could not tell what emotion had him in its grip. 'Earlier you were eloquent on the subject of my failings — not, I grant you, without reason — but your chief complaint seemed to be that I tried to buy you. Did it not occur to you that being conscious I could not offer you marriage — *could* not, not *would* not! — I dragged in all that I could offer simply to tilt the balance as far as possible in my favour? Or that, loving you as I did, I was too shaken by uncertainty, by my fear of nothing being enough, to put my case with grace?'

She looked at him with surprise. No, it had never occurred to her that a man of such positive qualities might still have doubts and diffidences. 'It wasn't lack of grace that mattered,' she said, her voice grown small.

But having loosed the rein of his sense of

grievance, he missed the importance of that and continued, 'You tell me I'm arrogant. Well, I never was so arrogant as to believe you would come to me as my mistress without some significance inducement.' Curt, matter-of-fact and ringingly truthful.

Perhaps for the first time she found herself looking past his outward showing of invincible strength and saw the man within: someone who, like herself, had needs and vulnerabilities and was as likely as she to fall into error. In other words, the evidence of his humanity. What did she love about him if it was not that?

In the same stringent tone, he said, 'You said you loved me . . . *had* loved me . . . ' It was less a statement, than a question.

It was too late, she decided, for anything except the truth. He had spoken of loving her only in the past tense. She said simply, 'I have loved you. Do love you. Will always love you.'

There was no relenting in the bleak coldness of his regard: if anything, it deepened as his lids narrowed over the hard glitter of his eyes.

'If I had found the right words in which to ask you to be my mistress, would you have consented?'

Almost inaudibly, she said, 'Yes.'

He stared at her unmoved, let the silence lengthen before saying,'So, you say you love me. Then if, upon your own terms, I ask you again to be my mistress, what will you answer?'

There was no *loving* in the question. This was revenge for affronted pride. She gazed steadily back at him. A strong man, but not without fault: the man she loved, but how deep did her understanding of him go? Bracing herself against the risk, she said, 'On my terms — yes.'

He bowed ironically. 'You have only to name them.'

'I ask only that you love me as I love you.'

For a moment the room was still, then his arms were hard about her and there was no coldness in the face looking down at her. '*Kezia* . . . ' He spoke with a deep, aching tenderness. 'Love you, I must — God help me, I have no choice! But I want you as my wife, not my mistress. In Heaven's name, let us marry soon before there can be any other misunderstandings. There have been enough for a lifetime!'

The kisses that sealed the compact took a long time, but surfacing at last, Kezia found a shadow lying across the glow of her happiness. 'The Egyptian girl?' she asked.

'Salide?' He sobered a little. 'The first time I went back to Egypt, I expected to marry her but I could not bring myself to do it. Instead, as a pledge of my commitment, I arranged for her to be taken into my mother's household. It bought me time . . . time to come back to Old Hall and try to persuade you to be my mistress before I married, because I was sure you never would consent if I had a young bride. Since I could not escape the trap I was in, I could see no other way to bind the woman I wanted to me.' He smiled crookedly at her. 'You know how successful *that* scheme was! After you left Old Hall I grew even more desperate to find a way of cutting free without destroying Salide's future.'

He broke off, drawing together his memories of what had happened. 'Nothing in life stands still. My brother, Malek, was back from Cairo. He's twenty now and more an Egyptian than I am. Though he went to Harrow as I did, he chose to finish his studies in Egypt. He's an ambitious young man, able and willing to take responsibility. To put it briefly, I asked if he would be prepared to marry Salide, accept headship of the family in Egypt and responsibility for its fortunes; I found him more eager than perhaps he should have been.'

He shadowed a smile. 'You see, women go unveiled in the home and Malek had seen, and I had, that Salide was a very lovely young girl.' His smile turned wry. 'Salide herself, given the choice between marrying Malek or marrying me was unflatteringly quick to choose Malek. Which left only her father and brothers to satisfy. Their interest, as it had been from the beginning, and as is usual in Egypt, was simply in the advantages that Salide's marriage would bring them. Once they understood that Malek was to take my place, own all that I had owned in Egypt, there was no difficulty. A free scattering of gold removed any lingering doubt from their minds — and gave me the opportunity to gain what most *I* wanted.'

'You do no know how nearly I failed to find the courage to come to you here in this room, how nearly I hurried away, convinced you could never forgive me for the terrible things I said to you.'

His eyes lit with laughter. 'If you think you could have left Old Hall without seeing me again, you are much mistaken. You would have found no carriage available. I had made sure of that!'

She gasped indignantly. 'You are the most — ' She closed her mouth on the rest of the sentence.

'You were about to tell me how arrogant I am, I think, Miss Aston,' he said silkily.

She laughed back at him. 'If you are not, you give an excellent impression of one who is.' And then, suddenly serious, added, 'You said once that considerations of fortune and status were necessary to you in marriage. I bring you neither. Have nothing to give you.'

A wicked gleam entered his eyes and his mouth curved into the curling gypsy smile she remembered so well. Laying a finger against her lips as he had at their first meeting, he said again what he had said then, '*Oh, but you have!*'

THE END